WHEN I DIE

When I Die

THE LEGEND OF JOE MUNDY

Monty McCord

FIVE STAR
A part of Gale, a Cengage Company

GALE
A Cengage Company

Farmington Hills, Mich • San Francisco • New York • Waterville, Maine
Meriden, Conn • Mason, Ohio • Chicago

LIBRARY OF CONGRESS CATALOGING-IN-PUBLICATION DATA

Names: McCord, Monty, author.
Title: When I die : the legend of Joe Mundy / Monty McCord.
Description: First edition. | Farmington Hills, Mich. : Five Star Publishing, [2018]
Identifiers: LCCN 2017047443 (print) | LCCN 2017050095 (ebook) | ISBN 9781432837259 (ebook) | ISBN 9781432837242 (ebook) | ISBN 9781432837303 (hardcover)
Subjects: LCSH: Law enforcement—Fiction. | BISAC: FICTION / Historical. | FICTION / Action & Adventure. | GSAFD: Western stories.
Classification: LCC PS3613.C38227 (ebook) | LCC PS3613.C38227 W48 2018 (print) | DDC 813/.6—dc23
LC record available at https://lccn.loc.gov/2017047443

First Edition. First Printing: March 2018
Find us on Facebook–https://www.facebook.com/FiveStarCengage
Visit our website–http://www.gale.cengage.com/fivestar/
Contact Five Star™ Publishing at FiveStar@cengage.com

For Ann, my inspiration, my oasis.
And for the little wrangler, Silas.

CHAPTER ONE

The two locked eyes on one another. Something would happen and happen soon. That was for sure. If nothing else, honor. Beads of sweat traced the creases on their faces, traveled downward, and fell from their chins. One wearily glanced at the other's hand and swallowed hard. Each wished he could read the other's mind. Both wished they were somewhere else. The younger man wondered how he got himself into such a pickle. His own wild bravado, he guessed. *Would this be the end?* He hoped that someone would step forward and demand a stop to it so he could save face.

The cold stares resumed. Onlookers gathered at a safe distance and watched with a combination of morbid curiosity and a desire for it to just stop. Some were unconsciously holding their breath.

"Don't you do it, old man," the young man blurted, finding his voice. He tried to recall his father's instructions, but they were blurry in his mind. He struggled to remember! Now! Soon it would be too late!

"Who you callin' old . . . *boy?*" the older man said with a grating voice. He locked eyes with the younger man.

The young man glanced up, met the older man's eyes, then again watched his hands. "Don't you do it," he said again, as a drop of sweat streaked into a corner of his eye. The young man tried to ignore the burning sensation. *Why today, of all the days, does it have to be hotter'n hell? This damned sweat . . . !*

"You think you have a snowball's chance in hell beatin' me
. . . *boy*? Why don't you stop jawin' and prove yourself?"

The younger one slowly raised his left sleeve and wiped the
sweat from his eye. A foolish move perhaps. He hated to do it,
but if he didn't, his vision wouldn't be clear enough. And he
had to watch for movement. Why didn't sweat run into *his* eyes?

"What's the matter boy . . . you losin' your nerve?" the old
man goaded.

When it came right down to it, yes, he was afraid of the older
man's experience. But, being younger, his mind was sharper . . .
wasn't it? "Make your move or quit yakkin', you old coot." *God,
why did I say that?*

The older man offered a villainous grin and made his move.
His hand flashed downward, picked up the red checker, and
hopped across three blacks.

"Damn!"

"Adam, I believe that makes six games in a row you let Gib
win," Siegler said, smiling.

"Believe I would have relented after four myself," Judge
Worden said, offering a stern look as he studied the checker-
board. He stroked his chin whiskers, which were one of four
prominent tufts of graying hair. The others had positioned
themselves at each side of his head and on top, but it was the
chin whiskers that received his immediate attention.

Gib said, "What do you mean, 'let him win'? He didn't let
me win nothin'. I beat him fair and square and that's all there is
to it! It seems he's a bit shallow on skill!"

Gib Hadley was the owner of the North Star saloon,
diagonally across the town's main intersection from the Martin
brothers' hotel. He was one of Marshal Joe Mundy's closest
friends besides Adam, his part-time jailor, and Byron Siegler.
Of course there was Sarah, too.

The group of onlookers inside Byron Siegler's general store

included Pastor Cadwallen Christmas Evans, Judge Elsworth T. Worden, Siegler, and Joe. The front doors stood open, in hopes that what little breeze there was would find its way inside. It was the end of August and Nebraska's summer heat was making everyone sluggish. No one wanted to exert themselves unnecessarily.

"Want to make it seven in a row, *Mr. Carr*?" Gib said, his grin wide this time. "Let's see now, how much is two-bits times six? Oh, yeah, I think you owe me a buck and a half!"

"I wasn't bettin' no money. Some delusionary you old coots get from time to time."

The onlookers laughed as Adam stood up shaking his head.

"To get your mind off your sorrows, Adam, those three crates need to be emptied," Siegler said, and pointed toward the back of the store.

"Anything to get away from this ol' fool's gibberish," Adam said. The men laughed again. He marched past them to work on the crates.

The spirits of Taylorsville's citizens were on the rise, despite the oppressive heat. During the depressing winter, an influenza outbreak had taken four souls, three children and one adult. A hired gunman out for revenge had seriously wounded Joe in a gunfight at the North Star saloon. Sheriff Wick Canfield's deputy had arrived in town to ambush Joe but shot Adam by mistake. Of course, Joe couldn't prove that Canfield was behind it.

As the small group began to depart, John "Smiley" Wilkie, the proprietor of the Palace saloon, wandered in. He dragged his feet like a nervous child. The small crowd stared at him and his filthy white apron. The wrecked and dirty bowler atop his head had seen better days. With his hound dog eyes, eternally scowling face, and greasy dark hair, many believed that it was impossible for him to produce anything remotely close to a smile.

Joe was the first to speak, "What do you want?"

Wilkie looked at the floor, then at Siegler. He mumbled something about a town board member until Joe broke in, "Speak up and quit mumblin'. Say somethin' or git." Wilkie was certainly no friend of Joe's. Judge Worden had given Smiley sixty days in Canfield's jail for suckering Joe with a chair rung when Joe carried Lucy Sauter back to the Palace. She had undertaken a drunken, naked stroll down the boardwalk. The thin scar on Joe's forehead served as a reminder of the fracas. Recalling that Smiley had gone to jail sporting two swollen eyes and a purple face gave him some satisfaction, however.

Siegler broke in, "What is it, John?" The saloonkeeper stood with eyes wide, and endeavored to recover his voice. "Siegler, you're on the town board." Wilkie forced out the words, as he studied the floor. "Doc is in his cups again and he's shooting up my place and I . . . I ask for action . . . I want him out."

"Doc don't own a gun, you horse apple. Why don't you just run along?" Joe said.

"Joe, John is a citizen and has lodged a complaint. As you are the marshal, we ask you to investigate the matter," Siegler said.

"Fine," Joe sighed. "This better not be some damned ghost chase. After you, if you please . . . *John.*"

As the two walked down the boardwalk near the Palace, they heard a gunshot, causing Smiley to flinch. The Colt appeared in Joe's hand without conscious thought. Smiley stood outside with his faced pressed against a window. Joe saw Doc standing on the bar, so he holstered the gun as he opened one of the tall doors and stepped inside. The usual stench of the place seemed even stronger than the previous day. A *palace,* it surely was not.

Thirty-three-year-old Doctor Thomas Sullivan was taking careful aim at beer mugs with a Colt conversion .44. The mugs sat on a table occupied by two petrified cowhands who looked like they didn't much want to be there. Joe wondered why they hadn't run out, but that question was soon answered.

"I shed, 'sit *very* shtill'! Or I could hit one of ya me mishtake . . ." Doc told them. He wore no coat and was wearing a gun belt loaded with cartridges, a second revolver stuck inside the belt. He was so frail that only his suspenders kept his trousers from plummeting to the bar. The gun fired again, the bullet splintering the table inches away from the errant mug. The long-haired cowhand at the table flinched, causing Doc to erupt as he cocked the hammer again.

"Shtill, I say! If ya move, I might hit ya instead of that damned glash . . ." He chuckled, "Then I hafta cut the bullet out of yer shtinker' hides!" Doc roared with laughter as the cocked revolver shook in his hand. He sucked in air to catch his breath. The beer mug full of whiskey in his left hand helped balance him between swigs.

Joe wondered if Sullivan weighed even a hundred pounds now. The doctor had steadily increased his drinking since he'd lost the three children under his care during the influenza outbreak. He once had told Joe that he moved out here to live peacefully and have a quiet little practice delivering babies. That hadn't turned out to be.

"Doc! What in hell you think you're doing?" Doc was startled by Joe's voice and let go a round that exploded one of the full mugs. Beer splashed over one of the cowhands. "That's enough, Doc." Joe marched toward the bar until Sullivan cocked the .44 again and aimed it at Joe's face. Joe froze. A long moment passed by before he spoke. "Well, Doc, what are you goin' to do? You goin' to shoot me?" Sullivan offered Joe a strange grin and took a slow swig of whiskey while watching Joe through the corner of one eye. The doctor's dark shadowed eyes contrasted with his pale white, stubbled face. Joe thought he looked sixty and tried to remember him sober.

The scrape of chair legs on the floor alerted Doc to movement. "Don't move! Not one damned pinch!" The desperate cowhand froze, hands gripping the chair arms. His mug of beer was still intact.

"Well, Doc, if you're bent on shootin' me, I don't want there to be no mistake. If I'm closer, you won't just wound me." Joe took a step closer and Doc, eyes growing wider, appeared even more on guard. "Okay now, shoot!" Joe yelled. At the same time he reached out and grabbed one of Sullivan's shoes and pulled. The pistol's hammer snapped in Joe's face without a report as Sullivan tumbled down onto the bar, and then to the floor. Doc's revolver landed near Joe's left boot. While a wide-eyed Sullivan gasped for air, Joe picked up the revolver. He held the hammer back, opened the loading gate, and turned the cylinder, ejecting each empty casing, and one live round. He dropped the empty ones onto the floor, and inspected the loaded cartridge. The primer was dented by the firing pin, but had failed to fire. *Not this time, I guess.* He replaced the cartridge and lined it up to fire. He swung it toward the abandoned table and pulled the trigger, exploding the mug of beer.

The skinny cowhand had moved to the front doors and was watching Joe. When the dud fired, Joe heard, "Sweet Jesus!" The cowhand stepped outside the door and retched on the boardwalk. Smiley swore at him until Joe grabbed the barkeep's collar and pushed him inside. "Whose guns are these?" Joe asked him, pointing at the two revolvers he had taken from Sullivan and placed on the bar.

"Them . . . them would be mine. Took them for a tab," Wilkie said, his lips almost quivering. Joe shook his head, leaned over, and dragged Sullivan to his feet, unbuckling the gun belt and letting it fall to the floor. He pretty much had to carry the doctor all the way to the church, where he asked Pastor Evans to keep an eye on him while he sobered up.

CHAPTER TWO

Sheriff Wick Canfield had stayed with Martha "Mart" Mellingham longer than usual. It was almost 3 a.m. when he negotiated the rear stairs of John Blessing's saloon. Blessing's wasn't the only saloon in Gracie Flats. But Blessing made a point to stay on Canfield's good side and insisted that he didn't have to pay for his time with Mart and threw in a free bottle of whiskey. Canfield knew he'd partaken of both a little too much, making the narrow stairs a challenge to navigate.

His powerful frame stumbled down the alley toward the hotel where he kept a room. Nature's call forced him to stop behind Avery's general store, even though an outhouse was nearby. As he unbuttoned his trousers, he spotted a small pane of glass in the back door that was broken out. Swearing under his breath, he fumbled with the buttons again and stepped closer. He could see someone moving around inside. Positioned beside the door, he swore to himself again. A few minutes passed before the door slowly opened and the thief stepped out into the darkness with a cloth sack in his hand. Canfield's drunken swing of his gun almost missed the intended target, but did manage to glance off the side of the man's head. He hit the dirt hard.

"There, you sorry bastard!" Canfield said as he re-holstered his gun and once again unbuttoned his trousers. By this time, he had to urinate so bad that he had trouble starting. But, when he did, he aimed the powerful stream at the unconscious man's head. "Teach you!" After finishing, he grabbed the sack in one hand and the thief's right arm in the other and dragged him toward the courthouse.

By the time Canfield deposited his prisoner on the floor of a cell, he was sweating profusely. With only one lamp lit, he fumbled around looking for the jail keys. After locking the cell, he tottered over to his hotel room.

It was nearing 11 a.m. when a clean but badly hungover Sheriff Canfield walked into his office in the tiny courthouse. He tossed his hat on the rack and saw Deputy Dick Nolan sitting beside the sheriff's desk reading a newspaper. "Mornin'. You look like hell."

Canfield offered nothing but a cold stare.

"Who's our new guest?" Nolan asked.

"Don't know," he said as he tipped a bottle of whiskey, winced as it went down his throat, and coughed. He re-corked the bottle and dropped it back inside his desk drawer.

"His head was bleeding pretty good and he stunk like piss, so I threw a bucket of water on him. Thought it'd help with the smell," Nolan said.

"Do you always talk so damned much early in the morning?" Canfield said.

Nolan went back to his newspaper, "It's eleven o'clock."

"Well, boy howdy, you sure do come in handy. I don't even know why in hell I carry this watch around when I have you to tell me the time."

Nolan tried to ignore Canfield and realized it wasn't a good time to converse.

Canfield picked up the cloth bag the thief had carried out of the store and emptied it on his desk. The first thing he inspected was a new Colt Single Action Army, a gun like his, in .44-40 caliber and a five-and-a-half-inch barrel. He looked it over and held it out, turning it like a woman admiring a new emerald

15

ring. He pulled open a desk drawer and placed it inside along with the two boxes of cartridges from the sack.

Nolan had put down his newspaper and was watching Canfield. Curious as to where the sack came from, he remained quiet until his boss decided to tell him.

Canfield rummaged through the other items, which included sixty-five dollars in cash, some dried meat, two cans of beans, four small potatoes, tooth cleaning powder, a small bottle of toilet water, and a new white shirt and tie. He stuffed the cash into a vest pocket and packed the rest back into the sack and shoved it under his desk. He picked up the jail keys and said, "Let's see who's brave enough to steal in my town." Nolan followed him into the block of three cells.

The prisoner was sitting on the cot holding his head in his hands. His wild, filthy hair hung over his ears. Most of the blood had dried. He wore a dirty blue, pullover shirt with black suspenders that held up brown trousers. Canfield opened the cell door. "Hold your head up!" The man didn't respond immediately, so Canfield hit him across the side of his head with an open hand. The man fell over on the cot, then struggled to sit up again. This time he looked at the sheriff. The man's overgrown beard and moustache made him look like he'd spent a long winter in the mountains. What little of his face that could be seen was wrinkled and darkened by the sun.

"What's your name?" Canfield asked. The man stared blankly.

He would look no different if he was laid out in his own coffin, Nolan thought.

Canfield hit him again and this time the man slipped off onto the floor. The two pulled him back onto the cot where he was struck again. "I won't ask you again." The prisoner held his hands up to defend himself.

"You know me, Wick, please don't hit me anymore," he said. Canfield grabbed the man's beard with both hands and yanked him up, where he studied his face. A slow chuckle rumbled out. "Well, by damn. Well, by damn right!" He pushed him backward and the man fell onto the cot and hit his head against the wall. They stepped out and Canfield locked the cell.

As they came into the office area, they found Nate Avery waiting. Canfield whispered to Nolan to keep quiet before addressing Avery. "Good morning, Nate."

"It's afternoon, Sheriff." Avery caught himself as Canfield looked at him. "I'm, I'm sorry, Sheriff, I'm sure you know what time it is."

Nolan shot an amused glance at Canfield.

It pleased the sheriff that the storekeeper was afraid of him. "I already know what you want. During the night, while completing my regular rounds, I found your back door was broken in. Been lookin' into it, followed some tracks out of town, but lost 'em. Did they get anything?"

Avery looked momentarily stunned at the sheriff's apparent efficiency. "I . . . I wrote down a list of what I know was taken," Avery said and handed the paper to Canfield. The list contained everything that the sack contained except the tie, and the storekeeper showed $105.25 in cash missing.

"Why the hell you leave that much money layin' around?" Canfield asked.

"I, uh, keep it hidden in a small can under the counter, for 'just in case.' " He hesitated, then added, "Truth is . . . that's all the money I have. Every cent. Don't trust bankers."

"Well, I'll see what turns up, Nate."

"Sheriff, business has been poor of late, what with Williamson's new store. I'll have to close if I don't get that money back," Nate said and looked at the floor.

"Be in touch." Canfield sat down and fired a cigar. Avery knew he had been dismissed, so he walked out.

"You know I don't question you, or what you do, or why, but

I gotta say I have a curious buncha questions about now," Nolan said.

Canfield's low, guttural chuckle rolled out. "With the election coming up and that damned Ike Raymond talking about running, I want more folks on our side. People feel sorry for 'im losing his son last winter. Nate will dance a jig in the street when *I find* most of his stuff, but I want him to sweat and whine a bit first. He'll probably want to manage my campaign!" He laughed out loud this time. "Right now, let's go back in there and find the rest of the money he's hidin'."

"You ever gonna tell me who he is?" Nolan asked.

Canfield laughed again, "In due time, Dick, in due time. Business first."

CHAPTER THREE

It was almost seven o'clock as Joe walked west down the boardwalk past the closed Texan and into the North Star. The informal, early morning coffee club whose membership included Hadley, owner of the saloon, Byron Siegler, Harold Martin, co-owner of the hotel, Pastor Evans, and Budd Jarvis, owner of the Texan, was in session. This particular morning, all were present except the pastor.

Joe walked over to a small cookstove and poured himself a cup and joined the others at a table. Since the shootout with hired killer Lute Kinney in the saloon, Joe sometimes felt a bit strange when he entered. He thought everyone looked at him differently there. He couldn't help a glance at the small wood and glass display case on the back bar that contained a matched pair of .44 caliber Smith & Wesson pistols. Since Kinney no longer needed them, Joe had given them to Gib to help pay for the damage done to the windows during the shooting. Instead of selling them, Gib had mounted them in the case he'd paid furniture maker and undertaker Iain McNab to build for that purpose. The pistols were a popular conversation piece and did seem to increase business. Not the increase of piano music, but an increase nonetheless. Gib had confided in Joe that about every day, at least one conversation among the customers included them and the fight. Thirteen bloody shots had been fired, but the number seemed to double with every telling.

"Mornin', Joe," Gib said. The others acknowledged him as

well. This same group, from the same table at which they now sat, had witnessed the shootout. A bullet hole in the front of the bar and one in the ceiling, Kinney's last two shots, were still visible. A dent in the big heating stove from one of Joe's errant shots was still there as well. Though the blood had long been cleaned up, dark stains on two separate areas of the floor, where Kinney and Joe had fallen, were still very evident. A customer had found one of Kinney's teeth not more than a month previously and traded it to Gib for a shot of whiskey. Gib had placed the tooth with the pistols inside the case.

"What's the word today, gentlemen?" Joe asked. He sipped carefully from the steaming cup.

Byron Siegler customarily guided the conversations through the news of the day with a copy of the *Omaha Bee* newspaper he brought along. "It seems that the First Cavalry lost thirty-four men in a fight with the Nez Perce in Idaho Territory."

"Wasn't you in the First in the war, Joe?" Hadley asked.

Joe nodded. "First Nebraska Volunteers and then cavalry out here." Joe looked at Harold Martin, whose hands vibrated incessantly. Harold was a high-strung character anyway, but now seemed terrified every moment, as if he was taking his last breath. Martin wasn't the same after sitting through the shootout. Joe learned later that Harold had slid down onto the floor with his hands over his head until it was over. In fact, he had laid there until the others picked him up and helped him back to his hotel. Harold hadn't uttered a single word to anyone for a full week afterward.

"I proudly served in Mr. Lincoln's navy, on the *Carondelet*. A beauty of an ironclad—"

"Devil in hell, Gib! You tell that same damned story every time a person parks his ass near your location!" Jarvis said.

"Well, pardon me, Budd, did you serve?"

"I damned sure did! Remember, I'm from Texas?" Jarvis said

with a frown.

Gib's face flushed when the revelation hit him.

Siegler interrupted the argument. "I was reading this about the army. Seems they were given approval to chase bandits into Mexico. Stock thieving in Texas is a bit out of control."

Jarvis joined in. "We're not the only ones gettin' our cattle and horses stolen. Believe it's gotten worse there since I left, though."

"You missin' some recently, Budd?" Joe asked.

"Damn sure have. I've got a couple my boys ridin', see if they can come across the curs doin' it. Might be Indians, considering what the freight teamsters said last week. Said a small band had killed a homesteader east of Gracie . . . probably Sioux."

As Joe listened to Jarvis talk, he noticed Doc Sullivan walking slowly down the boardwalk on the other side of the street. He swayed back and forth, bumping into building fronts as he continued east. He wore brown trousers with a dirty white shirt, one suspender draped down his leg, and no hat.

"Don't mean to interrupt, but there goes Doc, lit up again," Joe said.

Hadley got up, went to a front window, and watched as Sullivan stumbled his way down the block. "It's a dirty shame what Doc has become. All account of not savin' those poor souls from the sickness last winter. Don't he know he ain't no miracler."

"Something's going to have to be done, before he drinks himself to death," Siegler said. He slowly shook his head.

"I agree, Byron, but what?" Jarvis said, "We can't rope 'im and tie 'im up."

"I don't know, Budd, I wish I had an answer."

Hadley returned to his seat after refilling his cup. "Joe took him to Pastor Evans after the dustup at the Palace. Must have no more and got 'im sober when Doc dove headfirst right back into that bottle."

The men sat in thought. Doc Sullivan was a good man, a friend. But his drinking was a problem and they knew how important it was to get, and to keep, a doctor in a small town like Taylorsville. After Joe left the North Star, he walked across the street and on down to Judge Worden's office. He found the judge at his work table engrossed in what appeared to be a law book. Ink pen in hand, he scratched on a sheet of paper. Joe sat down in a nearby chair and waited.

"What can I do for you, Marshal?" he asked without looking up.

"Last winter you mentioned you were helping Sarah with a legal paper needed to end her marriage with George Welby," Joe said.

Worden looked up and removed his spectacles, "Ah, yes, on grounds of abandonment, a simple procedure after three years alone."

Joe nodded, "She was supposed to sign a paper . . . Did she?"

Worden moved a stack of folders on the table, then rifled through loose papers and held one up. "No, she never did, and I forgot about it apparently," he said. His frown indicated disappointment in the oversight. He turned the paper around. Joe saw the blank place where Sarah was to sign.

"I shall remind her the next time I see her."

Joe replied, "That's okay, I'll remind her. Thanks, Judge."

Dan Loman took pride in operating his own meat market. He still held a bitter resentment toward Ace Todd, Jarvis's prior manager. Todd's habit of buying stolen stock had earned Loman sixty days in Sheriff Canfield's calaboose. Loman was thankful to be alive, however, when he remembered what had happened to Todd. Canfield had reported to Judge Worden that while escorting Ace Todd to the state prison at Lincoln, Todd had tried to escape and the sheriff said he had no choice but to kill him. There had been no witnesses, of course. Dan Loman hadn't been there, but thought he knew the truth of it. Todd had secretly been working for the sheriff and probably knew too much of the man's illegal activities. That's what Loman believed, anyway.

He ran his favorite knife back and forth on a whetstone, and rubbed a thumb across the blade now and then to check sharpness. His thoughts drifted back to when Canfield had returned from the aborted Lincoln trip. He'd stepped into the jail toting a grin and told Loman that Todd died trying to escape. Loman had actually known little of the illegal dealings, but he'd felt sick, expecting Canfield to find an excuse to kill him too. He recalled thinking that even if they'd left the cell door wide open, they couldn't have dragged him out of there with a wagon team. Only when his sixty days were up, did he discover why Canfield had kept him around. And if there was ever a danger of forgetting, Canfield's man would be around to remind him. In fact, it looked like the next reminder was about to commence.

The little bell couldn't jingle when the man entered. The door was propped open for ventilation. He walked right in. About Loman's height, the man was a hundred pounds lighter. His sandy colored moustache mounted over thin lips, at rest, displayed a crooked smile due to a scar that ran from the corner of his mouth to the jawline.

"Afternoon . . . oh, I mean evenin', I guess it's evenin' now, isn't it, Mr. Banning," Loman said.

"Didn't come in this stink hole to converse, you fat bastard. What do you have?" Banning said. He walked behind the counter where Loman stood and looked around.

Loman allowed himself to swallow. He'd been thinking about this for a while and decided that this was the time. "Mr. Banning, uh, I can't spy on the marshal no more. I've done it since

I got out of jail and that's . . . that's long enough. I figure that's enough. You, uh, you tell Sheriff Canfield for me that there ain't no hard feelings, but I, I want to be left alone to run my business."

Banning was gently running his fingers over the handles of butcher knives resting in a wooden holder. He seemed to ignore Loman. He pulled out a cleaver and ran his thumb across the blade. "You . . . really want me . . . to tell Canfield that?"

Loman swallowed again and nodded. He labored to expel a mousy, "Yes."

Banning struck him in the face with a balled fist. Loman stumbled backward over a stool and landed on his back. He was choking for air as Banning knelt and shoved his knee into Loman's chest. As he regained his senses, he felt Banning grab his right hand and hold it against the floor. Loman struggled to sit up until Banning shoved the cleaver against his throat and pressed it enough to draw blood.

"Which will it be? Finger or throat, up to you," Banning said, matter-of-factly.

"Please, please . . . don't do this . . . I'll do what Canfield wants . . . please!"

Banning relaxed a little, and with a kind tone to his voice said, "Okay, take it easy."

As Loman relaxed slightly, the cleaver whacked into the floor, taking off his right little finger at the first joint.

"Ahhh! Goddamnit! Ahh!" Loman screamed.

"That's to remind you," Banning said softly in Loman's ear. "If you ever have doubts about what's expected of you." He stood up, leaving the cleaver embedded in the dirty floor, and sauntered out.

Chapter Four

Darkness found Joe making his rounds. He wore his suit coat though it was still plenty warm. As he walked by the new telegraph office across from the Texan saloon he saw Elijah Miller, the operator, with his head resting on folded arms on the desk. Except for the saloons, the rest of the businesses were closed. Joe continued on to the east end of the block, checking doors. As he crossed over to the other side, he remembered that he hadn't checked on Lucy for a while.

Joe would never forget how the prostitute had been severely beaten at the Palace saloon where she worked and lived. The memory of kicking open her door, knocking the attacker off Lucy, and shooting his partner was still clear in his mind. She'd suffered from serious vision and balance problems ever since. Without a family, she had no other option but to endure a sad existence working for Smiley Wilkie. The floors of the Palace were sticky and grimy, with dirty glasses left on tables. The smell was a combination of urine, sweat, liquor, and tobacco smoke. It was the last rung on the ladder of saloons. Cowhands and sodbusters from miles around frequented it, no doubt, because of Lucy working there.

Joe walked by Jarvis's Texan and Hadley's North Star, turned the corner north, and crossed the street. All three saloons had a fair number of customers, but the Palace attracted a lower level of clientele and trouble.

When he walked inside, Smiley looked at Joe and offered

nothing but hatred. Two men were taking turns dancing reck-lessly with Lucy, spinning her in circles and then stepping away. They laughed until breathless, as Lucy stumbled sideways and fell down. Then the other one picked her up and started all over again. She wore the same dirty dress that Joe had seen her in when he first arrived in Taylorsville the past November. Her brown hair tumbled around her face like a tangled mare's tail. Her dress was unbuttoned almost to her stomach, though he wasn't sure it had buttons anymore.

Joe pushed through the onlookers and saw that Lucy was crying. "That'll be enough!"

The dancer's partner was taking a draw on a bottle and Joe's order startled him enough to spill some down his cheek. "Damn! See what you made me do!"

"Party's over, you two clear out," Joe said, as he helped Lucy to a chair. "The rest of you go sit down." The onlookers gradu-ally stepped back to their respective tables.

"Who the hell's he think he is?" the scrawny dancer said, ad-dressing his partner. His dirty-faced grin exposed several miss-ing teeth and those that remained were dark around the edges. His black untrimmed hair resembled an abandoned bird nest.

"This ain't none of your business, so run away," the husky one said. Filthy suspenders were slung over the top of a sweat-soaked white union suit that served as his shirt. The man's belly lapped over the front of his belt and a Bowie knife hung from the side.

Joe pulled his coat open to expose the star. " 'Fraid it *is* my business, now get out. I won't tell you again." The saloon fell silent. Someone in the room whispered, "I'd leave, was me . . ." The fat man shot a quick glance sideways when he heard it, but faced Joe again.

"Oh, Denver, it's another one of those tin stars holdin' up a farmer!" the fat one said, and let loose a ragged laugh followed by coughing. " 'Member what happened to the last one, Denver?"

"Ya split him open and his innards plum fell on the floor, I 'member!" The man called Denver howled with laughter and slapped his knees. "He was a gutless law after that!" The men laughed harder.

Joe saw that Denver had a pistol stuck in the front of his belt and the fat one appeared to have only the knife. About that time, Joe heard two distinct clicks and felt cold steel on the back of his neck. He eased around and looked back.

Smiley's grin showed only on his mouth; the rest of his face was wooden. The sawed off double-barrel shotgun that he held against Joe's neck was the one he kept under the bar. Joe carefully turned back to face the two dancers.

"Ain't that jus' the shits, Mundy? Stickin' your nose in agin, and harassing me agin. You can't come in here and start causin' trouble, you oughta know better than that. Ain't that right?" Smiley asked the two dancers.

They chuckled.

"The town board ain't gonna like this at all. Ya know the whore is my property, she ain't yours. I can do whatever I damn well want with her." Joe's cold blue eyes narrowed a bit when Smiley poked him with the shotgun. "Unless, that is, you want to marry her? That it, Mundy, you want to get hitched up? If you do, I'm sure we can reach an agreeable price!"

Joe had never heard Smiley talk this much before. No doubt whiskey and the shotgun escalated his bravado.

"By the way, Mundy, meet my brother, Denver, and our cousin, Chug," Smiley chuckled again. "They's on their way to the Black Hills, stopped in to visit."

The two dancers grinned at Joe, raised their mugs, and drank. Chug said, "Guess we can see what he et for supper." He started to reach for his knife.

Joe heard another click, a faint one this time, and felt the shotgun move from his neck.

"It's okay, Marshal. I got my .32 stuck in ol' Smiley's ear. It won't make much mess, but it'll sure scramble up his brains a bit!"

Joe thought he recognized the voice and sure enough, when he looked back, there was Booth holding the shotgun in one hand and a shiny little revolver against Smiley's ear with the other. He stood almost two heads taller than the barkeeper. Joe had jailed Booth several months back. As he was a local farmer with a family, Joe had let him go instead of fining him for drunkenness.

Joe turned back to face Denver and Chug. "Ain't that the shits, Smiley?"

Denver moved closer to Joe's left. The fat man grinned slightly and pulled his knife. Joe didn't wait for the fat man to take a step. He drew the cavalry Colt with his right hand and shot Chug point blank in the chest, spun, and laid the barrel across Denver's face as he tried pulling his own gun. He heard a *crunch* when the heavy revolver's barrel made contact.

Denver fell down holding his face with a mixture of a groan and shrill whimper. Chug took a couple of steps back and looked with disbelief at the hole. It was smoking a little from unburnt powder and was beginning to leak blood. He fell to his knees, and looked again, seemingly amazed at the bloody hole. After a few seconds, Chug crumbled to the floor. The smoke around the wound got thicker and was about to ignite when a cowhand leaned over and poured the rest of his beer on it. Joe covered the crowd with the Colt to see if the two had any friends. When it seemed there was no other interest in getting mixed up in the affair, Joe glanced at Denver, who laid on the floor. The gash high on his cheek was bleeding well. Joe removed his pistol and threw it on the bar.

The front door opened and Adam and Jarvis rushed in, both carrying shotguns.

"You okay, Joe?" Adam asked.

Joe nodded and turned to Booth, who still held his little nickel-plated revolver in Smiley's ear. "You're not gamblin' again are ya, Booth?" he said, as he holstered his gun.

"Oh, no, sir. Found myself stopping for a beer before I went home with supplies," Booth said. "Can you believe I won this pretty little gun in a quick game of blackjack?"

"Takin' good care of your family?" Joe asked.

"Oh, yes, sir. Everything's fine, fine, fine. Crops lookin' good this year, too. In fact, got enough extra hogs to sell some finally." Smiley was careful to eye Booth and then Joe without moving his head, clearly wondering what he was supposed to do while they visited.

"Appreciate what ya done here, Booth, but you leave the law work to me from now on."

Smiley winced when Booth uncocked the little pistol and removed it from his ear. It seemed almost *too* small in his huge calloused hands. Smiley stood still, eyelids fluttering.

Joe stuck out his hand, "Thank you, Booth," he said.

"Marshal, you done me a kindness I won't never forget. This was nothin'." He shook Joe's hand and walked out.

Joe pulled the cavalry Colt and rammed it into Smiley's mouth, breaking off a front tooth in the process, and backed him up against the bar.

"Joe, what are you doin'?" Jarvis said. He approached Joe, but Adam stayed near the door eyeing the crowd. He lowered the ten gauge slightly to let them all know not to interfere.

Smiley's eyes were crossed as he stared down at the gun. "You pulled a gun on me, you son-of-a-bitch. You shoulda used it!" Joe said. He eased the hammer back on the Colt and Smiley's terrified eyes moved with the cylinder as it turned and locked into position.

"Joe, stop it. Don't do it!" Jarvis yelled, shocked at Joe's fiery rage.

Smiley started to shake.

Several moments went by before a calm, as quick as a breath, came over Joe. He straightened up and pulled the pistol barrel from the terrified man's mouth and holstered it. He then backhanded, Smiley sending the man spinning off the end of the bar and onto the floor. "If you care anything at all for your brother, you get him out of town right now," Joe told Smiley. "If I see him again, I'll kill him. Won't be any warnin', won't be any talk. He'll be dead."

"Adam, you and Budd can go now," Joe said in an almost soft voice. He took Lucy by the arm and eased her up the stairs to the middle of the three rooms.

"You're my knight in shining armor. Did you know that?" Lucy said as she sat down on her bed. Tears ran down her cheeks as she tried to look at Joe. He could tell that her gaze missed his eyes. "I knew you'd come to save me, I *knew you would.*"

"That's nice of you to say, Lucy," Joe said. "Your eyesight's worse, isn't it?"

Lucy nodded, "Balance, too. Can't get far without holding on to somethin' it seems. Headaches every day. Hell of a way to live, ain't it?"

Doc Sullivan had said there was nothing more he could do for Lucy, that the damage from her beating the previous winter was permanent.

"Is there not anything I can do for you, Lucy?" Joe glanced around the room. The bed sheets were filthy from cowhands who often didn't remove their boots while there for services. The stain on the wall from the past winter's shooting was still evident. The revolting stench in the room burned one's nostrils in the summer heat.

"Bet you didn't know that I fell in love with you the first time I laid eyes on you, when you first come in, and you met Sarah. Remember that day?" She looked down, no longer trying to act like she could meet Joe's eyes. A fly buzzed around her face but she didn't seem to notice, or care.

Joe nodded, "I do. My first day in town."

"I would have given anything to been the one you took to the hotel for a nice meal like you done Sarah, just anything. When Smiley's on me . . . I close my eyes and think of you. But look at me. Nobody would want a blind whore who can barely stand up, would they?"

"Lucy, I know of a hospital up at Omaha. I'll find out if they'll take you in."

She yanked her head toward Joe. "It's a place they put idiots, ain't it? I'm no idiot! Is that what you think of me?" Lucy broke down, tears streaking down her face.

Joe took her by the shoulders. "You're not like that, Lucy. This hospital is for folks who have it hard, you know, livin' by themselves. You deserve a better life, with folks who'll help care for you. You understand?" Joe said. "I have an old friend in Omaha. I'll wire him and he'll check into it for me. I'll pay for your trip if they can take you in, so you won't have to worry about nothin'. I'll let you know, okay?"

Lucy seemed to ignore Joe's words. "Would you kiss me?"

Joe was a bit surprised by her request. "Sure." He leaned toward her forehead.

"I mean on the lips. Oh! I promise I won't tell anyone!" she added.

Joe hesitated a moment, and then leaned down to her face. Lucy's lips responded to his firm kiss. He stepped to the door and stopped. "I'll let you know as soon as I hear back."

"Thank you, Joe," Lucy said and smiled.

Joe wasn't sure if the "thank you" was for the kiss or the hospital notion.

CHAPTER FIVE

Early the next morning Joe sat at his desk alone in the office. Adam had already gone to work at Siegler's store, but not before making a fresh pot of coffee. It was about light enough that Joe could see nothing but clouds in the sky. It would be a bit cooler. He gingerly sipped the steaming coffee and then uncorked an ink bottle. With pen in hand, he began scratching out a telegraph message to his old boss in Omaha. Joe had served two years as one of Daily's deputies before he ended up in Baxter Springs, Kansas.

August 20, 1877
Maj. Bill Daily, U.S. Marshal, Omaha, Neb.
Major,
Have good friend needs bed
St. Luke's Asylum. Find out and advise, thanks.
Joe Mundy, City Marshal, Taylorsville, Neb.

Joe reread the message, folded it in half, and slid it into a coat pocket. He blew out the desk lamp and was engulfed in near darkness. Tilted back in his chair, he thought about Lucy. *If I could have gotten to her quicker that night, her injuries might not have been so bad.* He closed his eyes and again saw his mother and father hanging from the tree. *Seems I shoulda done a lot of things. This time will be different. I will save Lucy.* He knew that her prospects were limited and hoped that the asylum could provide a bearable life for her. She had been partly right about the asylum and he felt almost as if he'd lied to her. It was a place for the insane, but also for the blind. He didn't know what else he could do for her. *Getting her away from Smiley will help.*

The telegraph office was still closed at that early hour, so Joe pounded on the door. Elijah Miller eventually came out from his tiny living quarters in the back, squinting his eyes and offering a large-mouthed yawn. The skinny brown moustache on his heavy top lip looked like an afterthought.

"Bit early, isn't it, Marshal?" he said as he wound the wire stems of his eyeglasses around his ears.

"Eli, figured you'd be up, with the apparatus and all," Joe said. He knew that the town's first telegrapher took his job very seriously.

"It is quite impossible to be awake *all* of the time," Miller said.

Joe nodded and handed him the message. "Right away, if you don't mind."

Miller nodded and yawned again as he sat down at the sender.

"Let me know soon as you hear back?" Joe said.

Miller nodded again as he read the note.

Joe walked west, crossed the street, and continued down the boardwalk to Sarah's laundry and bath business at the western end of the main street. Sarah was ready for breakfast, and as they walked down to the hotel, she told Joe all of the things she was hungry for.

"Sure you wouldn't like the chophouse more?" he asked.

"Why on earth would I want to eat there when you are willing to buy breakfast at the hotel?" She looked at him.

"Well, I remember one time you *really* wanted to go there *instead* of the hotel . . ." He turned away so she wouldn't see the glint in his eye.

"You're very funny, very funny." She tried to act annoyed but at the same time remembered almost a year ago when they first met. She'd been a working girl at the Palace and Joe had asked to take her to breakfast at the hotel the next morning. She remembered asking him why she should, and he had said, "Because that's *all* I'm asking of you, Sarah." It warmed her heart when she thought of that. Of course, things had changed considerably since then.

As they ate their eggs, bacon, and biscuits, Joe told her about the incident at the Palace and his conversation, and kiss, with Lucy. "I wired a man I worked for in Omaha to check and see if St. Luke's Asylum would take her in."

"Joe, that's a marvelous idea! But how are you going to get her away from Smiley?" she asked with a wrinkled brow.

"That . . ." he caught himself before continuing, "Smiley don't own her like he thinks he does. I hope he tries to prevent her departure." His steady blue-eyed stare gave Sarah unpleasant shivers. She didn't like it when he went cold like that.

After breakfast, Joe walked Sarah back to her laundry and then headed to the North Star. He found only Hadley and Jarvis inside.

"Gentlemen," Joe said and sat down.

"If you're waiting for me to pop up and get your coffee for ya . . ." Hadley began.

"I'd wait a long time, right? Had breakfast at the hotel, got my fill there."

"Oh, with that pretty Sarah! You two are becoming clockwork regular," Hadley chided. Joe ignored him.

"Was just tellin' Gib about the goin's on at the Palace last night," Jarvis said. "I was wonderin' what I'd a done if you'd blowed Smiley's brains out, few as they are."

"I wouldna blamed Joe one little bit after Smiley put that

scattergun to his head. What would them two fellers have done to Joe if Booth hadn't got the drop on Smiley, tell me that," Hadley said.

"I don't know, Gib, but I have a feelin' those two kin of Smiley's would have ended up dead," Jarvis said and offered Joe a grin. "That said, maybe someone should go with you from now on to the Palace."

"Not as long as I'm city marshal, Budd." Joe pulled his black hat off and ran his hand over his hair.

Jarvis expected that, so herded the subject elsewhere. "Haven't had a chance to tell you that one of my two range riders was wounded yesterday. Happened about seven miles west of my house. They told me they never even heard the shot before a bullet tore a hunk of flesh from Bony Wilson's side. He's okay, but as you might guess from his name, he ain't got any extra flesh to spare. I pulled 'em in, so no more ridin' 'til we can gather a large force to go out and shoot that bastard."

"And they didn't see anybody," Joe stated flatly. Jarvis shook his head.

Several minutes of silence passed by before Gib began another subject.

Late that afternoon, Joe sat at his desk cleaning both of his revolvers. The cavalry model was finished and so he started on the other, another Colt, with a barrel of just under five inches. It was the one he'd carried on his side while a deputy city marshal in Baxter Springs, Kansas. The one that he'd killed three men with who stood no more than six feet from him. Actually, it was two men and a fifteen-year-old boy. Adam sat near the open front door reading his book, *Howard's Book of 1400 Conundrums, Riddles, Enigmas and Amusing Sells,* which Joe hoped he wouldn't start reading aloud.

CHAPTER SIX

The gentle rock and comforting squeak of saddle leather relaxed him into dozing spells. His horse knew the way back to the TO-Bar so he could catch up on some rest. He awoke for a moment as Lightning plodded through the river. He eased up on the reins, removed his wide-brimmed hat, and scooped it full of cool water. After dumping it on his head, he used his shirtsleeve to wipe his face and let the six-year-old gelding drink. A birthday present when the sorrel was a colt, the horse had a white blaze on his face that looked like a lightning bolt. That made naming him easy. He spent a few extra moments taking in the beauty of the Loup River through squinted eyes. *Only the Lord could create a river this beautiful, and plunk it down right here in these hills. Someday I'll have me a place right on this very river.*

He nudged the sorrel in the ribs and resumed the daydreams, unaware of the distant eyes watching him. Thoughts about the day that Mr. Edson would give his permission to marry Trudy filled his mind. Mr. Edson had told him, *"not until you have money in the bank. My daughter won't wed a vagrant."* He worked for Edson most of a year now and knew there was a ways to go, but he *would* prove himself worthy of her hand.

He had a good start. At twenty-two, the experience working on his family's small eastern Nebraska ranch made him confident in his abilities with horses, cattle, and rope. He had never been afraid of hard work, either; his father made sure of that. He knew Mr. Edson was happy with the job he did, but rarely said so. *"Don't need 'em goin' soft 'cuz ya tell 'em they do good all the time."* He recalled Edson saying those exact words. Edson seemed to be a bit harder on him than the other hands, he assumed because of his affection for Trudy. He was okay with that as Edson was a good man. He dreamed of a cabin built with his own hands that he and Trudy would live in. He thought they would keep chickens and hogs as well as cattle.

The bawl of a calf cracked his eyes. Squinting in the bright sunshine, he saw a calf wandering around in a draw to his right. He guided the sorrel down the slope until close enough to see that the calf wore a Lazy-T brand. It belonged to Mr. Edson's neighbor, Abe Trumble. He looked around but saw no cow. Yawning, he untied the rope from his saddle and threw a loop, which missed the calf's head. The calf trotted off, then stopped and turned to look back. Too much beer at the Texan the previous night made his motions sluggish. He didn't get to Taylorsville often, but when he did, he enjoyed every minute of it. He was glad the older hands weren't there to see him miss because they looked for any small thing as an excuse to dig at him. The second try hit its mark and he proceeded on his way, pulling the protesting calf behind him. He abandoned the attempt to whistle a tune as his mouth was too dry. *How could I be dry and thirsty after drinking all that beer?*

He was approaching a rise when his left arm exploded, knocking him out of the saddle. The horse bolted, yanked the calf to the ground, and dragged it up the slope and beyond. He landed on his back, stunned. Then the pain hit. He gasped for air but little came. Stumbling to his feet in shock, his arm dangled like a wild rag at his side and blood streamed off the ends of his fingers. He lost his balance and fell as the ground beyond him erupted into a cloud of dust. He heard the shot that time. He was being shot at! Panicked, he scrambled to his feet again and ran toward the embankment in hopes of making it to the other side and to safety. Halfway up the slope his feet plowed wildly in the dirt and he fell. Pushing himself up with his right arm, he tore and scratched at the grass until he reached the top. Whimpers and tears escaped as he gulped at the air. As he stood to run again, the breath was knocked from his lungs. He watched a strange red spray shoot out in front of him and he felt himself falling again. Darkness came before he hit the ground.

Taylorsville's streets were quiet, especially the saloons. The only movement on the main street was a dog sniffing the boardwalk in front of the chophouse. Located next to the telegraph office, it was handy for Eli Miller to eat there.

Joe and Sarah sat in the nearly deserted hotel dining room enjoying supper. Joe sawed away on a beef steak while Sarah ate potato soup.

"Kinda hot out for soup," Joe said, looking at his plate.

"I like soup. It's good anytime, and cheaper."

"I'm payin' anyway," Joe said as he chewed. He stabbed a fork into a green bean.

"Thought I'd take it easy on your bill this time, as you usually pay when we eat here," Sarah said. She offered a smile to Joe who was again slicing through the meat.

She took a sip of water and said, "You must be hungry."

Joe nodded.

"You haven't heard back yet about the hospital for Lucy?"

"No, not yet. Should anytime, though," Joe said. Although he was anxious to receive the telegram, foremost on his mind at the moment was Sarah. He remembered the visit with Judge Worden and the paper Sarah hadn't yet signed that would end the marriage to George for abandoning her. He didn't want to do anything to spoil their time together, but this was bothering him. He didn't like wondering why she hadn't yet signed it.

"Is there something on your mind?" Sarah said. He stopped chewing and looked at her. Maybe she could tell he was fixed on something.

"Oh, Judge Worden asked me to remind you that you hadn't signed that legal paper to end your marriage. He sounded like he forgot about it, too," Joe said and picked up his glass.

"Oh, heavens, you're right! I've been so busy with my new business that I forgot all about it! I'll see him tomorrow, thanks for the reminder." Joe was relieved. She sounded sincere so it was off his mind.

CHAPTER SEVEN

Jenny, who worked in Budd Jarvis's saloon, ran through the front doors of the general store. Though small in stature, her attractiveness caught men's attention, but this time it was the panicked look on her face that they noticed first.

"Mr. Jarvis sent me to get Joe. It's Doc! Hurry!" She flashed Joe a warm smile, turned, and trotted back out on the boardwalk.

Some of the group let out a groan. This had come up before. The men followed Joe out of the store and walked behind him single file all the way to the Texan saloon.

Joe walked through the open doors of the saloon and saw Doc Sullivan standing behind the bar, waving a large knife in one hand and a whiskey bottle in the other. Budd Jarvis stood out in front of the bar, away from Sullivan's wild swings. Joe gazed at Hamilton "Ham" Bluford, Jarvis's barkeep, lying on the floor amidst pieces of a broken bottle.

"What's goin' on, Budd?" Joe said, as he looked Doc over.

"Damn Doc's gone off on a bender again. Ham tried to step in and take away his bottle and Doc hit him. He took Ham's knife and won't let nobody near him while he continues drinking my booze. He already owes me twenty-seven dollars."

"Twenty-nine!" Doc interjected and finished off the bottle in his hand. He then reached under the bar and retrieved a replacement.

"Why the hell didn't you stop him before he got this far?" Joe said.

"I got in from the ranch five minutes ago," Jarvis said, "when I sent Jenny for you!"

Joe walked slowly up to the bar and faced Doc, who drunkenly swiped the air with the knife while staring at Jarvis. Doc's gaunt face was sweaty and his eyes were set deep in dark sockets. He was in shirtsleeves with an unbuttoned vest, and looked like he'd been sleeping in his clothes . . . for about a month. His reddish hair shot out this way and that. Although never a large man, Joe thought he'd lost more weight. Sullivan would be nearly unrecognizable to anyone who'd seen him last fall, when the influenza outbreak started.

"You can't know how tedious this is getting, Doc," Joe said. "Party's over. Put the knife down."

Sullivan stopped waving the knife and pointed it at Joe. His eyes tracked more slowly than his hand and looked surprised when he saw Joe, as if it was the first time he'd noticed he was there.

"Come on, I'll walk you home," Joe said. One of the customers near the piano mumbled, "again."

Sullivan took another swig on the new bottle and swung the knife back and forth a couple more times and stopped. "I d-didn't kill you . . . yet." His words were slurred but understandable.

Joe knew that Sullivan referred to taking care of Joe when he had the influenza and later when he was shot by Lute Kinney. They had had this conversation before. The last time was this past Friday at the Palace saloon. The scene was the same, except for the knife.

Doc had started drinking heavily when the Sandersons' six-year-old daughter died of the sickness under his care during the winter. He drank worse after each subsequent death until he

42

could barely take care of himself, let alone anyone else. "The time's come, Doc. Time for you to quit drinkin'. You're comin' with me, one way or the other," Joe said.

"I oughta give you a lump or two," Doc replied.

"Why don't you come out here and do that?" Joe said.

Doc swigged another drink and took his time setting the bottle down, which fell over anyway. He laid the knife down and stumbled his way around the end of the bar, sliding up his shirtsleeves as he went. Some of the onlookers gave subdued cheers. One said aloud, "That's it, Doc! Knock him around some!"

Doc approached Joe. He took up a fairly accurate-appearing boxer's stance even though he was swaying back and forth. Instead of moving and bobbing around his opponent like a boxer, he bobbed up and down in one place. Some of the customers chuckled.

"Come on, Doc," Joe said, and reached out a hand. Doc swung with his right fist, which Joe ducked, but a quick left caught Joe in the jaw, sending him backward into a nearby table. He kept his balance, but lost his black hat.

"Atta boy, Doc! Give it to 'im!" One of the cowboys led a cheer from the crowd.

Sullivan tried another left but Joe dodged it and planted a firm fist in his stomach. Sullivan bent over, gasping for air. When Joe tried to take hold of his shoulders, he swung again, sending a glancing blow across Joe's cheek and nose. Blood ran down into Joe's moustache and onto his lips. Another cheer erupted from the crowd.

"You all cut that out or git!" Jarvis yelled and pointed at them with an index finger.

Joe buried his fist, more firmly this time, in Sullivan's stomach, which caused him to choke as he bent over. Joe picked up his hat and replaced it on his head. He grabbed Sullivan by the back of his vest but Sullivan stumbled backward away from Joe, easily slipping off the vest and regaining his unsteady stance. Jarvis glared at the onlookers, which kept them quiet this time.

"I don't want to hurt you, Doc, but this is getting irksome. Let's go," Joe said firmly.

Sullivan grinned and swung again. Joe got out of the way but Sullivan's fist hit Joe in the left shoulder where one of the gunshot wounds had been. He tried not to react to the pain that shot through his shoulder like a lightning bolt, and drove his fist into Sullivan's stomach again, dropping the doctor to the floor.

The crowd reacted with a, "Boo! Boo!" and Jarvis flashed them an angry glance. They fell silent.

Joe helped the gasping Sullivan to his feet. "Budd, if you can spare one of your hands, we should get Doc Finch down here from Gracie Flats."

Jarvis turned to the crowd, which was partly comprised of cowhands from his 77 Ranch. "Marvin, you were the loudest, you go get Finch, right now!" The hand groaned softly, pulled on his hat, and went out through the front door.

CHAPTER EIGHT

Joe sat at his desk reading a telegram that Eli Miller had delivered. The reply from U.S. Marshal Bill Daily indicated that he would be traveling through the area soon and would escort Lucy to Omaha. St. Luke's had a bed for her. For once in a long while, Joe felt that he had accomplished something. Being able to actually help Lucy elevated his mood.

Adam stepped into the marshal's office and started to offer Joe a greeting until he noticed Doc Sullivan passed out inside the flat iron jail cage.

"Gawd, Marshal, you didn't really arrest Doc this time, did ya?" Adam had finished his work at Siegler's and stepped into the marshal's office where he had a cot set up behind the cage. Joe employed him as a part-time, special deputy, mainly to take care of the jail. Other than that, he worked for Byron Siegler. Adam's being seriously wounded by Canfield's deputy was still fresh in Joe's mind, and he'd decided that jail work was enough risk for the twenty-six-year-old.

"I should," Joe said flatly. "I've sent for Doc Finch to help get him dried out and on glory's path. There's no way he can tend to folks in this shape. Lucky no one has called on him for a spell."

"There has been a few who wished for his help, but they went to Gracie Flats instead of seeing him," Adam said. He opened the lid on a keg of water and ladled out a tin cup full. He took a seat in an extra chair in front of Joe's desk and pulled out his book.

Joe wiped down his new '76 Winchester rifle, presented to him by the town board. They'd made a public presentation to him on a temporary bandstand that was erected at the intersection of town. The presentation had been part of the tenth anniversary of statehood celebration on March first. Siegler displayed the new model rifle in his store and it was much admired by the local men. Pricey for most, at $14.25, the town board felt that it would be a fitting way to show their appreciation for the work Joe had done in the short time he'd been city marshal. Besides being severely wounded by Lute Kinney, Joe had arrested Ace Todd and Dan Loman for dealing in stolen beeves at Jarvis's meat market. He suspected that Sheriff Wick Canfield was involved with stolen livestock, and probably a killer to boot. He hadn't yet been able to prove anything against the sheriff due to a lack of "surviving" witnesses.

Adam looked up from his book and watched Joe. "It surely is a beauty, ain't it?" he said quietly.

"Surely is," Joe said.

"Statehood day was special this year, you gettin' that rifle and all, but that was the shortest speech I ever did hear!"

Joe looked up at Adam, who grinned back. "Well, how many speeches have you heard?" Joe wasn't much for making public addresses and couldn't recall the few words he'd stumbled over when accepting the rifle. He slid by the uncomfortable memory by picking up some .45-75 cartridges and began reloading the rifle.

"Listen to this one," Adam said. "What is the difference between a watchmaker and a jailor?" Joe shrugged. "The one sells watches, and the other watches cells!"

Adam laughed and Joe smiled and gave a nod. Many times he'd considered burning that book of conundrums that Adam read from incessantly. The first time Joe considered destroying it was while he was recuperating at Doc Sullivan's. Adam had read to him *every day.*

"Figured you'd read that book through by now," Joe said.

"Oh, I have. It's so good I'm givin' it a second go-round!"

Before Joe could reply, a wagon pulled up in front of the office. The driver jumped down and tied up. As he stepped into the office he introduced himself.

"Marshal? I'm Tye Edson. I found one of my hands killed on my range about a half day's ride northwest of here." He nodded to the wagon. His dark brown pants showed dust and sweat soaked upward into the crown of his wide-brimmed tan hat.

Joe and Adam followed Edson out of the office and stepped off the boardwalk. Edson pulled back a blanket and showed them the body of a young man slightly younger than Adam. His left arm was covered in blood and laid at a strange angle. Another large bloodstain covered his white shirt and cloth vest.

Edson's eyes were wet and he wiped them on a sleeve. "Besides the arm, he was shot in the back."

Joe pulled the blanket back over the young man after looking at him. "What's his name?"

"Billy . . . Billy Parker," Edson said. He looked at the ground and then back up to Joe. The muscles in his face tightened, maybe to fight back more tears. "He was only twenty-two years old. My Trudy is going to be real sad."

"Come on inside, Mr. Edson. Adam here can take the boy down to the undertaker."

Edson nodded and stepped onto the boardwalk. "Thank you," he said to Adam.

Once inside, Joe gave Edson a cup of water and sat down behind his desk. "Trudy your wife, Mr. Edson?" Joe said.

Edson glanced at Doc snoring inside the cell. The man slowly shook his head and drank down the water. "No, my daughter. Billy asked for her hand, but I told him not until he could take

47

care of her proper."

"How did you happen onto him?" Joe said.

"His horse came running into the barn pulling a calf almost drug to death. Found blood on Billy's saddle. We backtracked easy enough."

"Know who might have done it?" Joe asked.

"The calf belongs to my neighbor, Abe Trumble. Recently branded. Musta strayed off. Billy was most probably bringing him back," Edson said.

"You saying this Trumble may have done it?"

"No. No, not at all. Abe and I are good friends. That's what I'm trying to say, I guess. I don't have no damned idea who would do such a contemptible thing like this. Billy had no enemies I'm aware of," Edson said. "He seemed to get on with everybody. He would have been good for my Trudy." Edson slumped in the chair across from Joe's desk. "Fact is, I can't think of a single soul I'd rather see her with," he said to the floor.

"I'll sure keep my ears open here, but you should report this to . . ." Joe stopped cold as his thoughts gathered.

"To who?" Edson asked.

Joe looked at Edson and said, "Sheriff . . . Canfield. Up at Gracie Flats." Joe's stomach turned and he wondered how he could send this good man to Canfield to ask for help.

"You're a lawman. I was hopin' maybe *you* would look into it," Edson said. The words came like molasses from a jar. "Why I came . . . here."

"You know I'll do whatever I can here in town, but," Joe hesitated again, "that's the sheriff's territory out there."

Edson looked at Joe with disappointment lining his face. "Don't like to speak ill of nobody, but there's some who wonder about Mr. Canfield."

Joe sighed. "I understand what you're saying. But . . . he is the sheriff."

"And it's not like he doesn't know we have a stealin' problem around here, especially after our last meetin'," Edson said. "Don't seem to care much."

"You met with Canfield then?"

"The new cattlemen's association did. We organized first of the year so we could fight the thievin' that's nearly breakin' us. There's only eight of us, but we asked Canfield to attend our first regular meetin'," Edson said, and sat the empty cup on the small table. "Several of them boys told the sheriff that if he didn't tend to the rustling problem, they'd conduct a campaign against formally electin' him this year."

Joe wondered how Canfield took that, as he was involved with stealing himself, or at least he had been. "What'd he have to say to that?" Joe asked.

"His face got kinda red, thought he might pop. We also told him that if he didn't do something about it, we'd hire a man for that purpose. He finally gave us the line of bullshit that we're used to from him. 'I'll do everything I can, but with only one deputy' . . ." Edson said, imitating Canfield.

"So he's got a new deputy? Wasn't aware of that," Joe said. He wondered if he'd have to kill this one, too. "Not trying to tell you your business, Mr. Edson, but some of the men that hire out as range detectives can be the unrepentant type."

"We wouldn't be lookin' for the preachin' type."

CHAPTER NINE

The next morning at dawn, Joe rolled over, kissed Sarah on the forehead, and slipped out of her bed so he didn't wake her. As he got dressed he glanced up to the tintype on the wall of Sarah and her husband, the one taken at St. Louis. He buckled on his gun belt and stared at George Welby's face. He wondered how a man could run out on his wife, especially one like Sarah.

Joe planned to look over Billy Parker's body before Edson took him home. He wanted nothing more than to find Parker's killer but he was limited by jurisdiction.

When he arrived on the main street, he stopped and looked over Sarah's new business. A faint golden hue saturated the town as sunrise neared, and another steamy August day set in. The business was located at the west end of the street before it turned and meandered south to Sarah's house and the church. Painted on the front of the building was LAUNDRY & BATH, in letters that curved upward and downward as they ran across the front. A sign painter from Loup City had been employed for that purpose.

Joe had devised the idea for the business, not only because such services were of value to the town, but it allowed Sarah to improve the quality of her life. Her husband, George, the first town marshal, had abandoned her and the town almost two years before Joe arrived. Refusing help from anyone, she'd had little choice but to take up the life of a prostitute, and work for John "Smiley" Wilkie.

Joe had been able to loan Sarah the money to start her business from the $750 reward he'd received from the Baxter Springs, Kansas, Businessman's Association for killing Lute Kinney. Kinney had been wanted for the murder of a family outside Baxter Springs. He'd come to Taylorsville to kill Joe on a vendetta mission.

After a few moments of admiring the building, Joe proceeded across the street to his office. He was glad to find Adam up and making coffee.

"Mornin', Marshal," Adam whispered. "Doc Finch was up half the night with . . . Doc . . . and he's still sleepin'." Doctor Walter Finch had arrived late in Taylorsville from Gracie Flats. The resolute physician had ordered Joe and Adam to help hold Sullivan down while he poured a horrible smelling concoction down his throat. The stench soon drove Joe and Adam outside. Joe had offered his cot to the visiting doctor and Sullivan remained in the jail cage, per Joe's orders.

"How's Doc doin'?" Joe asked quietly. He looked at Sullivan, who was asleep on the cell floor, the slop bucket near his head.

"He'd drink down some of that foul potion Doc Finch gave him, and back up it would come!" Adam said, slowly shaking his head. "Doc kept the last two down and then laid there and moaned. That stuff won't kill him, will it?"

"Guess we'll have to trust Finch on that, Adam," Joe said, as he splashed water from the keg on his face. "Goin' to McNab's to look over that boy's body."

"I'll be here 'til Pastor Evans comes in."

Joe noted that this was the second time he had stepped into Iain McNab's back room to view a body. The first time had been to check the body of Robert Carlson, whom he believed to have been one of Sheriff Canfield's stock thieves.

Billy Parker was laid out on the same heavily stained wooden table. McNab, the local undertaker, stood beside Joe as he inspected the body. Joe appreciated the dignity with which Mc-Nab treated the deceased under his care. The short man with flaming red hair and beard had a Scottish accent, evident on those rare occasions that he spoke. This was one of those occasions.

"What kind of animal would do this to a boy do ya 'spose?"

"Wish I knew, Iain," Joe said. He looked over the large, ugly hole surrounded by jagged tears, almost in a star shape, near the middle of the boy's chest. The notable damage told Joe it was indeed where the bullet had exited. He'd seen wounds like this at Shiloh. Large caliber bullets did extensive damage, no matter where they hit a person. Joe pushed the body gently over on the left side and saw a large but neat hole in the boy's back.

"Without doubt a big one," McNab observed solemnly.

"Yep, but wish I could narrow that down a bit," Joe said.

"If you be done, I'll get the boy ready then. Mr. Edson will be a buryin' him on his ranch."

Joe nodded.

Joe was the last to join the coffee club at the North Star.

"Did you hear about Billy Parker?" Joe said.

"Little Billy, works for Edson about ten miles north of my ranch?" Jarvis asked.

Joe nodded and took a sip of coffee.

"Sure, I know 'im. Damn good kid. What about 'im?"

"Somebody killed him out on Edson's range. Large caliber rifle, from a distance. In the back," Joe said.

Jarvis stared at Joe unbelievingly. "No, no, there must be some mistake," he said and looked at the table top and then back to Joe. "Why Billy?" He shook his head. "Know who done it?"

Joe shook his head. "No idea. Edson said the boy was bringing a calf home that belonged to Abe Trumble when it happened. Have any suspicions that might help?"

"Hell no! And it wasn't my range riders, either! They know Billy."

Joe nodded. He sat his cup on the bar and glanced at the two pistols in the glass case. "See you gentlemen later."

CHAPTER TEN

"That's such a shame, poor Billy. He and Trudy would have made such a sweet couple," Sarah said. She sipped from the porcelain cup and gently shook her head. "No idea at all who did it?" Sarah no longer got disdainful stares from others in the hotel now that she operated a *legitimate* business.

"Wish I did," Joe said, and sliced through a thick piece of ham. Billy Parker had been killed five days ago, the same day that Joe locked up Doc Sullivan to dry him out. Despite increasing pressure from Pastor Evans, Byron, and even Sarah, Joe refused to release Sullivan just yet. He expected Judge Worden to weigh in anytime.

The hotel dining room was full at the supper hour. They were so busy that Harold Martin helped deliver food to some of the tables. Joe watched Martin and wondered, with the way his hands shook, how he didn't spill anything. He wished Martin hadn't been at the North Star that fateful day. Martin found it difficult to speak to Joe since the shooting. It wasn't dislike, but he certainly felt differently about Joe

"Do you think Sheriff Canfield will do anything about it?" Sarah asked.

"He don't exactly have a shining record in that regard."

"Well, someone has to do something!" Sarah said, a little too loudly. A few of the other customers looked their way. Her statement was branded into Joe's mind.

They both noticed Adam making his way to their table. He

pulled off his hat and nodded, "Ma'am. Joe, there's a feller wantin' to see you at the office. Me and Christmas seen him walking into town from the east. I tol' him there's a freight wagon comes on Fridays that he coulda hitched a ride on. He didn't seem too eager at my idea."

"Say who he is?" Joe asked, chewing a piece of ham. He picked up a napkin and wiped his mouth.

"No, sir. Jus' said 'git the marshal, right now!' " Adam said.

"Tell him we're about finished here. Be there shortly."

After Adam left, Sarah looked at Joe. "Think that man walked all the way from Willow Springs?"

"Wouldn't know why he would," Joe said as they both stood. Joe escorted Sarah to her laundry business and then headed back across the street to his office.

When Joe stepped inside, the man sitting at his desk was silent. Adam was leaning with arms crossed against the old log cell that was now Joe's sleeping room, obviously not too happy with the stranger. Joe hung his suit coat and hat on a peg, stepped next to his chair, and waited for the stranger to abandon it.

"I hope I didn't *inconvenience* you, Marshal," the man said in a corrosive tone. When Joe didn't reply, the man sighed, stood up, and moved to the chair in front of Joe's desk.

"No inconvenience at all, Mr. . . . ?" Joe said.

"Smith," the man said without emotion. "I insist on a meeting with you *privately*, if you don't mind?" The man wore a new, tailored, black suit with a black short-brimmed hat, which would have been eye-catching had it not been covered with dust. A silver watch chain made an arc against the dark gray vest. The shine was barely evident on his new lace-up shoes.

"You may speak in Adam's presence."

The stranger looked exasperated. He patted his brow with a handkerchief and said, "And the *prisoner*? . . . I require privacy."

"Oh, never mind the prisoner. His mind comes and goes," Joe said with a wry grin. Adam held back a smile. Doc Sullivan sat on the bottom bunk of the cell and shot Joe a withering glance.

"Sir, in the case that you might be a lawyer, I have been held, without charges, for a week. I'm the town's only physician and I demand to be let out of this infernal cage!" Sullivan said.

After a moment, the stranger returned his gaze to Joe.

"See?" Joe said.

"I've not the time for this," he said, and reached into a vest pocket. He thrust a calling card at Joe that was embossed with an eagle. It read, "UNITED STATES DEPARTMENT OF JUSTICE—HARPER L. LANGSTON—SPECIAL AGENT."

"What's a '*special* . . . agent'?" Joe asked.

"I am directed by the U.S. Attorney for Nebraska under the authority of the Attorney General of the United States. I require your cooperation with information and then assistance in being re-provisioned!" Langston said.

"You *are* a lawyer then?" Sullivan interjected hopefully.

"I have been, but that's beside the point here," Langston said, without offering Sullivan the benefit of another glance.

"If I might ask . . . what happened to your provisions? Adam here saw you *walking* into town," Joe said.

Langston's sweaty face reddened. "During a stop at a farm east of here, a Mr. Raymond's place I believe, my horse and gear were stolen. That included a new .45-90 Sharps hunting rifle!"

Joe held back a smile, then said, "That's almost six miles to Ike Raymond's place; you walked all that way in this heat?" Langston didn't respond. "Well, I'm sure between the general store and Jarvis's livery, you can get outfitted again. So, what are you doing out here, anyway?"

Langston looked at Adam and then at Sullivan, who was

watching intently through a square hole of the cage straps. "This *is* a confidential matter, Marshal."

Joe's blank stare annoyed him.

He stammered a bit, but continued, "I have been assigned by the Justice Department to secretly ascertain the identities of those responsible for stealing horses from the reservation Indians, and for the illegal sale of whiskey. I am to provide the department with proper evidence for prosecutorial proceedings in U.S. court. We feel these same parties are stealing from whites in this region as well."

Joe rubbed his chin. "Let me see if I gather this all up. The government sent you out here to catch rustlers, but you walked into town, 'cuz your horse was stolen?" Adam closed his eyes and covered his mouth to stifle an outburst of laughter.

Langston sighed. "Enjoy the moment if you must, Marshal. But do know this: I am no fool. I was a detective with the New York police. I know my way around."

"No offense meant, Mr. Langston, but I guess you can see how it all looks." Joe feigned a smile. "And, if you don't mind me sayin', you'd blend in 'round here like a lightning bolt on a dark night."

"Thank you . . . for that," Langston said, feigning appreciation. "Before I ask you to direct me to a good hotel, I'm desirous to gather any names of suspected horse thieves in this area, and where they may be found, if known."

"Had trouble with some of them last winter, but they're dead, most of 'em, anyway. Course, there's others out there we don't know," Joe said. "Heard of a fella named Jim Riley, supposed to be ramroddin' the stealin' of Indian ponies. That's all rumor, though."

"Did you kill those who are dead, Marshal?" Langston asked.

"Only one. Had some help with the others." Langston studied

Joe's face. "Afraid I don't have any other names for you at this juncture."

Langston nodded, "I'll ride to Gracie Flats tomorrow to visit with the sheriff, Callfield, is it?"

"Canfield, Wick Canfield," Joe said. "Uh, about Canfield, there's some who feel he's involved with rustlin' himself, not firsthand mind you, but has men workin' for him. No proof. But, not so sure it's a good idea to talk to him about such matters. He could be considered a dangerous man."

"And *he's* the duly elected county sheriff?" Langston said with disgust.

"The county hasn't been officially set down as of yet. Canfield was appointed until that happens and a regular election is held," Joe said. "Comin' up as a matter of fact."

"Very well. I trust that you'll keep my identity to yourselves," Langston said, standing up. "Now, if you'll direct me to the hotel, a bath, and a meal, in that order."

"Adam will be happy to direct you," Joe said, standing. He nodded at Langston, who turned and stared at Sullivan. "He's not really a physician . . . is he?"

Joe frowned at him, "What do you think?"

Langston looked Sullivan up and down through the iron jail straps, shook his head, and walked out, with Adam following.

"That's very humorous, Marshal Mundy," Sullivan said dryly. "I shall most likely succumb to laughter."

CHAPTER ELEVEN

Byron Siegler relieved himself in the chamber pot and considered a return to bed. Footsteps pounding up the stairs on the rear of the building ended his thoughts on the matter. Siegler didn't have time to glance at Fern to see if she had been awakened by the sound because the frantic pounding on his door had surely got the job done. He grabbed his wife's Remington derringer from a knickknack shelf where Fern kept it and approached the door.

"Who is it at this hour?" Siegler demanded.

"It's me, John Wilkie, let me in. Please let me in." The pounding resumed and stopped. "He'll kill me for God's sake!"

Siegler unlocked the door and Wilkie knocked him aside and ran to the front windows that overlooked the main street. The early light was only beginning to filter into the living area. Wilkie crouched on the floor and pulled the curtain aside. Siegler saw the revolver in his hand.

"You have to protect me! You have to protect me from him!" Wilkie was screaming as he panted.

Siegler's wife peeked out of the bedroom, the only separated room in their residence above the store. Siegler waved her back inside.

"John, slow down and stop your yelling. Tell me what's happening. Who's after you?"

"It's the whore! It's the whore! He'll kill me! You have to protect me!" Wilkie's scream-whine and a pair of sobs turned

Siegler's stomach. He saw that Wilke's eyes were wet and thought he'd been crying.

Before Siegler could ask again, Wilkie screamed, "You *have* to protect me. You have a duty! You're the board!" He shot another quick glance over the sill, turned, and planted his back against the wall next to the window trying to catch his breath.

Siegler grabbed a whiskey bottle and sat a chair near Wilkie. "You're safe now John, calm down." He handed over the bottle and Wilkie took a long draw. Siegler then grabbed the bottle away before the man drained it. The drink calmed Wilkie very little. "Take a big breath, then tell me what's happened, John," Siegler said in the most calm tone that he could manage.

Wilkie looked up at Siegler. His lips quivered and a tear, or sweat, Siegler wasn't sure which, ran down his cheek. "It's no matter. You won't believe me. Mundy won't believe me just long enough to kill me." He sobbed. "I didn't do it!"

Siegler waited a moment until he calmed down enough to talk to. "John, we aren't getting anywhere because you haven't told me anything. Why do you think Marshal Mundy will kill you?"

Wilkie looked up again, "It's the whore."

"You mean Lucy? Where is she, John?"

"Palace," Wilke sobbed and drew his knees up to his face. He began rocking himself.

"John, give me the pistol for now."

Wilkie spun the muzzle toward Siegler but didn't cock it. "I have to protect myself if you won't."

"All right. Let's go to the Palace and see what this is all about," Siegler said. The response was immediate.

"You go. I'm staying here. You swear to protect me!"

"No one will harm you, I guarantee it. But I must know what's happened. You can't stay here. I'll take you over to Judge Worden and you can stay there until I see what this is all about."

Siegler said in a gentle tone. "I must have the pistol first, John, or I can't help you. No one will harm you if you're unarmed."

Wilkie was still for several minutes while Siegler waited. He sighed, hesitated, and handed over the gun. Before leaving, Siegler gave Fern the derringer and told her to lock the door after they left.

In the alley, Siegler and Wilkie had only to walk east behind the hotel and cross the side street to reach the judge's front door. While Siegler knocked, Wilkie kept his eyes on the main street. Worden came to the door wearing his old Prince Albert coat over a nightshirt.

"What in God's name is so urgent, so early?" Wilkie pushed by him and hid behind the bench.

"I'm sorry, Judge, but something has happened at the Palace and John is scared that Joe will kill him. Something to do with Lucy. I'm going to go check," he said, and whispered, "I'll get Joe first." Worden nodded.

Once out of sight of Worden's office, Siegler slid through a narrow gap between the empty building on the corner and the Palace saloon and trotted up to the rear door of the marshal's office. When identified, Joe let him inside.

"Forget where the front door is, Byron?" Joe frowned.

"John Wilkie came barging into our home a bit ago, scared like Satan himself was at his heels. He's asked me to protect him from you, but I don't know why. All he will say is 'it's the whore.' Pardon my use of that foul word." Siegler took a breath and continued. "I took him to Judge Worden and said I'd take a look. He doesn't know I came straight here."

"Well, this is a puzzlement. I guess we start by checking on Lucy." Joe strapped on his guns and the two went out the front door. The sun appeared bright, reporting that it would provide another steamy day in Taylorsville.

When they reached the front door of the Palace, Joe entered

first. He didn't immediately see Lucy, but spotted her as he went for the stairs. Siegler was close behind.

A cloth cord was around her neck, poorly, but effectively, tied to a post on the stairs. Lucy's bare feet were no more than an inch off the floor. Her head tilted slightly to the right, eyes half open. Joe didn't hear Siegler's, "Oh . . . my . . . God."

"Untie it!" Joe ordered. Lucy's torso lolled over as Joe wrapped his arms around her and lifted. Siegler climbed a few steps and released the clumsy knot.

Joe eased her to the floor. He loosened the cord and knelt to listen for breath. He knew there wouldn't be any. Her pasty face assured him of that. Sitting back on his heels, Joe studied her. She was wearing the usual old dirty, buttonless dress with one distinct difference. She had apparently used a needle and thread to stitch short sections, which closed the dress all the way to the neck. The stitching was crooked and had gaps, but overall it was effective. Her hair was neatly piled into a bun and pinned, her face clean. She had done what she could to look her best on the last day of her life.

Although Joe tried his best to blame "Smiley" Wilkie, he could see that Lucy had prepared herself, and hung herself. Neither man talked. Neither asked, "oh why did she do it?" Both knew of her miserable existence at the Palace. Joe surveyed the scene, looking for a chair or something that she had stepped off of. There wasn't anything close by.

"Wait a minute! What did she stand on?" Joe said. Siegler had also been looking over the area alongside the stairs.

"Joe, Wilkie didn't do this. You see how she made herself up. As nice as she was at little Katy Sanderson's funeral last winter," Siegler said. "And why would he kill her? She was a source of income for him."

The men were quiet again.

"How about this?" Siegler said. He stepped up to the side of the banister as if measuring his height, and then walked around and climbed the stairs. He went through the motions of tying the cord to the post, then around his neck. He then raised a leg over the rail and eased himself down to the floor.

Sure. Why hadn't I thought of that? Of course Byron is right. But Joe still wanted to arrest Wilkie. *But it would be a waste of time.*

"I'll go for Iain," Siegler said. "Will you wait here?"

Joe nodded. "Smiley with the judge?"

"Yes, but we'll talk to him after I'm back," Siegler said and walked out.

Joe enjoyed the early morning hours, when he hadn't been walking the town late. To watch the sun's brilliance gradually infiltrate the blackness of the office was something special to see. But this morning was different. He sat in a chair and stared at Lucy's lifeless body while he waited for Siegler to bring back the undertaker. *Guess I didn't save you after all, Lucy. Why couldn't you wait for Omaha, see how that went?* Joe was sure that she would have found it a much better life than Taylorsville. "I'll see that you have a nice funeral, Lucy," Joe said out loud.

After Iain McNab took Lucy's body, Joe and Siegler walked down to Judge Worden's office. When they entered, only the judge was present. "Where's Wilkie?" Joe asked.

"One moment, please," Worden said. He went into the back room, and after several moments, returned with the saloon man. Wilkie stayed mostly behind the judge until he was pushed into a chair. The judge sat down at his work table and watched.

Joe's stare was enough to make Wilkie shake. "Tell me everything that happened with Lucy," Joe said, with nearly gritted teeth. "And don't leave out one damned thing."

Wilkie glanced at Judge Worden and then at Siegler. "Go ahead, John, tell Joe what happened," Siegler said.

It took all of a minute before his quivering lips made a noise.

Wilkie turned again to Worden, "I didn't do nothin' to her . . . you gotta believe me. I . . . found her like that."

"Tell us every detail from when you first awoke this morning, Mr. Wilkie," Worden said.

"I woke up and had to piss, but my pot was full. Stupid bitch hadn't . . ." he caught himself and whipped his arms up to fend off an imaginary attack. "I mean, I mean, Miz Lucy hadn't emptied it, so I went downstairs to use the outhouse. That, that's when I found her. She was hangin' off the side of the stairs. I swear to God! I didn't do it! I swear!" he started to wail as if defending himself from a death sentence.

"Did you come to me as soon as you found her, John?" Siegler asked.

"I did! I did! Right then, and . . ."

Joe cut him off. "Did you try to get her down? Was she still breathing?"

Wilkie looked at Worden, "I didn't, she was already dead. I know that!" He was shaking.

"Can you add anything?" Worden looked toward Joe and Siegler.

Siegler reported, "Judge, Lucy had made herself up nicely, washed her face, pinned up her hair, and sewed her dress closed, all the way up to her neck. It appeared that she wanted to look presentable at her funeral."

"Do you concur, Marshal?" Worden asked.

Joe's narrow eyes met Wilkie's until the barkeep looked to the floor.

"Your Honor, she wouldn't have done this if *he* hadn't treated her like he did."

"That very well may be, Marshal, but I asked if you agreed with Mr. Siegler's observations?" Worden said.

"Yes . . . I do." Joe felt each word drag across his teeth like a chain.

"Very well, we'll have a coroner's inquest at ten o'clock, I want you three back here at that time. I'll assemble a jury and we'll make it quick."

Though it was evening, the temperature hadn't budged from its daytime high. To make matters worse, the air was so thick, it seemed one could moisten his mouth only by opening it. The front and rear doors of the marshal's office were standing open. Joe and Adam sat in chairs on the boardwalk that were tipped back against the front of the building.

Joe reviewed the day, a very bad day. He had walked from the judge's office straight to Sarah's house to tell her about Lucy. Sarah had been a friend to Lucy since they both worked at the Palace. Sarah didn't believe it at first, and searched Joe's eyes for the truth. Then she broke down. Joe usually took pleasure in holding her in his arms, but this time she cried.

The coroner's inquest was brief, with the jury finding that Lucy had taken her own life. That made it official on the legal papers. All tidied up. Except for the funeral.

When Joe returned to the office, he opened the cell door to tell Doc Sullivan about Lucy's suicide. Doc had eased himself onto the lower bunk and, head in hands, cried for several minutes.

Joe eyed flickers of light in the southwestern sky while Adam read from his book of conundrums. The outside lamps of nearly every business, including the marshal's office, were lit to compensate for the premature evening darkness.

"What is the height of folly?" Adam read out loud. "Spending your last dollar on a purse!" Adam laughed and Joe tried to ignore him.

When Joe turned his head from the sky and looked east, he noticed Judge Worden and Pastor Evans cross the intersection and climb onto the boardwalk, coming their way. The judge walked with a shiny black cane.

"Evenin' Judge . . . Christmas," Joe said. He had been expecting a visit from Worden as more and more folks were clamoring for Doc Sullivan's release. He'd managed to hold Sullivan eight days so far, to dry out. Doc Finch had only stayed three days, but told Joe he was hopeful. Joe and Adam had been tasked with giving Sullivan four more doses of the foul-smelling potion. Each time, they had held him down, pinched his nose, and poured the medicine down his throat. Adam claimed that he learned some cussing words he'd never heard before, thanks to Sullivan.

"Good evening, Marshal. Looks like we have storms brewing," Worden said. He was not looking at the sky where Joe watched the lightning.

"I 'spose you mean here in town," Joe said.

"I have been trying to contain them as long as possible, because I knew that your dubious endeavor was meant only to help the good doctor. But, I'm afraid the time has come to release him."

"Bless you, Joe, for what you've done for Doctor Sullivan," Evans said. "We cannot stand to see the poor man caged like an animal any longer. I've read to him from the scriptures every day, and I believe that he's allowed the Lord to take the reins of his burden." Evans clasped his hands and looked skyward. "But if we hope for what we do not see, we wait for it with patience."

"And," Worden said, "this *is* a margin outside of the law."

"Not sure it's been long enough to take," Joe said, his gaze on the southwest.

"Only the Lord can help now, if Doctor Sullivan will allow Him. It's out of our hands, Joe," Evans said.

Joe nodded and slowly tipped the chair forward. He tugged at a pant leg until a brass ring appeared, protruding from the top of his tall boot. From the ring dangled the cell key. The three men walked into the office and Joe unlocked the cage door. Sullivan, who'd heard the conversation, was standing.

"Bath's on me, Doc. Sarah's still over there," Joe said. Sullivan ignored Joe.

"Thank you, Judge, Pastor," Sullivan said as he walked out.

"I'm going to finish my stroll now. Pastor Evans, would you care to join me?" Worden said.

"Thank you, no," Evans said. "I'd like to visit with Joe for a moment." Worden tipped his hat and left the marshal's office. As they stood in silence they could hear the judge's footsteps punctuated by the tap of the cane.

Joe walked to the open front door and leaned against the jam. He glanced at Worden as he walked west down the boardwalk, then watched Doc Sullivan who walked slowly down the middle of the street, seeming unsure of his destination and then he stopped. Sullivan turned and looked at Siegler's store.

"Joe, I hope you hold no ill will with my conferring with Judge Worden on Doc Sullivan's behalf," Evans said.

Joe's eyes were fixed on Sullivan. "No. No, course not, Christmas."

"We only . . ." Evans started to speak as Joe walked out.

Joe saw Sullivan stop in the street for a moment before going into Siegler's store. Joe sauntered into the store and into the middle of an argument between Sullivan and Earl, Siegler's clerk.

"There a problem?" Joe said cautiously.

Earl stuttered, "Doc wants to make a purchase, Marshal, but he don't have any money. Mr. Siegler's the only one who can approve credit."

"Joe, this is *none* of your concern," Sullivan said.

"What was he wanting? I'll cover it," Joe said.

Earl meekly held up a new bottle of whiskey, his eyes darting between Joe and Sullivan.

Byron Siegler appeared from the back room. "What's going on, Earl, I heard loud voices?"

"I was starting to close up when Doc came in to buy a bottle, but didn't have any money," Earl said.

Before Siegler could reply, Sullivan lunged at Joe. His first swing missed, but he followed up with two more, both taking effect. The two men scuffled through the open doors and into the street. Sullivan appeared to be possessed by the devil himself. On top of Joe, he pounded at his face. A hard punch to the kidney dislodged the doctor so Joe could stand up. With one eye already swelling and blood running from a small gash in the left eyebrow, Joe went at Doc but tried to keep his punches to the stomach. He didn't want to hurt the man, but for every two hits Joe would land, Doc came back like a paddle wheeler with three or four. With a proper boxer's stance, Doc kept smashing his fists into Joe, one to each side of the face and then to the stomach. One to the midsection had Joe gasping for air. He knew his physical condition wasn't up to snuff yet and this proved it. Out of self-preservation, Joe delivered a hard right, which Sullivan ducked with ease, but the doctor didn't see the left coming. With a similar punch from Joe to the midsection, Doc gasped for air as he went to his knees.

The combatants didn't notice that a crowd had formed. No one was cheering either party. Only mumbled questions could be heard amid the rumbles of thunder. Brief lightning flashes illuminated the street and buildings around them. While Sullivan caught his breath, Joe used the chance to unbuckle his gun belt and hand it to Siegler, who was watching open-mouthed.

Doc stumbled, but had regained his boxing stance when Joe sent a fist into his chin. Doc spun and took a couple of steps backward, but kept his balance and weighed into Joe with a blur of thrashing fists. Joe planted another in the kidney, which made Doc buckle slightly, and continued with a punch to the nose, one to the chin, and one to the stomach. Doc sucked at the air when Joe hit him again. He remained standing and tried to throw punches, but they were ineffective.

"Call it quits, Doc, this is enough," Joe said in heaving breaths.

Still gasping for air, Doc threw a wild swing and fell against Joe. Both landed in front of the boardwalk in front of Siegler's store. Sitting up, Doc held onto Joe with his head against Joe's chest, going through the motions of punching him. Joe realized that Doc's gasps had turned into mournful sobbing. He looked at the crowd. Their faces expressed individual feelings: Sarah's, sadness; Siegler's, astonishment; Adam's, disbelief; and Pastor Evan's, understanding. The rain started to fall, gently at first, and then in torrents. Joe let Doc cry as they were soaked by the rain.

CHAPTER TWELVE

A night with Sarah was like a miracle elixir, Joe thought. After Pastor Evans took Doc home in the rain, she gave Joe a *private* after-hours bath. Sarah cleaned up the cuts on Joe's face and rubbed his sore ribs and muscles. He left her bed a short time before the sun made any serious attempt at lighting the day, the day of Lucy Sauter's funeral.

At about ten o'clock that morning, Iain McNab's wagon and team, adorned in black ribbon, started rolling west down the main street. In the back was a plain pine box with a black wreath, also made of ribbon. Joe and Adam stepped off the boardwalk in front of the Texan to join Pastor Evans, Doc Sullivan, the town board members, and Sarah. Joe was proud to pay for Lucy's funeral, but would rather have paid for her trip to Omaha.

The town had closed and citizens of all ages had followed the procession for little Katy Sanderson's funeral the past winter. Nothing of the kind happened for Lucy, a mere saloon prostitute.

As the small procession passed the main intersection of town, no one else had joined in. Joe ordered Iain to stop and glanced around. "Where are all of you God-fearin' people? We're burying one of our own here today!" He yelled at the empty streets. "Afraid your neighbor will see you paying last respects to a human being?"

Sarah walked back to Joe and took his arm, which he shook

off in anger.

"Joe, never mind them. Come on . . . for Lucy."

He slapped his hat against the side of his leg and with gritted teeth rejoined Sarah and the procession. "They all appear in church every Sunday, holier than thou," he said.

With the burial complete, Joe escorted Sarah to her house. When he reached the main street again, he saw a tandem-seated carriage with two men pull away from the telegrapher's office. Joe and Adam stepped onto the boardwalk in front of the marshal's office and watched the carriage continue toward them.

Joe's sour mood lightened a bit when he saw his old boss and friend. "Welcome to our little town, Major."

The man stepped up and took his extended hand. "Joe, it's been too long. This is Wayne Tripp, my office deputy."

"Adam Carr. Helps me out," Joe said as he motioned to his side.

"Adam, this here is as fine a man that lives, meet Major Bill Daily. He's the United States Marshal for Nebraska. I once worked for him."

Adam had been surveying the man, who appeared to be in his late forties, if he hadn't yet reached fifty. His eyes widened, and he vigorously shook Daily's hand. "Nice to make your acquaintance, Marshal Daily."

Joe showed the men into the office and Adam served coffee. "I'm sorry to have brought you out here for nothing, Major," Joe said

"Your friend decide against moving to the asylum?"

"In a matter of speaking. We just buried her," Joe said. "Hung herself."

"Real sorry to hear that, but it's no trouble. We had business in Broken Bow, anyway," Daily said. "Would you mind if we sent Wayne and Adam to have a beer, like to talk to you."

"Sure thing," Joe said. He flipped a silver dollar off his thumb to Adam, "Beer's on me."

After they were alone in the office, Joe poured them each a shot of whiskey.

"How have you been, Major? It's good to see you again."

"Joe, it's good to see you as well. You were one of my best deputies." Daily sipped the whiskey and sat the glass back on Joe's desk. "I'm under a lot of pressure these days. The reservations are losing horses right and left, some say by thieves in this region. Folks in Omaha are afraid the fragile peace we've managed with the Indians will end soon, and we'll be back at war with them. There's already been some warriors split off into raiding parties. Only two settlers killed so far, but that's too many."

"I heard about that. Troops from Fort Hartsuff chased them almost into Dakota," Joe said.

"I'm trying to do what I can, but two of my men up and quit. Headed for Deadwood Gulch to find the gold everyone else can't find," Daily said, and emptied his glass. "The justice department is sending a man out here to find out who's stealing . . . as if he can simply ask folks and they'll tell him." He shook his head. "They've said I'm not doing anything about it. Those people in the justice department are trying to make me out a fool."

"I met this man, a New Yorker, not long ago. Came walkin' into town. He was all loaded for bear, except someone stole his horse and all of his gear!" The two men were silent as they looked at each other until Daily broke out in heavy laughter, with Joe joining in.

Daily grew serious, downed a second shot of whiskey that Joe had poured, and said, "Joe, before you say no, hear me out. I need a man here in this area. A good man I can trust. Someone who can get a hold of things before they get out of control." With that he reached inside his coat, drew out a folded sheet of paper and a badge, and placed them on the desk in front of Joe.

Joe didn't reach for the them. He could read the six-pointed star from where he sat: DEPUTY U.S. MARSHAL was stamped on it.

"I remember the government was more interested in workin' the deputies than payin' them. Usually two months behind. One of the reasons I quit," Joe said, and sipped his whiskey.

"I'm well aware of that, Joe. And it hasn't changed much to be honest. I've already signed the commission, all you have to do is sign it, to make it official. You don't have to quit your job," Daily said. "Put them in your drawer and promise me that you'll think seriously about it and then sign it."

Joe mulled it over in his mind and realized that the added position would give him legal authority anywhere. *That would be useful right about now.* He leaned forward, picked up a pen, dabbed it into the ink bottle, and signed his name.

"Excellent! Thank you, Joe," Daily said. "Truthfully thought you'd be a harder sell than that." He then asked Joe to raise his right hand and administered the oath of office.

"To square with you, someone is shooting at cowhands here abouts. Killed a twenty-two-year-old, a good boy. And a farmer."

"I know you will find them," Daily said. "I wouldn't want to be the shooter."

Joe poured them each another drink and the two men toasted.

After Marshal Daily left for Omaha with his deputy, Joe sat and thought about what he would do about the killer.

"If Marshal Daily's hair was whiter, he'd kinda look like ol' General Lee, except of a taller variety. He was a major in the army?" Adam asked.

"No, he took over as Indian agent on the Otoe reservation during the war and the man he replaced was an army major. They gave him that same title," Joe said. "President Grant himself appointed the major as marshal of Nebraska back in '72."

"So he appointed you then?"

"I had worked a short while under Joe Hoile before the major took over," Joe said. "And, he just appointed me again."

Adam's eyes widened. "You ain't quitting the town, are you?"

"No, I'll hold both positions. Not lookin' to take over my job, are you?" Joe said with a slight grin.

"Not on your life! I'm happy helpin' out with the jail and whatnot for now."

"I'd like to keep it between us. I'll tell Byron later."

Joe told Adam that he was taking the bay out for a ride and planned to stop and visit Ike Raymond. Although Joe didn't really doubt Langston's identity, he wanted to see what Raymond had to say about the theft of Langston's horse and gear. As he walked the bay down the main street, Siegler stepped out of the store on his way to morning coffee at the North Star.

"Coming down for coffee, Joe?"

"Not today, Byron. Goin' out to visit Ike Raymond a bit," Joe said.

"Oh, would you mind taking a sack of flour to him?"

Joe agreed and rode out after tying a ten-pound bag of flour behind the saddle. He kept the bay to a walk and enjoyed the early morning air. It wouldn't be long and the heat would set in again. The ride would offer another opportunity to shoot the new Winchester. The cobbler had made a longer saddle scabbard to accommodate the longer barrel of the big rifle.

Rounding a short bluff and a stand of trees near Raymond's farm, Joe heard a powerful gunshot in the distance that echoed through the hollows. It took a little extra leaning and stretching to clear the rifle from its sheath, but Joe did so, then gently touched his spurs to the bay's sides. As Raymond's shack came into view, a second shot boomed. Joe noticed a steer on its side, legs thrashing, in Raymond's shoulder-high corn patch.

Closer to the steer, he saw a spot of blood above the shoulder. A third shot exploded the flour sack behind Joe, spooking the bay, who shied to the left, then started forward. That was unusual for the bay, Joe thought, but his horse had never seen an exploding sack of flour before. The shot seemed to come from bluffs to the northeast. He slid off the bay and led him to cover in front of the shack. The white cloud of flour settled over the bay's rump, making him look like an appaloosa.

Joe pushed through the door of the shack carrying the Winchester and a box of cartridges. No one was home. He found a small window in the back wall and peered out. He studied the bluffs, which were at least two-hundred yards, maybe more, from the shack. A puff of black powder smoke on a ridge, to the right of a bush, caused Joe to duck. The bullet slammed through the window and tore a splinter from a table behind him. Joe unfolded his pocket knife and sliced away at a gap in the wall boards to widen it. He figured it would be safer to look through than the window. The first thing he saw from his new vantage point was Ike Raymond lying facedown, about twenty feet behind the house. Joe couldn't tell if he was dead or not, but could see blood on his back. His eyes moved back to the ridge in time to see another puff of smoke, followed by the inevitable *whack!* that knocked a small chunk of wall out below the window.

Joe levered one of the big .45-75 rounds into the chamber and waited for the next shot, which came about thirty seconds later. He went to the broken window and rested the rifle on the sill. He sighted in on the spot where the shots had come from, and elevated the rear sight. The recoil of the first shot always surprised him, as it was much rougher than his old .44 rimfire carbine. Joe saw a spray of dust below the shooter's position and stepped away from the window, barely in time to miss the next bullet that tore through the wall.

A few minutes passed with no more shots. Joe decided he had to move Raymond inside. After unlatching the rear door, Joe again rested the rifle on the windowsill and fired three more rounds as fast as he could accurately sight. After the expected return shot, Joe left the rifle leaning against the wall and ran out. He grabbed Ike Raymond under the armpits at the same moment an eruption of dirt peppered his face. No sooner did he slam the door shut, than another bullet hit it almost dead center, splitting a board in half. Joe knelt and watched the farmer's bloody chest. It was motionless. He held his ear near the man's mouth, but heard nothing.

Joe reloaded the rifle and wrapped Raymond in an old blanket, hoping to protect the body somewhat until he could return. He thought about Raymond's nine-year-old son, Grant, who'd died from the influenza the past winter. Someone had said Grant was the last member of Raymond's family after his wife had died.

The shooter was possibly the same man who'd murdered Billy Parker, and Joe wanted him. With the rifle in his right hand and the reins in the left, the bay carried Joe at a run up the hills in an effort to maneuver behind the shooter. When they were close to the ridge Joe slowed the bay to a trot and scoured the area. He watched every bush and draw for over an hour, with no sign of the shooter. He did find tracks in the grass and followed them in a northeasterly direction. With the shooter on the move, he knew an ambush was possible somewhere in the hills and ravines that covered the area.

Chapter Thirteen

"Joe's been gone two days now and I'm concerned," Siegler said. The town board met at its usual place in Siegler's store on Friday morning with Gib Hadley, Adam Carr, and Sarah Welby looking on. "I sent a bag of flour with him since he was going to visit Ike Raymond on Wednesday morning. He said he'd be back before nightfall."

"It's not like him. He usually tells you what he's doing," Jarvis said, looking at Siegler.

Harold Martin sat at the small table, wringing his hands. He glanced back and forth from Jarvis to Siegler and then to Hadley.

"Adam, did he tell you why he wanted to see Ike?" Siegler asked.

"He jus' wanted to hear how—" Adam stopped, and wondered how to proceed.

"Wanted to hear what? Speak up, Adam!" Jarvis said.

"Uh, he, uh. Well, there was this, Mr. *Smith,* and he told Joe that his horse and gear was taken while he was at Ike's place. Why he had to walk into town that day. Joe wanted to talk to Mr. Raymond about it," Adam said. He carefully checked the others, hoping to keep the secret of Harper Langston's identity safe.

"He sure as hell don't think Raymond took the horse, does he?" Jarvis said.

Adam shook his head.

"Well, now that we have a telegraph, we could wire the marshal at Willow Springs and see if he's seen 'im," Siegler said. "I don't know what else to do."

"Might not be a bad idea, Byron. I'll do that after this meeting," Jarvis said. "You know anything more about this, Adam?"

"No."

"Can't you form a search party at least?" Sarah said. They all heard the desperation in her voice. "If he's not at Mr. Raymond's place, maybe he could say where Joe went from there!" Her voice got louder as she talked.

"Hell, I'll ride out there with Adam and check," Hadley said. "We'll go right now."

Before leaving Taylorsville, Adam strapped on the navy Colt that he kept in one of Joe's desk drawers. He also took the liberty of pinning on the special deputy star that Joe let him wear when his help was required. Hadley brought along his sawed-off shotgun from the North Star.

On the way to Ike Raymond's place, Adam and Gib speculated as to Joe's whereabouts. Neither had a clue, of course, but it helped to pass the time.

They saw the buzzards long before arriving at Raymond's shack. Gib looked at Adam. Turkey buzzards often circled above anything dead, anticipating their next meal. Both knew something was wrong and didn't talk anymore.

Relief washed over them like a waterfall when they saw the dead steer in the cornfield.

"Worrying for nothin', wasn't ya," Hadley said, and smirked.

"Wasn't worried a'tal, you ol' fool," Adam said. "But whose steer is it? Ike never had none, even his milk cow died last winter."

Hadley pulled his hat off, wiped a sleeve across his face, and scratched his head. He knew Adam was right. "Yeah . . ."

The pair tied up at a porch stanchion and knocked on the

door, which was ajar. Adam drew the navy Colt while Hadley pushed the door open. It squeaked eerily until it banged into a chair. They walked in slowly and saw the boots protruding from inside a rolled-up blanket.

"Oh, God. Don't let it be Joe," Hadley said softly, looking upward while he said it.

Adam's first thought was that it might be Ike Raymond, but after hearing Hadley's quick prayer, he started gulping air as his heart raced. He'd come close to losing his friend once before and didn't like considering it again. The two stood and looked down at the blanket.

"We're gonna have to uncover him," Hadley said. He glanced at Adam out of the corner of his eye. Adam stood motionless, eyes fixed on the blanket.

"Well, hell," Hadley said and leaned over. When he pulled the blanket clear and saw Ike Raymond's face, there was relief and sadness for them both. They saw the bloodstain on the man's shirt. Hadley wrapped him back up and stood.

"Wonder what happened?" Hadley said.

Adam looked around the one-room shack and first noticed the broken window. Then he saw the bullet holes in the wall and something on the floor. He walked over and found four empty cartridge cases.

"Forty-five, seventy-five," Adam read from the base of one of the cartridge cases. "Joe's rifle."

"He wouldna shot Ike," Hadley said, puzzled.

Adam pointed out the wall and broken window. "I think someone was shootin' at 'em and got Ike. Joe was shootin' back."

Hadley nodded in agreement. "We gotta take him back and tell everyone what we found here."

"I'll help ya mount Ike up behind you," Adam said.

"You're the damned deputy, he's ridin' with you!"

★ ★ ★ ★ ★

Siegler was standing in front of the Texan saloon talking with Budd Jarvis and a cowhand when they saw Adam and Gib ride up to McNab's. Siegler and Jarvis hurried to the east end of the block to meet them.

McNab helped slide Ike Raymond's body from behind Adam's saddle and they took him inside. Adam told Siegler and Jarvis what they found.

" 'Fore we left, I looked over that dead steer. Had a Circle A brand," Adam said.

"Ike didn't own a brand," Jarvis said. "What the hell was it doin' there?"

"Layin' there stinkin' up Ike's cornfield," Adam said blankly. The others stared at him.

"Anyway, we got a reply to the telegraph message. Marshal Twilliger in Willow hasn't seen Joe, either," Siegler said.

Chapter Fourteen

Gib Hadley swept dust from the boardwalk in front of the North Star saloon for the fifth time that Saturday. It was an excuse to keep an eye on the road into town. The temperature had topped one-hundred degrees during the afternoon, with enough wind to blow dirt onto and into everything. His front doors stood open, like many along the quiet main street. Most folks were taking supper; others sat quietly in the saloons drinking lukewarm beer.

Hadley stopped to take a breath and wipe his face with a cloth that he kept on him for that purpose. As he leaned on the broom and gazed east out on the road, he saw a man walking with a horse following several feet behind. As the man got close to McNab's, Hadley recognized Joe and the bay. He stepped to the edge of the boardwalk and waited for Joe to approach. He was amused to see the bay keeping pace with Joe, the reins wound around the saddle horn.

"You're a damned sight for sore eyes," Hadley said, looking over the grimy marshal. Joe stopped and looked up at Hadley. He pulled his black hat off and wiped his forehead on a filthy sleeve.

"I think you're supposed to *ride* the horse, I think that's how it's done," Hadley said. His snide comments were his way of telling Joe that he was relieved to see his friend in one piece.

"It true, there's gonna be a saloon here someday?" Joe said, and nodded at the North Star.

Hadley smiled. "Get your dirty carcass in here. I'll pour a beer down you so you can think straight."

Joe turned to the bay, who was drinking from the water trough, and snapped his fingers. He motioned over to the hitching rail in front of the saloon and the bay walked over to it. Joe left the reins on the saddle horn and the bay stood at the rail.

Hadley watched in amazement. "You ever want to sell that bag of bones, I've got five bucks layin' around here somewhere."

"Don't let him hear that, he'll start thinkin' he's worth somethin'," Joe said, and stepped onto the boardwalk.

Joe emptied the first mug of beer without stopping, so Hadley refilled it. "So you gonna tell where you been for three days?" Hadley said. "I've heard that some folks around town here was worried." He didn't look at Joe while he wiped down the bar.

Joe's lips moved into his barely noticeable smile. He'd learned that the more Gib liked a person, the harder time he'd give them. He told Gib about Ike Raymond's killing and the dead steer, and his pursuit of the shooter. "I'm not the best tracker ever lived, but managed to stay on his trail to near Willow Springs. Stopped at the mouth of Jones Canyon. Looked like the place was designed for an ambush."

"Discretionary is the best particle of valor, I always say," Hadley said.

Joe nodded and sipped at his beer. "There'll be another time."

"Yesterday, me and Adam rode out to Raymond's lookin' for you. We brung Ike back and planted him with McNab. From what you said, Adam about figgered out what happened. He's no dummy."

"No, he's not," Joe said. He dropped a couple nickels on the bar and headed for the door. "Have to get cleaned up and back to work, see you later." Gib followed him out.

Joe stepped off the boardwalk and glanced at the bay. "Let's go." The bay turned his head and followed him toward the office.

"Why don't you give that damn horse a name?" Gib asked.

"Thing like that'd make him think I liked 'im." Joe said without looking back.

Gib shook his head as he watched the bay follow Joe down the street. "Damn horse," he mumbled.

Adam was sitting in one of the chairs in front of the office watching as Joe approached, the bay following behind. "Guess we can all quit worrin' about you," he said with a sour note.

"Sorry to leave you like that, couldn't be helped," Joe said. He noticed that Adam was wearing his special deputy badge as he waved the bay to the rail. Joe slid the big Winchester from the scabbard and carried it into the office, placing it in the rack next to the ten gauge.

"Gib and I figured out what happened at Raymond's place. Did ya catch up with the shooter?"

Joe shook his head as he sat down behind his desk and pulled out the whiskey bottle and a shot glass from the bottom drawer. " 'Spect he's the one who shot that kid. There'll be another time." He drank down a couple of shots and stood up.

"I'll be at Sarah's. Appreciate it if you'd take the bay down to the livery. Have Mose clean him up good and give 'im a rubdown. He's plum tuckered."

"Glad to, Marshal," Adam said. He left his badge on Joe's desk and followed Joe out.

When Joe was on the other side of the street, he looked back at Adam.

Joe's part-time deputy smacked his lips at the bay and started walking west toward the livery. When Adam noticed that the bay was still standing at the hitching rail, he stopped and walked back to the horse, waved at him, smacked his lips, and started walking away again. The bay didn't move. Adam went back mumbling, took the reins from the saddle horn, and led the bay down the street.

Joe smiled slightly and continued on to Sarah's house.

Joe and Sarah laid on the bed, their naked forms covered only by a bed sheet. Sarah gently wiped sweat from her forehead.

"That bath must have revived you," she said. "And I thought sure you were tired!" When there was no answer she turned her head toward Joe, who was sound asleep.

CHAPTER FIFTEEN

It was almost midnight by the time Courtney Banning finished telling Sheriff Canfield about shooting a young cowboy who was stealing a calf on Tye Edson's range; then Banning went on to tell about his visit to Ike Raymond.

"He rode up right as I dumped old man Raymond. Pulled my glass out to see who it was, and it was him, all right. So, I thought you might pay even more if *he* caught a bullet." Banning sipped whiskey from a coffee cup and let go a belch.

"You *claimed* to be an expert rifle shot, I don't pay shit for misses," Canfield said.

"*I am* an expert, the army made sure of that," Banning said. He held his eyes on Canfield. "They taught me how to kill at a distance. Who knew it would be a worthwhile skill after the war?" He grinned.

Canfield nodded and chewed at the end of a dead cheroot.

"I thought I hit 'im, but he exploded in a cloud of white dust, like some sort of ghost. We traded shots and the son-of-a-bitch chased me clear to Willow Springs. I went up Jones Canyon. Got up on a ridge and waited, but he never came in."

"Mundy's too smart for that," Canfield said.

Dick Nolan was seated in a chair beside Canfield's desk. "Never had any use for long-distance ambushers, even in war. No honor in killing unless you face your enemy."

Canfield looked at his deputy. "Well, Dick, that was very touching. Now shut the hell up!"

Banning smirked at Nolan and held his eyes for a few moments.

"Took me all day to herd that damned steer to Raymond's place. After I went up and found a spot, the steer wandered into Raymond's cornfield. 'Bout then the old man came out to see what it was, and pow! Then I dropped the steer. Wasn't his brand, so he must have been a rustler!" he said, laughing.

Nolan stared at the man. "Sheriff, I thought you hired him to shoot stock thieves, so you could be officially elected. Show the ranchers that you're doing your job?"

Canfield stopped grinning and pulled the stubby cigar out of his mouth. "Quit beatin' around the bush, Dick, what the hell's on your mind?"

"Everybody knows Ike was no thief. It was a needless killin'. Stirs up too much trouble, especially since it sounded like Raymond was going to jump into the sheriff's race," Nolan said.

"Dick, if you're gettin' too weak-hearted for this work, take off that badge and leave. No hard feelin's," Canfield said.

"That ain't it. We moved *our* men farther east, so anybody thievin' around here won't be our men. He should be findin' and shootin' them, not innocent farmers."

Canfield shook his head. "Ike was fixin' to run against me in the election. He was stringin' together some followers too. If he'd won, me, *and you,* woulda had a lot harder time makin' the living we've become accustomed to. This tax-collectin' business is pretty good, especially when I add on a little." He grinned.

Nolan shook his head. "It don't take a lot of smarts to figure out *you* may have been the one who wanted to eliminate the competition for sheriff."

"Dick has a point there," Canfield said slowly, and looked at Banning. "Killing Ike took care of my competition, that's fine, real fine. But, you missed Mundy like some damned amateur."

"You oughta fire him," Nolan said.

"Mr. Banning is going to take over the men. That'll get him out of this area 'til things cool off." He looked at Banning. "You'll want to make sure our acquisitions are handled quickly. The buyer up to Atkinson is workin' out well," Canfield said. He lit a new cigar and took several puffs. "I'll ride with you up to Long Pine to introduce you to the boys."

"What about the trouble they had with some of them pony boys?" Banning asked. "That Jim Riley don't want us operating up there. Says it's his territory."

Canfield puffed the cigar again. "Yeah, too bad they wouldn't throw in with us. Too bad our boys had to kill one of 'em that got in the way."

Nolan spoke up, "You talkin' about Dave Middleton? Goes by 'Doc'?" Canfield and Banning looked at each other.

"That's what he goes by now. Riley's his real name, changed it when he come up from Texas. Seems some rangers wanted to see him," Banning said.

"Knew him when I lived up at Long Pine. Came through there a lot. Drank with him a few times. Wouldn't be messin' with him, I was you." Nolan said.

"He gets in my way, I'll shoot him like a dog," Banning said.

Canfield grinned, "That's the spirit, Courtney." The grin turned to a slow laugh.

Nolan continued, "He killed a soldier at Sidney twice his size. And, he likes to help himself to horses from the reservation. Takes balls big as church bells to steal from the Sioux."

Nolan glanced at Canfield, who'd quit laughing.

"We'll operate any goddamn place we want to. They don't like it, we'll bury 'em where they fall," Canfield said.

Nolan poured himself a cup of coffee and stared at Banning as he drank. He thought the man was "tiched" in the mind. What he and Canfield saw next convinced him of it.

"Did Loman have anything for us?" Canfield said.

A low rumble started down deep inside until a laugh broke out and stopped as fast as it began. "That pile of shit was gonna quit ya, Wick, but I asked him real nice to keep us informed." He reached into a pocket and brought out a bloody handkerchief and tossed it in front of Canfield. Nolan stared while the sheriff unfolded it and saw the end of a human finger.

"Chrissakes," Nolan said with disgust and looked at Canfield. Banning roared with laughter again.

"Get it off my desk," Canfield said with a coldness Nolan hadn't heard before.

Banning grinned and did as he was told. "I appreciate the offer of headin' up the men, but I'll pass, Wick. I like the work I'm doing for you right around here," he said. He leaned over and took a cigar from a wooden box on Canfield's desk, bit off the end, and spat it on the floor.

Nolan was stunned, not only that Banning said this, but helping himself to a cigar without asking. He glanced at Canfield, who stood up and pulled a wooden match from a vest pocket as he walked around the desk. Canfield stood beside Banning and handed him the match. He struck it on the edge of the sheriff's desk and puffed as the cigar came to life. As Canfield scratched his chin he walked around behind Banning, drawing a slender knife that was concealed behind his back.

Nolan watched, but didn't see the knife until Canfield grabbed Banning around the mouth and slammed it into his chest. The cigar bounced to the floor as he grabbed Canfield's hand. The sheriff worked the knife up, down, and around as Banning whimpered and kicked the desk. It took only a few seconds before he stopped moving and Canfield withdrew the bloody knife. After wiping the blade on Banning's shoulder, he returned to his desk and sat down.

Nolan stared at Banning, whose chin rested on his chest. Blood oozed down his vest and dripped on the floor.

"Get rid of that," Canfield said, glancing at Banning. "And take all his gear to my room."

CHAPTER SIXTEEN

Sarah and Joe sat on the last bench in church and listened as Pastor Evans delivered one of his most eloquent sermons. Adam sat on the other side of Sarah and all three were happy to see Doc Sullivan in the front row. He appeared to be clean and well dressed, though he seemed to have aged ten years over the past months.

Every seat was taken, so three cowhands had to stand at the back. The women whisked handheld fans in front of their faces, and the men dabbed at sweat with handkerchiefs.

"... *trust that by the grace of God, I have overcome my natural disposition to anger and revenge* ..."

The day before, Joe had met with Siegler, Jarvis, and Martin to explain why he'd been missing. Jarvis wasn't happy that he left town for three days, but understood why. He also informed them of his appointment as a federal deputy. *At least Jarvis didn't want to fire me . . . again.* They were saddened by the killing of Ike Raymond, and like Joe, didn't believe that he had stolen the steer found on his property. There was some debate about burial plans, now that his land would have to be sold. Jarvis suggested that they dig up Ike's wife and boy, Grant, so they could all be buried together in the Taylorsville cemetery.

"... *enabled to forgive my greatest enemies, and pray that they may be forgiven of God* ..."

Joe's mind wandered. He badly wanted the killer with the rifle. He considered that the man might be a stock detective Tye

Edson's association employed to stop the thefts.

"Who is he?"

Sarah leaned toward him and whispered, "What?" Realizing that he'd spoken out loud, he shook his head at her and looked away. He could feel her stare for a few moments before she returned her gaze to Pastor Evans.

Joe retrieved his thoughts and considered that it may have appeared to the shooter that Billy Parker was trying to steal the calf. But the shooting of Ike Raymond was different. A stray wandered onto his property, so he was shot down?

"How'd he know it wasn't Ike's steer?"

Sarah, Adam, and two women seated in front of them turned to look at Joe. "Excuse me," he whispered, as his face reddened.

Pastor Evans looked upward and raised an open hand, *"Lord, lay not this sin to their charge! I have no wish that any of them should suffer . . ."*

Both killings disgusted Joe. Some stock detectives were successful in stopping thefts and when possible, captured the thieves. He also knew that some weren't as honorable. Joe realized that he alone had to stop the shooter, if only he could find him.

". . . but that they may all be led to repentance, and settle their matters at the mercy seat . . ."

The door squeaked when it opened. Joe turned to see who'd come in late and was amazed to see Sheriff Canfield step in and lean against the rear wall. He looked over the crowd until he locked eyes with Joe. Noting that this was the first time Canfield had set foot in Taylorsville since winter, Joe wondered what was important enough to bring him into church. It seemed a poor fit for the apocryphal sheriff.

". . . hope also that the multitude of my own trespasses will be covered and forgotten . . ."

Adam leaned forward to get Joe's attention and nodded

toward the back. He had noticed Canfield as well. Joe nodded his acknowledgment.

"Bow your heads, please," Evans said. *"Be he merciful, ever as your Father who is in heaven is merciful. There is no virtue more beautiful in its character, or more important to the Christian, than that thus enjoined by the Son of God. Amen!"*

As usual, Pastor Evans met each person at the door as they filed out. Joe, Sarah, and Adam were among the first. They noticed Canfield had stepped out before the sermon finished.

"You outdid yourself again, Christmas," Joe said, taking the pastor's hand.

"It is eternally a topic of paramount importance, Joe. If we, as human beings cannot, *or will not,* find forgiveness . . . what are we?"

Joe nodded as he walked outside.

Sheriff Canfield and another man were aboard their horses a few yards in front of the church. Since he also wore a badge, Joe assumed the other man was the new deputy. Joe complied with Pastor Evans's request that no guns be worn in church, so he felt especially vulnerable standing in front of Canfield unarmed.

"Marshal Mundy, like a word."

"Meet you at my office, Sheriff," Joe replied.

After seeing Sarah to her house, Joe and Adam walked up to the marshal's office. While Adam unbarred and opened the rear door to allow some circulation, the others sat down.

"Marshal Mundy, this is my deputy, Dick Nolan," Canfield began. They nodded at each other.

"What brings you to town, Sheriff?" Joe said.

"Well, the murder of Ike Raymond, of course!" Canfield said, "I certainly wasn't going to ignore this wickedness. Wanted to ask if you had any information that might be useful in finding the guilty party."

"What about Billy Parker's murder?" Joe asked, as he tilted

his chair back and rested a boot on his desk.

"Billy Parker?"

"Murdered on Tye Edson's range a while back," Joe said.

"Oh, you mean the rustler caught right in the act. One thing sure, his thievin' days are over," Canfield said. "No need to look into that except maybe to shake the hand of the one who done it." He chuckled and looked over at Nolan.

"Billy Parker was twenty-two-years-old, a hand of Edson's. He lassoed a calf to take it back to the owner, a friend and neighbor of Edson. Some *hero* shot 'im in the back, from a ways away."

Nolan turned his head and looked at Canfield.

Joe spoke more slowly, "I'm going to find him and I'm going to kill him." They locked eyes. Joe thought Canfield's facial expression could best be explained by the saying, ". . . *didn't know whether to shit or go blind.*" He stared at Canfield.

The sheriff recovered his thoughts. "Well, I don't know about all that—"

"S'pose not," Joe interrupted.

Canfield's face reddened, which contrasted with the black hair that swept toward the back of his head. The two stared at each other in an eerie silence. Canfield broke the stare first with a glance at Joe's waist. That told Joe the sheriff was checking to see if he was armed. Joe hadn't yet buckled on his gun belt since leaving the church.

"If you do, it will be *legal,* or I *will* arrest you for murder," Canfield said without his normal smirk.

"Be sure and let me know about your success in finding *this* murderer," Joe said. Canfield's face reddened more and his deputy looked over at him again. Joe stared at Canfield.

A few moments later the fake joviality that Canfield was known for reappeared.

"Well, I'm not surprised that you have nothing to offer that may be of help, so we'll take our leave." The sheriff touched his hat and the two stood. Nolan nodded at Joe, who sat and watched them leave. They mounted their horses and trotted east down the main street.

"Hell, o'mighty. Things was gettin' a might tenseful," Adam said, as he wiped a sleeve across his face. "Why didn't you put your gun back on knowin' you'd be talkin' to *him*? And sittin' there all relaxed like that."

Joe's lips curled slightly. "Take a breath, Adam," he said, and dropped his boot back to the floor. He brought his hand up from his lap. Adam's eyes widened when he saw the Webley R.I.C. in Joe's right hand. Joe had taken the nickel-plated .455 from Clyde Davey, Canfield's last deputy, as he lay dying.

"Where'd you have that hid?" Adam said, amazed by the almost magical appearance of the gun.

"Thought it might be handy if I hung it on a nail under the drawer here."

"You like to be ready, don't you?" Adam said.

"Don't hurt."

CHAPTER SEVENTEEN

Joe had been visiting with Ham Bluford and Jenny at the Texan for several minutes. No customers were there at that early hour.

"Sure glad that Doc got straightened out. He was aimin' for a cliff," Bluford said.

"Yeah, hope he stays off the stuff," Joe said. "I guess your head got healed up?"

Bluford nodded. "Had a headache for a week."

"I'll bet. Well, see you later." Joe left and dropped in to the North Star next.

The conversation covered several mundane topics and stopped. Several minutes of silence passed by before Gib commenced on a different subject. "Did you two know that Ike Raymond was gatherin' support to run for sheriff?"

Joe stopped the cup at his mouth and looked at Gib. He lowered it to the table and shook his head.

"Yeah, word was floatin' around in here last night that he'd been talkin' to folks to see if they would vote for him. Believed Canfield wasn't serving the citizens any more," Hadley said. "For once, I knew somethin' you didn't." He looked pleased.

"Ike was a damned farmer, he wasn't no lawman," Jarvis said, dismissing Hadley's revelation.

"Maybe, but sounded like lots of folks were willin' to give him a try!" Hadley said. "Canfield wasn't a lawman before, either."

"So what's that got to do with anything?" Jarvis grumbled.

It had already struck Joe. He knew Sheriff Canfield wasn't afraid to eliminate anyone who was a real or perceived danger to him. *Why didn't I know about Ike's political ambitions? If Canfield killed him, or had him killed, who in their right mind would run against him now?*

"It might have to do with Canfield," Joe said, looking down at his cup.

"You think Canfield killed him . . . oh, uh, yeah, he *could* have done that!" Jarvis caught on.

"You two are sharp as sticks, ain't ya?" Hadley said, shaking his head.

Late that evening, Joe sat alone in the office sipping on a shot of whiskey. He was thinking about the murders of Billy Parker and Ike Raymond, and the shooting of Budd Jarvis's man. The smell of Canfield's involvement was strong. Once again Joe found himself trying to figure a way of arresting the sheriff. Still, he had no evidence. If the murders were the work of a hired killer of Canfield's maybe Joe was again, or still, on the sheriff's list. *He sure did his best to kill me out at Ike Raymond's place.* Before that thought had evaporated there were two knocks at the front door as it opened.

Doc Sullivan didn't immediately say anything. His clothes, although clean, still looked too big for him and he could pass for a man much older than the thirty-three he really was.

"Evenin', Doc," Joe said. "Help yourself to the coffee; it's not fresh, but it's hot." Other than at church, Joe hadn't seen Doc Sullivan since their fight in the street.

Doc picked up a tin cup from the little table that sat by the stove and poured. He sat down in front of Joe's desk and said, "I owe you an apology—" Joe held his hand up. "No, let me finish. Even though I didn't like it very much, and in fact hated you at the time for keeping me in that . . . that cage, I know you were trying to help me. You probably saved my life, and I thank you for that."

Joe watched Doc as he spoke what was on his mind. "And . . . I'm sorry that I attacked you . . . at Byron's store like that. There was no call . . ." Doc left it hanging in the air. "As the storm came on us that night . . . in the street, all of what Pastor Evans had been preaching to me got through to my brain." Doc looked at the floor as he talked and Joe knew how ashamed he was. "A few knocks to the head from you didn't hurt, either, figuratively." Doc hesitated a moment, dabbed at the tears in his eyes, and then continued. "I will say that if I knew any other way to make a living, I'd do it. But I don't. I am thankful for the friends I have, including you and Pastor Evans."

Joe could see how hard this was for Doc, and how necessary it was to unburden himself from it. He let a few seconds go by before speaking. "I'm glad you're doin' better, Doc. We've missed you. I do have a question, though. Where'd you learn to fight like that?"

"While I was at Harvard Medical School in Boston, there was a local boxing club."

Joe raised his head slightly, "Ahh, that explains it."

"Not the sport of choice for a man who depends on his hands, I suppose, but I proved to be somewhat successful at it," Doc said and placed his cup on Joe's desk. "You didn't handle yourself too badly, either, in an unrefined, back-alley sort of manner." They both smiled at each other as the tension broke.

Joe downed his whiskey and watched Doc glance at the shot glass. Their eyes met. "Must be hard not taking a drink."

"It is a constant struggle, but I hope, and pray, that I'm mostly past all that. I do wish to pass along something before I go, nothing good I'm afraid. I did what I could for the man you hit in the Palace. The fractures in his face prevent him from speaking well. Told him to go to Omaha for a surgeon. Anyway, he rode out earlier today."

"I know, Adam told me," Joe said. "Smiley's brother, Denver."

Doc hesitated before continuing. "I'd forgotten a few things, many things actually, over the past weeks. Something that I did remember was that Dan Loman came to see me and he made me promise not to tell you or anyone else about his *accident.*"

"What happened, Doc?"

"He cut off the end of his finger," Sullivan said. "He caught me when I could still stand, so I sewed it up the best I could under the circumstances.

"Hazard of the butcher's job, I 'spose," Joe said.

"I've been thinking about this, and his story does not fit. Yes, he said he accidentally cut it off while chopping, but asked me several times not to mention it to anyone. What bothers me is, it's the end of his right little finger. Dan's right-handed, so wouldn't it be a bit difficult to do that?"

"Difficult, but I don't 'spose impossible, Doc," Joe said. He studied Sullivan's face.

"If you're right-handed, it's not possible. If, for some reason he was using his left hand to chop, it would still be about impossible," Doc said. He went through the motions to illustrate his point.

"Hmm, yeah," Joe said as he contemplated the motions. "So, you think maybe someone helped him lose part of his finger?"

"It does raise the possibility. And how Dan acted that day also bothered me, upset, he seemed real upset."

"Doc, I believe it would spoil my whole day and part of the next if I cut off a finger," Joe said.

"I think you should talk to him, a casual visit, then ask about his finger. See what you think," Sullivan said.

"If it'll make you feel better, I'll see him in the morning."

★   ★   ★   ★   ★

Joe was up well before dawn and on his second cup of coffee when he heard Adam stirring. The cot behind the jail cage squeaked as he climbed out and Joe offered a "good morning" greeting. Joe sat with his boots on the desk contemplating Dan Loman's injury. If someone attacked him, who and why?

"You're up kinda early, ain't ya?" Adam mumbled as he stood, yawned, and stretched.

"Aren't you," Joe said.

"Ain't I what?"

"It's not 'ain't ya,' it's 'aren't you,' " Joe said.

Adam stared at Joe. "You're doin' that on account *I ain't* awake yet, *aren't you?*"

Joe offered a slight smile as Adam poured coffee. He sat his cup down and walked out the back door on a mission. When he returned, he picked up his cup and sat down in front of Joe's desk.

"You hear about Dan Loman losing part of a finger, got it cut off?" Joe asked.

Adam shook his head, " 'Spect that's what comes from working with sharp knives." He sipped the coffee and yawned again.

"This is between you and me. Doc came by and told me he took care of him, but suspicions someone did it for him on purpose," Joe said and drained his cup.

"Why?" Adam said with a near whisper and yawned again.

"Why what?" Joe was amused by Adam's drowsiness. "Why is it a secret, or why does he think someone did it for him?"

"Yes," Adam said and took another sip from his cup.

Joe explained that Doc Sullivan thought that Dan had acted very strange and kept asking him not to tell anyone about the injury. Before Adam headed for Siegler's store, Joe told him he was going to visit Loman and find out what had happened.

CHAPTER EIGHTEEN

The sun was up, but no direct sunlight entered Dan Loman's meat market since the building faced west, almost directly across the street from Jarvis's livery. When Joe opened the door, a little bell sounded, which appeared to frighten the proprietor.

"Mornin', Dan," Joe said. "Didn't mean to startle you."

"Oh, oh, that's okay, Marshal. What can I do for you?"

"Beautiful morning, huh, Dan?" Joe said and looked out through the front windows. He noticed a rider on a sorrel with one white sock trot by. Joe hesitated a bit as he watched the rider; something caught his eye for a short moment, and then the rider was out of view of the windows.

"Huh? Oh, yeah, I guess so. Yeah, I guess it is, what can I get you, Marshal?"

"How about another quarter pound of that good bacon. Adam and me like to fry up some in the office with a biscuit."

Without replying Dan went to work. He weighed and wrapped up what Joe thought was more bacon than he'd ordered.

"I think ya gave me more than a quarter pound."

"That's okay, Marshal, now if you don't mind, I have this order for the hotel to finish. Good day to you," Loman said and turned back to his work.

"I think I should pay you for this, Dan, still the eight cents?" Joe said.

"Oh, uh, on the house today. Thanks for stopping in," Loman said.

"Say, what happened to your finger there?"

"Oh, nothing. An accident." Loman again turned back to the chopping table.

Joe changed his tone. "You must take me for some hollow-headed fool. I don't like that."

Loman turned around even more nervous than he was before. "Oh, oh, no, Marshal, I don't think that. I don't think that at all, really. I was chopping awhile back, and wham! Ha, ha. It happens sometimes, just quick like that."

"So, you're a lefty, huh?" Joe asked, tone still in place.

"Huh, what? Oh yeah, I guess I am. I mean, yes, I am, so . . ." Loman left his words hang, apparently thinking it was best to stop talking.

"You run a good business here, Dan. Lots better than that jail cell you were in up at the Flats with Sheriff Canfield lookin' after ya," Joe said. "I'm glad this is working out so well for you. But, it seems some don't care if you win or lose, right? Shame."

"Wha', what, Marshal? I guess I don't know what you mean?"

Joe looked toward the door and through the front windows again and turned back to Loman. "Who cut off your finger and why?"

"Oh, oh, no one . . ." Loman stopped when he saw Joe hold a finger up to his lips.

"Now start over, and let the truth out," Joe said. "Be quick about it!"

Loman's eyes widened farther. He glanced to the door and out into the street, then looked down. "Did that damn Doc tell you? I told him not . . ."

"Doc? What's he got to do with this? I've got eyes, it's not laborious to calculate!"

"If Canfield finds out I told you, he'll kill me. He'll send his man to kill me, as sure as we're standin' here."

"Who's his man?" Joe said.

Loman hesitated, and met Joe's eyes. Even though there was no one else in the market and the front door was closed, he whispered, "His, his name is, Courtney Banning. He's a very mean son-of-a-bitch."

"This Banning works for Canfield I take it? Why'd he do that?" Joe glanced at Loman's finger stub.

"I'm sorry and ashamed to tell you this, Marshal, but when I was let out of jail, the sheriff told me to report to him what you was up to. 'Anything and everything,' he said. Even who you was sleeping with. I'm so ashamed."

"Why'd he want to know all this?" Joe asked.

Loman shrugged.

"And Banning came around to collect the information from you?"

Loman nodded.

"Why'd he take off your finger?"

"I was tired of sneaking around watching you for something to report. Tol' Banning that I was done with that. He hit me, and when I was on the floor, I thought he was going to cut my throat, but instead whacked my finger."

"So, you're still 'on the job' so to speak?" Joe asked.

Loman nodded. "He said he'd kill me. I'm sorry, Marshal."

"Doesn't the truth set you free?" Joe said. "It better be the truth, then you and me will be okay. In fact, you will continue spying for Canfield. And, occasionally I'll let you know what to pass along to our esteemed sheriff. Understood?"

Loman nodded, "That's a good idea. I will!"

It seemed to be of some relief to Dan Loman, for which Joe was glad. He dropped coins for the bacon on the counter and wished Loman a good day.

CHAPTER NINETEEN

Joe and Adam stepped inside the church where Byron Siegler, Harold Martin, and Budd Jarvis were already seated. The wood frame building with windows along each side served also as a school and now as the meeting place for the town board. The school children had been dismissed by Pastor Evans, who was serving as teacher until one could be found. Siegler's general store became too crowded to hold board meetings as more folks became interested in town affairs.

Among the onlookers were Thord Sanderson, the blacksmith; Doc Sullivan; Gib Hadley; Pastor Evans; Judge Worden; Klaus Volker, the jeweler and clock repairman who had made Joe's badge; and Aldo Fisk, the cobbler.

Siegler stood at the pulpit, while Jarvis and Martin sat in the first row of benches. The onlookers sat here and there on the other benches. Joe and Adam sat at the back.

"Meeting come to order," Siegler said. "The first topic of discussion today is Marshal Mundy, who has been appointed as a federal deputy." Jarvis and Martin turned and glanced at Joe with a somewhat surprised look on their faces. Apparently Siegler had not told them beforehand.

"Thankfully, he has agreed to continue as city marshal but on occasion his government work may take him away for short periods of time. I feel that the board desires to keep Joe on . . ." He stopped and looked at the other board members. Jarvis turned and looked at Joe again and then nodded his approval along with Martin. "So that can be entered into town records." Martin dabbed a pencil on his tongue and scratched onto the open record-book on his lap.

Siegler continued, "The main topic, then, is who do we have to step in during these periods when Joe is gone? Joe has informed me that Adam has had enough experience to fill in."

Aldo Fisk raised his hand and Siegler acknowledged him. "Nothing against Adam, he's a fine man, but sometimes rough people come in. Are you sure he could handle them? He was almost killed *with* the marshal last winter. Marshal Mundy has had his hands full of late, where someone did get shot again."

"Joe would you step up and give us your opinion?" Siegler asked.

Joe left his black hat on the bench in front of him and walked up near the pulpit. "All along I've been tellin' Adam everything I can think of about the job and handling folks. Mostly it's checkin' doors of businesses at night and checkin' the saloons for any problems. And keep an eye out for fires. I think being shot last year taught Adam a few things. Hard lesson, but well learned."

"What about gun work?" Jarvis asked.

"He's well practiced with his pistol," Joe answered.

"I'm sure he is against a bottle or tin can that won't shoot back," Jarvis said.

"That's true, Budd. There's no real learning that until you're knee-deep in it. Hopefully it won't come to that. I'll make my absences as few and short as I can."

"We have no one else with any experience," Martin said. Joe watched the pencil shake in his hand.

"Adam, is there anything you wish to add here?" Siegler said.

Adam stood, hat in hand. "No, sir, not really. Only I'll be plum proud to fill in for Joe when he asks." Adam's words were firm and clear. This seemed to help assuage some of the doubts in the minds present. Adam raised his right hand and said, "I swear to uphold the law, so help me God." He glanced at Joe, who nodded.

"I've already done the official swearing at the office," Joe said to Siegler. A couple of the onlookers chuckled.

"The town can afford one dollar per day as special deputy, but only when necessary. If Marshal Mundy has an extended absence, we may ask him to help pay Adam's wages. Does the board approve that expenditure when necessary as I've outlined?" Siegler asked.

Jarvis and Martin said yes and Martin made more scratches in the book. "Very well, thank you, Adam, for accepting this responsibility. And if you want help, you can find myself, Budd, or Gib."

Joe and Adam stepped out of the church as the board proceeded into other affairs that didn't concern them. The sky had been taken over by dark clouds with a sea-green tint and a breeze had kicked up.

"So you know, nothing has really changed except now you have official board approval . . . and *they'll* be paying you instead of me," Joe said.

"Wait a damned minute, you won't pay, too?" Adam's stone look turned into a grin. Joe looked at him and shook his head.

Joe let Adam make the rounds of town with him after they had some bacon, biscuits, and coffee at the office. Later in the evening, they sat on the boardwalk in front of the office and watched the clouds as they turned darker. Wind gusts started to blow dust in their faces, so they hauled the chairs inside and closed the door. The clouds brought down the steamy temperature, so it wasn't completely uncomfortable to have the office closed up.

After firing the lamps, Adam sat down in front of Joe's desk and pulled out his book of conundrums. Joe sat at his desk and poured a shot of whiskey as dull lightning flashes lit up the office. He avoided meeting Adam's eyes on the chance he might think Joe wanted to hear him read from the book. But, best-laid plans . . .

"Oh, listen to this," Adam said. The dreaded words came at last, Joe thought to himself. "Why is a professional thief very comfortable?" Adam looked at Joe like he expected a guess. Joe stared at him.

Undeterred, Adam continued, "Because he takes things easy!" He smiled as Joe emptied his glass and poured another.

Thunder rumbled through the sky and seemed to vibrate everything in its path, only delaying the next reading.

"Why was Eve made?" He looked at Joe's blank face. "For Adam's Express Company!"

Well after dark, the rain came. Heavy, wind-driven rain plastered everything outside. Small streams of water crept in under the front door. The thunder and lightning only temporarily beat out the sound of the rain. Adam had settled down and was reading to himself as Joe sipped whiskey and looked through old wanted posters. The Regulator struck eleven times and Joe considered turning in for the night. That thought was interrupted when Budd Jarvis stepped into the office wearing a glistening brown slicker. Water poured off of his big Stetson and his face was drenched.

"Hello, Budd, what are you doin' out in this downpour?" Joe asked. A very serious look appeared on Jarvis's face as he hung his hat and slicker on wall pegs.

"Joe, I want to talk to you alone, right now," he said and looked at Adam. "Sorry, Adam, this is something I have to say only to Joe."

"Kind of a nasty night out, don't you think? You can talk in Adam's company," Joe said.

"No, this is between you and me," Jarvis said.

Joe could tell that there was something very important on Jarvis's mind and hoped it wasn't an argument regarding Joe's added position. Jarvis had voted to approve keeping Joe on.

"Okay, Adam, put on Budd's slicker and step out under the porch awning, we won't be long," Joe said. Adam was somewhere less than excited about the idea, but did as Joe asked. "Could ya make it quick before I drown out there?" He stepped out and closed the front door behind him.

Budd sat down on the chair that Adam had vacated. "Have you seen him?"

"Who, Budd?" Joe said.

"I've got some serious talking to do right now, and I'll have to start at the front," Jarvis said and leaned forward in his chair. "George Welby is back."

Chapter Twenty

Joe was stunned and wondered if he'd heard Jarvis correctly. Thoughts of Sarah came into mind. Actually, *all* kinds of thoughts came to mind. "Well . . . that *is* a surprise. You sure it's him?" He poured Jarvis a shot.

Jarvis nodded. "I was down an alley and saw him ride by on a sorrel with one white sock. He didn't see me. Looks a little rough, his face, from hard livin' I 'spose, but it was him all right."

Joe repeated Jarvis's words in his mind, and what it meant. He also remembered the rider that trotted by Loman's Meat Market when he was inside talking to Dan. The rider that caught his eye for a moment, and riding *that* horse. "Well, I'll have to make sure Sarah doesn't shoot him," Joe said. "He has it coming, though, far as I'm concerned. Anyone who runs off and leaves his wife to fend for hers—"

"I'm real glad you feel that way because I'm going to kill him," Jarvis said.

Joe stared at Jarvis and wondered what was going on here. He also wondered if Jarvis had already been too deep in a whiskey bottle. "What are you talking about, Budd? You can't kill him, and why would you want to anyway?"

"Only me and him know what I'm going to tell you . . . and my wife, Rosella. This is between you and me." Jarvis studied Joe for a moment. "About three years ago, I decided late one evening that I wasn't going to stay here in town like I often do, so rode on out home. I knew Rosella would be asleep by the time I got there, so I was very quiet so's not to wake her. I heard a noise and thought she must be up still, so I went up to our room. I found Welby with her," Jarvis's face tightened for a moment and then he continued. "He jumped out the window as I was shooting at him. Don't have no damned idea how I could have missed him. Went to the window and fired my gun empty and still didn't hit the son-of-a-bitch. I ran back downstairs, grabbed my Winchester, and fired it dry as Welby rode off." Jarvis stopped to study Joe and took another sip of whiskey. "Never saw him again and nobody else did, either."

"That . . . I did not know." Joe couldn't think of anything else to say and rubbed his forehead. He'd never met Budd's wife, and only knew what Adam said about her, "of a fitful nature" he'd said, and that Doc Sullivan took some medicine to her or gave it to Jarvis to give to her, on a regular basis.

"And that's why I'm going to kill him. And why I'm asking you to stay out of it," Jarvis said.

"Budd, you know I can't stand by and let you or anyone else do something like that," Joe said. "You know that."

"Don't worry, it will be a fair fight, I'll make sure of that."

"Budd, you can't come in here and tell me that you *plan* to kill someone and then say you'll make it a fair fight. The cat's already escaped the bag. Frankly, I'm surprised at you."

"So you won't stay out of it?" Jarvis asked.

"The board hired me as a peace officer, and that's my job," Joe said, "Nobody ought to be above the law."

"You do a good job, too, be a shame if the board fired you," Jarvis said and stood. "Appreciate it if you'd keep this about Rosella between us."

"You have my word."

Joe watched Adam shuck the slicker and Jarvis put it on as he walked out. Adam slapped his soaked hat against his leg before hanging it on a peg. He wiped his dripping face with a kerchief. "Guess I won't have need of a bath this week. It's getting worse out there, I think this may be a bad one." He poured a cup of coffee and sat down. "Budd was acting all fired strange. Have a difficulty?"

"Some personal steam he wanted to blow off, I guess." Joe blew out the lamps at the same moment something outside crashed, grabbing their attention. They looked out the front windows and with the assistance of lightning, saw part of a porch awning on their boardwalk. It had struck and snapped one of two posts that supported their own awning and it hung flapping in the wind.

"Where'd that come from?" Adam asked. Before Joe could answer, a new blast of wind ripped off the wounded awning and it vanished. "Damn!"

A couple of roof shakes blasted their way through one of the office windows, showering them with rain and glass. "We better stand in the log room 'til this blows over!" Joe yelled. The small room, now Joe's sleeping quarters, was the original jail cell before the town purchased the new flat iron jail cage from Cincinnati, Ohio.

The noise of the storm grew louder and they heard more crashing sounds.

"Is it taking the town apart?" Adam said as they listened to a distant rumbling.

"It may be, sounds like a cyclone," Joe said.

"Whaat?"

"I said, it sounds like a cyclone!" Joe repeated. He couldn't see Adam in the dark. If he could have, he would've seen a pale face with wide searching eyes.

The front door whipped open and hit the wall, shattering its own glass. Wanted posters and other papers blew off Joe's desk and were soaked by the rain. The desk lamp smashed to the floor, adding to the broken glass. They sat on Joe's cot with their backs against the wall. Joe reached out and closed the heavy log door that usually remained open. They could still feel a wet wind blowing through the slot cut in the door, which had been used for serving prisoners' meals.

They next heard a terrible, unnatural grinding noise and a rumbling that sounded like a thousand locomotives. "What the hell is that?" Adam cupped his hand and yelled into Joe's ear.

"Cy-clone!" Joe yelled. "You never been in one before?"

"Whaat?"

"Nothing!" Joe said.

A few long minutes later the roar stopped like a clock. Joe looked through the slot, saw lightning flashes, and heard rain. He stood up and pushed the door open. Glass crunched under their boots as they walked through the office and looked outside. It wasn't as dark as before and they could see the outlines of the buildings across the street.

"Well, looks like this part of town is still here," Joe said. "Let's take a walk, see if everyone is okay." Adam wandered east down the boardwalk and Joe stepped off into the muddy street to look in on Sarah.

CHAPTER TWENTY-ONE

That night, Joe's sleep had been periodic and not restful. As the sunrise approached, he stood in the office doorway and watched. It was like a theatre curtain ascending to reveal a stage play of the war.

"Gawd, what a night. Couldn't sleep worth a damn after we got back last night," Adam said as he walked up beside Joe.

"Me, neither." They watched as the scene unfolded before them. Debris in the form of garbage, wood shingles, signs, and a multitude of other items littered the main street. A dead steer laid on its side at the west end of the street in front of Sarah's business. Joe had found her at home when the storm quit. Her house only lost shingles and a couple of windows so she was lucky. But she was scared, so Joe had taken her to the hotel and continued to look for others who might want assistance.

Joe kicked short, broken-off pieces of lumber away from the door and into the street. The windows of buildings across from the marshal's office, on the south side, seemed to be unbroken.

As they stepped out onto the boardwalk, Gib Hadley approached. "I see you two are okay. What a damned night that was! Ain't seen a mess like this since the war."

"Glad to see you're breathin'. Considering everything, I think we were all lucky," Joe said.

"I come down to tell you that your sign and awning are in my front window, should you like to fetch them sometime," Hadley said. "It'll take the three of us."

On the way to the North Star, they surveyed the town. Buildings on the north side of the street had lost most of their windows and were covered with mud. Awnings, on those who had them, were damaged in varying degrees. Those sign boards attached only to a pole in the street were gone. Townspeople were out in force picking up debris, loading it into wagons, and sweeping boardwalks. They were so efficient one might have thought that they all had prior experience with that sort of thing.

The three stopped in front of the North Star and stared at the porch wreckage that hung halfway inside the saloon, where one of the large glass windows used to be. "City Marshal & Jail" could be read on the mud-plastered sign, if one already knew what it said.

"Real fine, ain't it," Hadley said. "See the Texan? Muddy, but untouched. But that doesn't bother me. No, not by a dog's bark! What bothers me is that piece of buzzard bait over there all fine and dandy." He stepped to the side window and pointed across the side street to the Palace. It was almost eerie how clean and undamaged it was. Of course, it faced east.

"Budd has an awning, maybe that helped from gettin' his windows busted," Adam observed. "And . . . you don't."

Hadley frowned, and shot back, "Well, you did, too, but now you don't!"

"If you're all done visiting, how are we going to get this out of your window, break it up first?" Joe said.

As Joe and Hadley discussed the best way to approach the wreckage, Adam glanced up and saw Sarah walking out of the hotel with a man. Someone he thought he recognized. He looked at Joe, who was bent over trying to pry the sign loose. He looked again and squinted, trying to see if Sarah had her arm in his.

"If you're done restin', maybe you could see fit to give us a hand, Mr. Carr?" Hadley said. Adam looked again and the couple had walked into Sarah's laundry business. Not knowing for sure whom he saw, he decided to keep it to himself.

They were able to retrieve the sign and pull the awning wreckage into the street. Adam washed off the sign and leaned it up against the office front under one of the windows. Joe had gone over to visit with Siegler while Adam cleaned and swept the office. With the door glass and both sets of front windows gone, he wondered what they'd do if another storm came.

As Adam leaned on the broom thinking, he looked southwest down the street and noticed Sarah and that man come out of the laundry and walk around the corner to the south toward her house. Sarah wasn't smiling but was walking with him. *It is him. I don't believe it. George Welby in the flesh.* Adam wondered why he'd come back and if Joe knew.

CHAPTER TWENTY-TWO

"This is sure a blow to our town. This storm will cost everyone," Siegler said and shook his head.

"My office will need windows for now. Adam and I can rebuild the awning," Joe said. "Looks like you fared well here."

"Yes, thank God. Business has been slow, but I suppose it will pick up now, especially with orders of lumber, shingles, and windows." As they left Siegler's office they noticed a cowhand talking to Earl, the clerk.

"Bony came to town to ask for help. Some farmers south of here were hit bad by the cyclone. Booth is missing two of his children," Earl said with urgency. Bony Wilson, one of Jarvis's hands, was a slender drip of sun-beaten rawhide in high heel boots, spurs, and a bent-up brown hat. His gunshot wound was almost healed.

"Adam and I will ride out to Booth's right now," Joe said.

Joe and Adam rode at an easy canter across rolling hills that began to flatten out into rich farmland. They slowed to a trot, and then stopped.

"We should be able to see Booth's soddy," Joe said. It was more of a question than a statement.

"I don't see it, but I only been through here once before," Adam said. Joe touched the bay into a trot and Adam followed on Siegler's appaloosa.

After fifteen minutes of searching, the two rode up to the

remains of the soddy. There was no roof and only one partial wall still stood. The stoic wall was partly melted from the rain. Marylee Booth sat on a bucket rocking a child. The little girl, who looked to be four or five, Joe thought, had a tight hold around her mother's neck. Both were covered in dried mud.

Joe stepped down from the bay and pulled off his hat as he knelt in front of them. He didn't see any remaining personal belongings when he glanced at the soddy's footprint. "Ma'am, I'm Marshal Joe Mundy and this is my special deputy, Adam Carr. We've come fr—"

"I know who you are, Mr. Mundy," the mother said. She used the back of one hand to clear dried dirt from her eyes. "You once did my husband a kindness, thank you."

"And he did one for me as well. Where is Booth?"

She broke down and pointed east. "They're looking for Lacy and Jake," she sobbed. "A neighbor, Mr. Klein, and Booth." She held onto the little girl and rocked her faster.

"We'll find your children, Mrs. Booth, how old are they?" Joe said.

"This is Mary, she's five. Lacy is six, Jake is the oldest, eight," she managed to say between wrenching sobs.

Joe stood up and remounted the bay. "I'll cross to the other side of that crick and start looking. Get Mrs. Booth a bucket of water and then come along east on this side." Adam nodded.

Joe had searched through tall prairie grass and butchered cornfields for about three hours when he decided the bay should have a drink. He turned the horse back toward the creek, which was about a mile north. Joe searched every crevice and clump of weeds as they went. The bay walked up close to the shallow creek and stopped. Joe stepped down and splashed some water on his face. He pulled a canteen off the saddle horn and took a drink. He looked at the bay, who stood, head half lowered as if he was inspecting the creek water.

"You gonna drink or not? We don't have all day," Joe said and slid his hand across his horse's neck. The bay turned his head away from Joe at the rub and pat. "What's wrong with you?" The bay kept his head facing away so Joe looked in the distance in the same direction. He knew the bay well and trusted his instinct. But, this time he didn't see anything.

"Okay, time's up," Joe said and remounted. The bay uncharacteristically resisted being reined away from the creek. Joe knew the bay sensed something. He didn't see anything, but oftentimes, you didn't *see* Indians. A few were still causing trouble across the frontier, which had kept the soldiers at Fort Hartsuff on their trail. Or, was the mysterious shooter taking up a position? Joe pulled his rifle from the scabbard and climbed down once more.

The bay kept the same stance as Joe walked east through weeds with the rifle in hand. Twenty minutes of searching resulted in finding nothing. Now, a little perturbed, Joe replaced the rifle and took hold of the reins. He started to walk away, pulling on the reins, but the bay wouldn't budge. The horse then lowered his head a bit more as if he saw something. Joe looked where the bay was looking, and as he started to glance back at the horse, he caught movement. On the opposite bank of the narrow creek was a small animal, the same color as the dirt bank it laid on. Joe stepped through the water to take a closer look.

The bay whinnied when Joe was close. It wasn't an animal at all, but a small child curled up! He sat down on the bank and picked up a little girl. She was barely moving. Joe soaked his bandanna in the water and dabbed at the crusted dirt chunks in her eyes and mouth. She didn't look well to him but he couldn't detect any broken bones. None he could see anyway. With most of the dirt wiped from her face and arms, the little girl started to cry. He held her close, patted her back, and whispered to her.

"How about we take you home to your momma and daddy?" She still cried but at a less furious pace. "My name is Joe. Is your name Lacy? She ignored the questions but Joe persisted. "Would you like a ride on my horse? You know, he's the one who found you," Joe said. Lacy nodded as the crying almost stopped. He stood up with her in his arms and was amused to see the bay drinking from the creek.

When Joe and Lacy arrived back at the ruins of the Booth soddy, Bony Wilson was there. While Bony stood rocking Mary back and forth, Mrs. Booth ran up to the bay crying and took Lacy from Joe. "Oh my God! Is she okay?" She settled down after a minute and Joe said, "I think she is, but Doc Sullivan should look you all over. Bony, you bring little Mary there and the missus and Lacy can ride with me."

Before they started back to Taylorsville, Adam rode up at a gallop. "They found Jake! They're taking him straight to Doc's in Booth's wagon. Has a broken leg, but other than that looks fine," he said, which sent Mrs. Booth into tears again.

When they tied up in front of Doc's house, Joe noticed a broken window and many shingles missing from the roof. Mrs. Booth carried Lacy inside, followed by Bony with Mary. They saw another man and woman who both wore an assortment of bandages.

Booth had been standing by the examining table with Jake as Sullivan tied splints to his leg. He ran to meet his family, tears sliding down his crusty face.

"Marshal Mundy found our Lacy on the crick bank!" she told her husband. He took Mary from Bony and hugged his family. He whispered the words, "You're one up . . . on me."

Joe smiled and adjusted his hat. "Thanks to Bony for coming in for help. Wouldn't have been good for these little ones to be out in the night." He saw the cowboy's face flush.

Bony looked at the ground, "Gotta get back, we're still a' lookin' for strays."

CHAPTER TWENTY-THREE

The next morning Adam had washed the mud off the front of the office and the process of rebuilding the office awning had begun. Jarvis donated a new pole support, which replaced the one broken off. Joe was up on a ladder nailing shingles when the Booth family pulled up in their wagon.

"Good morning, Marshal," Booth said. His wife sat next to him with Mary on her lap. Jake was laid on a pile of canvas in the back with Lacy next to him.

"How you all faring?" Joe asked.

"Only cuts and bruises, except for Jake. But we're thankful, it's a miracle it wasn't worse for us. Mr. Siegler loaned us a tent until we rebuild our house. He was kind enough to give me credit on supplies, too."

"You need any help at home, let us know."

"My neighbor, Klein, and me will be helping each other, but thanks anyways, Marshal. We stopped to thank you for finding our little Lacy," Booth said. "We better be goin' home now."

"Anytime, Booth. You folks take care," Joe said.

After Booth's wagon rolled out of town, Adam decided it was time to tell Joe what was on his mind. "Ah, yesterday when we was at the North Star, I saw Sarah walk into her bathhouse with a feller, and, ah, I saw the same feller come out later—"

"Yeah? Wanna hand me more nails?"

Adam hesitated a moment and continued, "What I'm tryin' to say is, the man was George Welby."

"Yeah," Joe said. "He's back."

Adam looked up and down the street with a wrinkled brow. "You mean, you already knew?"

"Yep."

"Did ya hear me say Sarah was with him?" Adam asked.

"Yep."

He planted hands on hips, looked up and down the street again, and returned his gaze upward. "Well, what are ya gonna do?"

"About what?" Joe asked and drove in another nail.

Adam looked up and scratched his head. He waited for the pounding to stop and said, "About Sarah's . . . well, I mean about Welby coming back!"

"Don't know," Joe said. "Hand me another shingle."

It had taken another hour to finish the awning. Joe's thoughts ambled from Sarah, to George Welby, and to the killer with the big rifle. He stopped to admire his sufficient, but not altogether flawless, work. He was glad that no more attacks had occurred, but wasn't confident that they were over. He also thought about the upcoming election and doubted anyone would run against Canfield after the murder of potential candidate Ike Raymond.

Joe finished drying his face and pulled up his suspenders. Adam was already through washing up. "How about we go over and have breakfast, I'm buyin'."

"Let's get goin' before you change your mind!" Adam said and smiled.

Joe sipped his coffee and watched Adam mop up the last of his breakfast with a biscuit. He sat back in his chair and sighed, "Boy, that was a spot needed fillin'."

"Act like ya haven't eaten in a week," Joe said. The hotel dining room had only five other customers, some still eating, some who were finished, and one who hadn't been served yet.

Joe paid Harold Martin, and he and Adam stepped to the door. As Adam reached for the knob, the door opened and Sarah stepped in, followed closely by George Welby. Adam stood there, glancing at them and then back at Joe. Welby had a partial black eye and scratches on his sunburned and weathered face that might have been caused by fingernails. He wore a brown suit that was presentable, but certainly not new. Joe thought he looked a lot rougher than the portrait hanging in Sarah's bedroom. She looked down, and then back up to Joe.

Before she could speak, Joe greeted her and pulled off his hat, "Good morning, Sarah."

"Ah, Joe, this is . . . this is George . . . my husband." She turned to George, "This is Joe Mundy, the . . . city marshal." Her discomfort was palpable.

"Pleasure to meet you, Marshal," Welby said and offered his hand. Joe looked at it and stepped aside so they could enter. Sarah looked away from Joe and walked into the dining room. "Well . . . good day," Welby added in a brusque tone.

That afternoon at the marshal's office, Adam watched Joe open the day's mail. No words had been spoken between them after leaving the hotel. He tried to read his book but couldn't concentrate. He stared at Joe in hopes of starting a conversation. He wondered how Joe could sit there calmly after seeing George with Sarah. Adam wished that he could read Joe's mind. He got up and slowly paced the floor. He stopped and leaned onto the door windowsill with his arms hanging outside. He saw George Welby walk out of Sarah's bathhouse, mount his horse, and trot north past the livery. He commenced to pacing once more.

"Somethin' on your mind?" Joe said, without looking up from the business at hand.

Adam stopped, "Yes! And you know what it is!" He surprised himself with the outburst. "Are you going to sit there while Sarah is with George? Who just left town by the way, so this would be a fine time to go talk to her." He took a breath and stared at Joe.

Joe laid an envelope on the desk and sat back in his chair. He looked at Adam, "George is her husband."

"No, he ain't. She signed that cancelled marriage paper, don't ya remember?"

Joe smiled. He picked up some unnecessary mail and dropped it into a trash bucket beside his desk. "The judge says she never signed it. I reminded her, but she hasn't signed far as I know."

Adam stood there speechless and gawked at Joe. "But, I thought you two . . . you know, were a couple? I know you care about her."

"She's a fine woman," Joe said. "I assume that's about all what's on your mind."

Adam wasn't deaf. He caught the cold tone that indicated the conversation was over. He threw on his hat and walked out.

CHAPTER TWENTY-FOUR

Joe watched Adam leave the office as he pulled open the bottom desk drawer and withdrew a shot glass and whiskey bottle. After gulping down two shots, he poured a third and once again leaned back in his chair. He tried not to dwell on the new events with Sarah. Catching the ambush killer was foremost on his mind, at least he tried to keep it there.

"Mundy! . . . Mun-dy! You sum' bitch! Get out here. Right now, you coward!"

The voice was a bit distorted, but Joe understood each word. He drained the glass, carefully replaced the bottle cork, and stood up. He could see Smiley's brother, Denver, standing in the middle of the street. As Joe had told him not to ever come back to Taylorsville, he was surprised that he had the pluck to return.

"I'll come in for ya if I have to, you coward!" Denver yelled.

Joe stepped out onto the boardwalk. Denver had two pistols, one Colt Navy .36, which was poked under his belt, and a Remington Army .44, which he held down at his side.

"I wouldna bet you had the guts to face me 'thout help. I'm the man who's gonna kill ya!" Around his lower jaw was a cloth bandage, which was tied behind his head, and he grimaced with each word. Evidence of his first run in with Joe at the Palace saloon. "You killed our cousin, Chug, and you gave me pain, pain all the damned time, you cur! Now it's time to pay up!"

Joe heard hurried footsteps on the boardwalk to his left. With a quick glance he saw Smiley hurrying up the street, shotgun in hand.

"You ain't killin' my brother, Mundy! I'm not lettin' ya!" Smiley screamed.

Joe concentrated on Denver, and depended on his senses to cover Smiley. He took a slow breath.

"You ain't gonna hurt nobody again!" Denver yelled.

Adam stepped out of a store behind Smiley and picked up a scrap board that was lying on the boardwalk. He swung and caught Smiley on the right side of his head, sending the barkeep headlong into the street.

As Joe drew his cavalry Colt he offered Adam a quick glance. Denver saw what Adam had done to Smiley and raised the .44 in his hand, not toward Joe, but Adam. It was already cocked.

Joe's first shot hit Denver in the upper left side of the chest. The bullet's impact caused Denver to stumble backward and shoot wildly in Adam's direction. Unarmed, Adam slammed himself down on the boardwalk. He laid there and watched Joe cock the hammer again, in no apparent hurry, then shoot again, but missing his target. Denver fired two more shots as he wavered; the first whizzed safely by Joe, the second burned a bloody crease across the side of his neck. Joe was slow and deliberate as he fired again, the .45 caliber bullet finding a stopping place inside Denver's body. Joe cocked the cavalry Colt again as Denver collapsed onto his back, knees bent, feet still planted almost where they were when standing.

Townspeople and others stepped out and gawked at the man lying in the street. Some stared at Joe, who still stood in the same place. He ejected the three empty cartridge casings onto the boardwalk and pulled fresh rounds from his belt to reload the Colt.

"Help! Please help, we need a doctor!" A man's plea came from the new millinery that had recently opened. It was the business Adam had been in when the trouble started.

Doc Sullivan had watched the fight from inside Siegler's general store. He trotted across the street toward the call for help. Elva Escott, with her husband, Cleve, owned the new business. She got in the way of Denver's first wild shot at Adam, catching the .44 ball in her upper left hip.

Joe stepped inside the store and knelt down beside her. "Doc's comin', from across the street."

"Oh, I'll live, Marshal, thank you," Elva said and grimaced. "I'm glad we haven't replaced our windows yet from the storm, or we'd have to do it again!" She offered a crooked smile. Joe stepped out as Doc took over.

People were milling closer around Denver's body so Joe and Adam walked up to send them on their way. "Take his guns and belt to the office, I'll wait for Iain."

Adam did as he was told without saying a word. As he unfastened the gun belt, he saw the two bullet wounds. Joe watched three young boys in front of the office grabbing up Joe's empty cartridges. He wasn't sure what to make of that, but the groaning sounds of Smiley coming to changed his thoughts.

He walked over and grabbed Smiley by his vest and vaulted him into a standing position. The barkeep shielded his face with his hands. Joe slapped them away. "Don't get in my way again . . . ever." He shoved Smiley back in the direction he'd come. "Leave it!" Joe snapped, when Smiley leaned down for his shotgun. Wilkie left it without argument and continued back to the Palace.

Joe left the office door open when he walked in. He sat down at his desk, poured a shot of whiskey, and sipped.

"Mind if I have one?" Adam asked.

"Didn't think you imbibed?" Joe poured another glass and handed it to Adam. "You okay?"

"Don't like being shot at, that's for sure. But what bothers me is the way you were so slow at shooting back," Adam said, and sipped the whiskey. "Did you know you were doing that?"

"Shooting fast isn't accurate. Slow and deliberate, in a hurry, is best."

"You've told me. But, well, it looked like you were, well, never mind," Adam said. He concentrated on the whiskey. He decided not to pursue his concerns that Joe deliberately courted death. Was it because of Sarah? Maybe he was all wrong, but it stuck in his mind.

"You should have Doc look at your neck," Adam said.

Joe nodded and picked up Denver's .44 Remington and examined it. "I want you to give up that Navy, and start practicing with this."

"Why?" Adam asked and drained his glass.

"It's quicker to reload when you have an extra cylinder to carry." Joe half cocked the Remington, pulled down the loading lever, and pulled out the cylinder pin in quick succession. When the cylinder fell out, Adam was hooked.

"That is easier and quicker than reloading that old Colt," Adam said.

"And ya got a .44 caliber instead of the .36." Joe reassembled the pistol and handed it to Adam. "Have this belt reworked to fit you, it's in better shape than yours."

Adam nodded as he practiced taking the Remington apart.

CHAPTER TWENTY-FIVE

Byron Siegler and Pastor Evans were the first to arrive for morning coffee at the North Star. They sat down with Hadley and sipped from the steaming cups.

"Ya saddled with a problem, seems to me," Hadley said. He examined the frown on Siegler's face.

"I am, Gib. Doc and I saw the shooting yesterday and something has bothered me about it."

"Well, okay. Could it be someone was killed?" Hadley asked, leaning over the table. He often added to the conversation with the finesse of a cannon.

"Of course that's part of it. More bloodshed in our town, which we didn't have necessity of. But I've realized that it was the way Joe fired his gun. Very slow, too slow to be safe, it looked like to me, especially with someone standing there shooting at you," Siegler said. "I don't know, Gib, it almost looked like it didn't matter to him if he was shot or not. I can't explain it."

Pastor Evans was content just listening to the conversation.

Hadley rubbed his chin hair. "I know . . . I do know, that if ya shoot too fast, ya won't hit nothin'. Sure way to gain a third eye." Cannon blast.

"I would imagine that's correct. Did you know George Welby is back? And it appears he's taken up with Sarah again?" Siegler asked.

"Heard that tick was back in town. Didn't know Sarah took him back." Hadley rubbed his chin hair again. "Never thought we'd see him again after what, three years? Why in hell would she have anything to do with him? Lucky for him, she didn't kill him!"

Evans nodded, "The sanctity of marriage is God's will. But, I admit, it troubles me, seeing them together again. Does anyone know what Joe thinks about it?"

"You can ask him now if ya want," Hadley said, and nodded toward the empty window.

Joe approached the door but was summoned by Eli Miller. When he returned to the North Star, he held a telegraph message in hand. He studied the message while holding a cup in the other hand. The men shifted their eyes from the piece of paper to the ugly red line on the side of Joe's neck.

"Well, ya gonna tell us what it says or is it some kinda secret?" Hadley asked.

Thoughts interrupted, Joe looked up. "I've got to find a soldier who decided he was done with army service. 'Cept the army wasn't done with him yet. It says, 'To US Marshal Omaha, Wanted desertion this post night of 2nd instant. Private Melvin Thackett. Check home Brown's Station. Captain G. S. Carpenter, Commanding, 9th Infantry Fort Hartsuff.' "

"A stinkin' deserter! Hope ya bring him back lyin' over his saddle," Hadley said.

"Now, Gib, you certainly don't mean that. I've no love for deserters, either, but the Lord and our laws will guide him to a fair trial and a just punishment." Evans finished his coffee and set the cup down.

"Where is Brown's Station?" Siegler asked. He would rather have asked about the Welby situation, but decided against it. *Maybe someone else will bring it up.*

"It's about a two-day ride northwest on the river," Joe said.

"Don't think I've ever heard of it," Siegler said. "When will you leave?"

"It's a stage station. Head out as soon as I can get my gear. Adam will be fine 'til I get back."

Adam stood and read the telegraph message as Joe packed his saddlebags. He pulled the Winchester from the rack, checked its load, and laid it on his desk. Joe opened a desk drawer and handed Adam the special deputy badge. Adam's hand shook a little when he pinned it to his vest.

"Lot of responsibility, a town. I know you'll do fine," Joe said. He unpinned his own badge and laid it in the drawer. He retrieved the federal star and slipped it inside one vest pocket and the message in another. "You need help, you know who to see."

Adam nodded, "Be careful. He may not want to come back."

Joe offered a slight grin, "You know how *persuasive* I can be."

Adam watched Joe walk west down the boardwalk toward the livery with his gear and wondered how he couldn't have Sarah on his mind.

Mose watched Joe saddle the bay. The black man had a round, but not fat, face. Though his head was covered by very short white hair and he had a few face wrinkles, he didn't look old. Budd Jarvis had hired the black man to run the livery after his former man was arrested by Joe and later killed by Sheriff Canfield. Mose proved to be very capable with horses and gear. Joe liked him.

"Tek real good care of yoursef, Mr. Mashal," Mose said.

"Mose, I told you to call me Joe."

"I knows ya did that, Mashal." He handed Joe the saddlebags and bedroll.

All set, Mose walked along with Joe outside. "It's jus that some folk you meet may not be of a same mind as yousef, suh."

"Joe." He shook Mose's hand. "Thanks for taking such good

care of the bay for me."

The old man nodded. "It truly be a pleasure . . . suh. Might I ask why ya not name that fine ammal yet?"

Joe mounted up and smiled at Mose. "Seems you aren't the only one wants to know that." He started to offer Mose a wave when he noticed Sarah walking toward him. Joe's eyes searched behind her and around the end of town, but didn't see George. He stepped down and waited. He removed his hat when she stopped in front of him. She shot Mose a nervous glance.

"Thank you, Mose," Joe said.

"Sure nuff, suh," he said and walked back into the livery.

Sarah strained a smile, which flickered on and off. "I wanted to talk to you, and uh, saw you were leaving, so . . ."

Joe waited.

"I'm sorry about, well, that I didn't tell you right away about George coming back. Before you ran into us, I mean."

Joe nodded but did not speak.

"You must think horribly of me." She stalled to give a chance for a reply but none came.

Sarah cleared her throat, "When he showed up, I let him in and then lit into him. I hit him over and over. He never even tried to protect himself. I often thought I'd kill him if I ever saw him again." Tears dripped from her round cheeks. "He told me why he left. I really wanted to kill him then. But . . . he's my husband. And, after what I did, *had* to do . . . And that's the problem." She wiped away tears with her hand.

"Problem?" Joe said. It was a firm voice not often aimed at Sarah. He didn't like how he sounded.

"The problem is . . . the problem is, you made me love you! And I still do," she sobbed, holding a handkerchief to her nose.

Joe replaced his black hat and remounted the bay. "Can't have it both ways, can we?"

She reached into her reticule, withdrew three one-hundred

dollar bills, and handed them to Joe. He didn't reach for them. "George told me to give you this. We, he will have the rest of what I owe you next month . . . I told him how kind you were to loan me the money to start my business."

"He must have a good job to make that kind of money. What's he do, rob banks?" He shifted a bit in the saddle.

"He scouts land for the railroad. They pay well," Sarah said, tears streaming.

"Give it to Adam for safekeeping." He loosed the reins and the bay started walking. As the bay shifted to a trot Joe heard Sarah.

"Joe . . . I'm sorry! . . . I love you! . . . I'm sorry!" He could still hear her sobs so he touched the bay into a canter.

CHAPTER TWENTY-SIX

Sheriff Canfield tapped a finger on his desk as he waited for Nate Avery. He'd told Dick to let Avery know that he had recovered some of his stolen items. He puffed on the cheroot and counted the cash that was stolen by the thief he arrested. After searching the prisoner, the rest of the missing one-hundred and five dollars was found in a shoe.

It was about 3 p.m. when Nolan returned with Avery, hat in hand, as they entered the sheriff's office.

"Nate, come on in, sit down," Canfield said.

"Deputy Nolan told me that you found my merchandise and money," Avery said, smiling. "I can't thank you enough, Sheriff!"

"Well, don't thank me too much, didn't get everything, but it's better than nothing, isn't it?" Canfield said.

"So, you caught the thief?" Avery asked.

"I did, tracked him down."

Nolan looked at the floor.

"Is he here in jail? Can I see the son-of—. Excuse my profanity," Avery said.

"No, afraid he's not here, but don't you worry, he won't be stealing anything again," Canfield chuckled.

"Oh . . . you mean you . . . ?" Avery swallowed hard and his face turned a bit ashen.

"Here, show you what I got." Canfield shifted the conversation. "Here's two cans of beans, tooth cleaning powder, toilet water, shirt, tie, and seventy-four dollars. That's all was left of your money and sorry to say he didn't have the pistol and cartridges. The meat and taters were bad so tossed them aside." Canfield handed Avery the cash and bagged up the other items.

"Sheriff, I never thought I'd see my money again, I don't know how to thank you!" Avery stuffed the money into his pocket.

"Glad I got what I could. I'll be honest here, Nate, I could use your help with the election."

"But nobody else is running, are they? But I'll be glad to help, Sheriff. I'll be talking to everyone I know and tell them what you did for me," Nate said.

"Fine. Fine, Nate, all I ask." Canfield stood and shook the storekeeper's hand. "In case someone should jump into the race."

After he left the office, Dick sat down in the chair next to Canfield's desk. "Surprised you gave that much money back."

"Dick, I'm no street thief. Call it an investment in the future!"

"Think it's all worth it? Besides, like he said, no one else is running against you," Nolan said.

"Always better to stack the deck, you never know." Canfield leaned back and piled his boots on the desk. "You remember that meeting with the so-called cattlemen's association?"

Dick nodded, "Tye Edson and friends."

"He said some things that were downright disrespectful of my office. That's why I replaced our . . . *stock detective,* yes, I like the sound of that."

"Banning was no detective, he was a low-minded killer," Nolan said. "Can't figure why you replaced him with that stinkin' thief we had in jail. Can he even shoot that big Sharps? Ever goin' to tell me who he is?"

"It's not important who he is. I have a criminal complaint in my drawer ready to file on him for breaking into Avery's store. He does not want prison time," Canfield said and smiled.

"You really think *that* will keep him from just quittin' the territory?"

"No, I'm not that dumb, Dick. I offered another incentive for him to think about. That one made more of an impression." Canfield laughed.

"I hope so."

"And, I haven't forgotten the disrespect directed at me by those cow herders. It's my aim to see some of them find greener grass. And they will. Some will have to be buried under it first, though," Canfield said. "I've wanted a place of my own."

As she watched Joe disappear with the bay, she wiped again at her tears and turned around. She wanted to be alone. George wasn't in town so she headed for her house. She could be alone there. Her front door within range, the tears wouldn't stop. She looked past her door and caught sight of Pastor Evans as he stepped inside the church. She stopped, hesitated, and continued on.

When she stepped inside the church, it was stone silent. She stopped at the back row of benches and stared at the cross on the lectern. Her gaze was broken when Pastor Evans stepped out of his living quarters.

"Hello, my dear, I thought I heard someone, come in!"

Sarah hesitated again, then walked with determination toward the pastor. "I'm *not* here for a sermon. I just want someone to listen to me, damnit!"

The veteran preacher was a bit taken aback, but experience told him that one of his sheep required his shoulder. "Come over here and we'll sit on the new chairs that our county has supplied. They're a little more comfortable than those primitive benches."

Sarah seated herself a proper distance from Evans. "I'm sorry for speaking like that to you, Pastor. It's, it's, I'm so upset, and

I don't know what to do." She couldn't stop the convulsive sobs that burst forth. Pastor Evans placed a hand on hers and waited.

"Now, child, tell me what's heavy on your mind? No sermons, I promise. Speak," he said.

"I still love Joe, that's the problem," she blurted as her sobs died. "But George is my husband. By law, and by God's law, is that not so?"

"That is correct my child . . . go on." Evans was patient.

"The reason he left almost three years ago, is, he was caught by Budd Jarvis with his wife, at their ranch house."

Evans couldn't prevent the rise of his bushy eyebrows.

"When he came home . . . and told me, I attacked him. If I could have found my damned scissors I would have driven them through his heart. I hit him, and tore at his face. I think as much for leaving me as his seeing Rosella." She stopped to wipe her eyes and nose with a handkerchief. "I was so glad to see him anyway, to know that he hadn't just forgotten about me. And then, Joe. How can I love both at once? *Tell* me that!"

"Sarah, what you've been through, why, many wouldn't have survived it. You are a strong woman, a survivor. Look not to me, but to God for guidance. The one who deserves your love is known to Him."

"I know Joe is the one . . ." she said, and wiped her nose again. "But, I am married, have been for many years, to George. When I remember what *I've* done, how can I punish George?"

"My dear, *he* had a choice. You didn't, not really. You did what you had to, to survive on your own. Do not feel the weight of guilt upon your shoulders, for you have no room for it."

"What do I do?" Her voice was tiny.

"I know you desire no sermons, young lady, but He can help. Pray to Him for guidance, and you *will* find the answer, and the peace, which you so richly deserve."

"I've thought about a future with Joe, many times. But, I also knew all along, in the back of my mind, that the way he is, and the job he does . . ." She let out one more sob. "That he might not come back alive some day. That wouldn't be much of a future, would it? I know he wouldn't do anything else, and I would *never* ask him to!"

"I think, my dear, you have known all along what is the correct path to take. George has some soul searching to do and must seek repentance for what he's done. God does not take kindly to that sort of behavior. But, yes, you are married forever in His eyes. Always stand up for what is right, and against what is wrong. I think you will do well."

Chapter Twenty-Seven

With one day's ride complete, Joe was anxious to start early. He enjoyed the quiet beauty of the countryside camped along the bank of the Loup River's north branch. Except for coyotes howling half the night. But, even they were soothing to hear while his thoughts bounced around. He realized that he was used to Sarah being regular company. Marriage? Hadn't thought that far ahead, he supposed. But things were different now. *Wouldn't have bet George would have ever come back. Why I'm not a gambler.*

After retying his roll behind the saddle, he mounted up. The bay pranced, ready to go. He thought he would make Brown's Station by late afternoon. He hoped Private Thackett was present, and there wouldn't be any trouble. Last he knew, there was an older couple who ran the station, but never knew their names.

As the bay walked along the river, he started humming a tune. The horse turned his head and shook it. "What, you don't like that song?" Joe patted the bay's neck. "You know, Sarah gave me an idea as to who I am. When we get to the station, I mean." His eyes scanned the hills and valleys watching for others, including Indians, but also to take in the lush, green beauty of the sandy hills.

After many miles Joe stopped the bay in a shallow valley. He withdrew the pocket watch. "About five o'clock. Should be there in about twenty minutes."

By the time Joe rode into the stage station, he was prepared. "Hello!"

A straggly gray-haired man stepped through the open door of a good-sized soddy with a long-barreled shotgun in hand. "What's yer business?"

"Is this Brown's stagecoach station?" Joe said.

"Well, it's not the state capitol! What's yer business?" the old man asked again.

"My name's Frank Tyler. I'm with the railroad."

"Which one?"

Hmm. Worthy question. "Why, the Union Pacific, of course!" Joe said, proud of his performance.

"What are ya doin' out here then?" the old man asked, shotgun still at the ready.

"Scouting the area for a possible line to the Black Hills. If it's built, it will mean money for the region, yes, sir," Joe said and looked around.

"You can put yer horse in with the team, they's feed there." The old man pointed to the sod-covered lean-to where the relief team was kept.

"Thank you kindly," Joe said.

After unsaddling the bay and making sure feed and water were at hand, he looked at the other horses. Two were different than the rest. One, a tall sorrel, looked like he'd be a good runner. The next in line was a bay. Salt streaks covered him; he'd been ridden far and fast. Joe continued to inspect the horse until he found the brand. A "U.S." appeared on the shoulder and he noticed a McClellan saddle perched on a side rail. Entering the soddy, Joe stopped inside the door to let his eyes adjust. He dropped his saddlebags on the floor. To the right were two barrels topped by a short plank. A few bottles sat on it next to a small keg. To the left were two crude tables with benches and beyond that four roughly cut plank bunks. The dirt floor was packed smooth. The northwest corner was concealed by two hanging blankets that served as privacy walls. At the second table sat the old man, shotgun on the table in front of him. The striking v-pointed beard and piercing eyes of the man who sat next to him caught Joe's attention. A wide-brimmed tan hat laid in front of him.

"I didn't catch your name." The bearded man spoke, not taking his eyes off of Joe.

"Frank Tyler, Union Pacific Railroad, at your service, sir!" Joe said and thrust out his hand. The movement startled the bearded man. In a quick move, he hauled out a revolver from under his hat and cocked it.

"Whoa, friend. Only a handshake. Didn't mean to startle you, by golly!" Joe said as he stared at the pistol muzzle and grinned.

"Got anything with your name on it? Like a calling card, or a letter."

"No, sir, they haven't given me any cards yet. But if you wire Milburn Cade, in Omaha, he'll verify who I am, okay?" Joe said.

"You see any telegraph wires around here?"

Joe acted flustered and gave out a nervous chuckle. "Oh, uh, no, sir, I sure don't."

"All right, relax. He's okay," the old man said. He stood up and leaned the shotgun against the wall. "I been around these railroad men before. Help yourself to a beer or water. I'll start some grub."

Joe followed his lead and walked straight to the beer keg and poured a tin cup full. He looked back at the bearded man who still sat with his pistol out. "Can I get you one, Mr. . . . ?" Joe asked.

"Smith." The man slowly holstered the pistol and shook his head. Joe stood at the crude bar set up and watched the old man drop four good-sized beef steaks into the frying pan. *Four steaks for three people?* He hoped that Private Thackett was behind the hanging blankets.

"It'll be five dollars for bed and grub," the old man said.

"That's a little expensive, isn't it?" Joe said, and glanced around the soddy.

"You're free to go someplace else. Take it or leave it."

Joe frowned, "Well, okay. There's nowhere else for miles." He dug into a pocket and handed over five silver dollars. The old man smiled, produced a small leather pouch from inside his pants, and deposited the coins.

The bearded man stared at Joe. "Why don't you leave that shooter on the bar and sit down?" Before arriving, Joe had slipped off the cross-draw holster with the cavalry Colt and stashed them in a saddlebag. He kept the shorter-barreled Colt holstered on his hip. He didn't want to look overly armed for a railroad employee.

"Now leave our guest alone, will ya. I got a payin' customer here." The old man scolded the beard as he patted the concealed pouch. Joe raised the cup at the old man in a toast and grinned.

Joe returned to the table with his cup refilled and got comfortable. The old man stepped closer while the steaks were frying.

"So, tell us about this new line you're buildin'."

"Well, it's not definite, not yet, anyway. But if my report is successful the U.P., that's Union Pacific, will build a line, starting from the main line at Kearney City. You know Kearney, down near where the old fort is? We'll build it in a northwesterly direction through Broken Bow, and maybe right through here, if my report recommends it," Joe stopped and grinned again. "The line will end in Deadwood Gulch. It's sure to be a money maker for the railroad. You could travel there quickly and haul mining supplies, well any supplies." Joe wished that Adam could see his performance.

The beard didn't seem interested in the news. "Ain't those steaks done?"

The old man ignored him. "So, if you say it's good to come right by my station here, they will?"

"I don't have the power to make the final decision, you understand, but they do value these reports. I believe they would," Joe said and sipped his beer. "The bad side of it, though, there wouldn't be any more need for a stage line here. But, I'm sure you could hire on with the railroad."

"Think of that, I could work for the railroad," he said as if daydreaming. He returned to the stove in deep thought. "Okay, come and get 'em, I ain't your servant."

Joe glanced at the beard, who was staring at him. He got up and walked over to the stove where the old man handed him a tin plate with steak and beans. Picking up a knife and fork on the way back to the table, Joe ignored the beard and dug in. When the beard got up to get his, Joe slipped out the Colt and held it between his legs.

The old man brought two plates with him to the table and before he sat down, he hollered, "Come on, son, grub's ready." Out from behind the blanket wall stepped a young man wearing a calico shirt hanging over blue wool, army trousers. He looked like he just woke up.

"This is my son, Melvin, Mr. Tyler." Joe shook his hand. "Mr. Tyler, ya think Melvin here could get a job on the railroad? He's a fine boy. Fresh from his completed service in the army."

"Well congratulations, Melvin. Served my time in the war, no more of that for me, though!" Joe said. "Where were you posted, Melvin?"

The boy looked down at his meal and to the old man and then to Joe. "Fort Hartsuff, Mr. Tyler. I was in the infantry." He went right to cutting a chunk of meat and stuffed it into his mouth.

"Damned shame he never got to see his mama again. Ya see, she passed last month, while Melvin was still at the fort," the old man said, and swiped at his eye. "Fact is, he hadn't seen her in two years. They was too busy chasin' them savages."

"Sorry about your missus, and your mother, Melvin," Joe said. The old man seemed like a decent sort, how decent, he would find out soon enough.

The beard seemed to relax a bit and enjoyed the food and conversation.

"How did you like it in the infantry, Melvin?" Joe asked. The boy stopped chewing and glared at Joe. *Quite a reaction, about the same as if I'd asked him to cut his own throat.* "We walked a lot, same with your company, I bet," Joe added.

Several moments ticked by until the boy regained his composure and nodded, a few too many times, and kept chewing.

"Speak up, son, Mr. Tyler can't hear the rocks knocking around in your head." The old man looked at Melvin and frowned. "Taught you better than that."

Melvin swallowed the mouthful, "Yes, sir, a lot of walkin'. Bein' deployed as mounted infantry was the best times."

"I fought at Gettysburg, Mr. Tyler. I'll never get it out of my mind, that war," the old man said. "I was proud to serve, don't get me wrong. The proudest time of my life, to fight for my country. I was a sergeant by war's end." He seemed lost in times past.

"Where did you serve, Mr. Tyler?"

Joe finished his beer and said, "First Nebraska Volunteers, fought at Fort Donelson and Shiloh. Only made corporal, though. Then they sent us to Fort Kearny as cavalry to fight the Sioux and Cheyenne."

"Evil beings if there ever was any," the old man growled.

"They can be tricky, ain't that right, Doc?" Joe asked the beard.

"That's ri—" Those startled eyes opened wide as he reached for his holstered pistol.

"Don't," Joe said in a firm tone. The beard froze as Joe pulled the Colt from between his legs. The old man and boy glanced at each other.

Joe shoved his fork over to the beard. "Now, Doc, I hear you're a real dangerous man. Let's see how careful you can be. Pick up those two forks with your left hand, and using your left hand, unbuckle that rig and let it fall to the floor. But don't let even one of those forks drop." Joe pulled back on the hammer. The final click of the cylinder was clear in the silence. "I haven't killed anyone this month, try not to be the first."

The beard stared at Joe for a moment, then picked up both forks. He fumbled a bit while he unbuckled his gun belt, pulled it away, and dropped it on the floor.

"You a bounty hunter?" the beard asked.

Joe slipped out the deputy U.S. marshal star and held it up by the bottom point.

"Horse shit. A U.S. marshal. I knew you weren't no railroad man."

"Sorry to disappoint," Joe said. "What do you prefer to be called, Jim Riley, Doc Middleton, Doc? What?"

The beard offered a cold stare. "Everybody calls me Doc, I guess."

" 'Fraid I have some disappointing news for you," Joe said and handed the old man the telegraph message. The old man's face drooped worse as he read it. He carefully refolded it and handed it back to Joe. Tears welled in his eyes. He then backhanded his son, which hurtled him from his seat at the table. Resting his head against his folded hands, the old man started to cry.

"They execute deserters, don't they?" he asked without looking up at Joe.

"I don't know. My only job is return him to the army for a court martial," Joe said.

"What about me?" the beard asked. "I got some money, it's yours. More than you'll make in a year."

Joe ignored his attempted bribe. "You're coming back to Taylorsville with me. I have two posters on you."

"You think you can bring in two prisoners by yourself? On a two-day ride?" the beard said and smiled.

"Seated, or layin' over your saddle, up to you. I get paid the same." Joe stared back at Doc.

"You going to give me any trouble?" Joe looked at the old man, who raised his head.

"You take my . . . Melvin back and hang him."

"Did you know who this gentleman was?" Joe asked.

"I only know him by Jim Riley. What's he wanted for?" the old man said wiping sleeves across his eyes.

"He's apparently stolen more reservation ponies, and others, than we can count. And, the army wants him for killing a soldier at Sidney."

The old man looked at Doc. "Good for you, you steal all their ponies, they shouldn't be allowed any!" the old man said.

Doc's gaze remained on Joe.

"I won't give you any trouble, Marshal. I have no more family," the old man said.

"You still have a son," Joe said. The old man looked at him.

Joe got up and walked to his saddlebags by the door. He pulled out two sets of handcuffs and one set of leg irons. He kept the Colt pointed at Doc as he dropped the hardware on the table.

He looked at the old man. "Put the leg irons on, one on

each. Stand them up, then cuff them around this support pole." The old man completed the chore without speaking. The roof support pole was in the ground, how far, Joe didn't know. But if they pulled it out during the night, it would loose dirt down on them all. Joe didn't plan on sleeping much anyway, as trusting the old man wasn't a good bet.

CHAPTER TWENTY-EIGHT

Joe slept a grand total of an hour and a half during the night. He got the two prisoners and the old man up before first light. The old man agreed to saddle the three horses. Cold coffee, beans, and biscuits were served as Joe didn't want to lose any daylight.

Joe used a lariat to throw a double loop around Middleton's midsection and wrapped it around his saddle horn. Each prisoner was handcuffed, the leg irons fastened between the rigging dees of each saddle. This required the two horses to travel close together, side by side.

The old man stood outside the soddy door with glassy eyes. Melvin, dressed in his army shirt and trousers, sat on the stolen army horse, but wouldn't look at him. Dried blood surrounded the nose on his solemn face.

The old man walked over to Joe and looked up. "Nothing you told us was true, was it?"

"The railroad story wasn't."

"So, you did fight at Shiloh?" The old man seemed to search for something to salvage from recent events.

"I did," Joe said. The old man extended his hand and Joe shook it.

"Okay, men, move out," Joe said, and touched his hat brim to the old man. The two prisoners gave their horses an easy kick and they started walking with Joe following at the end of the lariat.

Throughout the day, they followed the river in a southeasterly direction, sometimes at a trot or canter. Joe watched Middleton's smoothness and ease in the saddle, which countered Melvin's jerky bouncing. It got hotter as the day wore on and Joe knew that the kepi Melvin wore offered little protection from the sun. He made short stops to water the horses and they used those opportunities to drink from their canteens. At the last water stop after noontime, Joe handed Melvin and Doc a piece of jerky.

"We gonna get a chance to rest?" Middleton asked. "Ahead only about five miles is Brewster Gap, nice little saloon there."

"Sure will, when we get to Taylorsville. Have beds all ready for you."

"You can't expect us to stay in the saddle all night?"

"You've had plenty of experience riding all night," Joe said, "Isn't that right? Of course, Melvin there, he's thankful to be horseback. Right, Melvin?" The young soldier ignored him.

Actually, Joe had been considering an overnight stop at Brewster Gap . . . until Middleton suggested it. He knew the outlaw's so-called "pony boys" included several men who would probably be looking for their leader. And, Joe knew Middleton had friends scattered around the countryside who would help him escape if the opportunity arose. He hoped for a cloudless sky to make another bright moonlit night.

"Turn south through this canyon," Joe told his charges.

"We're not even going through Brewster Gap?" Middleton asked.

"We'll head south about four miles and then turn east. We should be back at the river by dark." Joe thought it wise to avoid the settlement altogether.

By late afternoon they made the easterly turn. Walking the horses, Joe wondered what Melvin was thinking about. His future looked grim. Joe knew if it was wartime, the young man would be summarily executed upon arrival back at his post. It wasn't, so maybe the guardhouse and a later dishonorable discharge. Speculations, that's all they were, he told himself. Before he formed thoughts of Sarah once again, they heard a powerful zip through the air close by, then a distant gunshot. The horses jumped and shied to one side. "Get over here!" Joe yelled and pointed to the outcropping of a steep hill. They kicked their horses, dashed behind it, and dismounted.

"You two, sit down in that crevice in front of me where I can see you." With his Winchester in hand, Joe crawled up to the hilltop. He placed his hat on the ridge and lowered his head. A few moments later he peered over the edge again. A bullet smashed into the ground in front of him, sending dirt into both eyes. Temporarily blinded and using his sleeves to clear his eyes, the rifle slipped out of his hand and slid down the hill. Middleton grabbed it barrel first, then he heard the familiar cocking sound of Joe's Colt. He froze, one hand on the rifle and looked up at Joe. As Joe wiped at the eye that was still closed he said, "Be a bad gamble." Middleton hesitated and released the rifle barrel and stepped back into the crevice.

Joe grabbed his hat and retrieved the rifle. He scaled the hill again and believed he saw where the puff of smoke originated, so he fired two quick shots. He saw the dust cloud of one of the shots, short of the target. He aimed again, higher, and fired again. The round kicked up dust at the hilltop where the shooter was. He watched a few moments until a lone rider raced away to the south.

Joe stumbled down the hill to the bay, reloaded the rifle, and slid it back into the scabbard.

"Thought maybe your boys had come to rescue you," Joe said as he motioned them to remount.

"Wasn't mine. There was only one," Middleton said.

"You're right about that. Move out." Joe knew this shooter, by style anyway. He considered the distinct possibility that *he* was a target. *Hope to meet one day soon.*

At dusk they overtook the river. Joe had washed his eyes while the horses drank. As hoped, a three-quarter moon was bright, set in a crystal clear sky.

Joe knew it had to be at least 3 a.m. and he was having trouble keeping his eyes open. Canteen water to the face helped revive him somewhat, but fatigue pulled at him. The comforting rock of the bay didn't help. He noticed Melvin leaning to the left, with chin on chest.

"Melvin . . . Melvin!" Joe yelled.

The boy jerked upright and looked around. He readjusted the kepi and looked at the sky. Middleton glanced at the young soldier and shook his head.

It was obvious to Joe that the outlaw wasn't having any trouble staying awake. He knew it couldn't be much longer. He kept his mind busy considering his response to a rescue attempt. There was a lot to consider. He thought about the possibility of the pony boys trying to stage a jail break back in town. Maybe he'd hire an extra guard or two. He thought, too, about Sarah. It was apparent that their relationship, or whatever it was, was over.

The night sky was beginning to fail as the three trotted into Taylorsville. Joe preferred the gait to help keep himself awake. He tied up in front of the office, which had a lamp burning inside. Joe saw Adam asleep at the desk and yelled at him through the vacant windows.

"Get down," Joe said. He stepped up to Middleton, loosened the lariat around his waist, and let it drop to his feet. "That way."

"Marshal. It's sure good to see you!" Adam said, keeping his voice low.

"How's everything here?"

"Oh, fine. The only trouble was an argument between two cowhands at the Texan. Ol' Ham and me, we threw 'em right out. He can be a forceful fella if he wants to be. Boy, do I have news to tell you!"

Before they closed the jail door on the two new prisoners, Joe noticed a bearded man sleeping on the bottom bunk. "Who's he?"

Adam held up one finger. The new prisoners put their hands through the narrow door slot used for serving food, and Adam removed their handcuffs. He nodded toward the rear office door with a wide grin. Joe could tell he was anxious to unburden himself. They stepped out back and shut the door.

"You'll never believe who that prisoner is in there. Special Agent Langston brought him in this afternoon!"

"Who?" Joe was more concerned about climbing onto his cot.

"None other than, are you ready? The most wanted outlaw in the state, Doc Middleton himself!"

Chapter Twenty-Nine

With only two hours' sleep, Joe had already been to the telegraph office to send a message to Fort Hartsuff informing them of Private Melvin Thackett's arrest. Back at the office he was able to look over Langston's "Middleton." To an intoxicated eye, there were some distant similarities, but that was it. He was not *the* Doc Middleton. Joe knew he was very fortunate to have stumbled across the real one by accident. He'd met him in Kansas a few years back when Middleton first came north from Texas. He went by Jim Riley then. The sketches of him on reward posters were only fair renditions, however. Joe did relish the thought of breaking the news to Harper Langston.

While waiting for Adam to return, Joe watched two men installing new windows in the office front. And, dark green window shades were installed for the first time. These could be pulled down to cover the windows if desired. Byron Siegler had sold out his first shipment of glass and other materials and more were on order. Citizens volunteered to form work crews to help repair storm damage.

"All finished, Marshal. Bet you like having windows again," one of the workers said.

"I do, indeed. Thank you, gentlemen." Joe stood out front and admired their work.

Adam crossed the street and stepped onto the boardwalk near Joe. "Thought you'd still be sleeping. You sure look like you need it."

Joe nodded. "Before we go back inside, somethin' you should know. The fella I brought in with Private Thackett is Doc Middleton. He is not the one Langston brought in."

Adam stood open-mouthed and then a grin formed. "I'd sure be willing to watch him take in that news. How'd you find him, anyway?"

"Run on to him at Brown's Station by luck," Joe said. "Where is Langston?"

"He left the hotel early," Adam said and grinned again. "Said he'd be back tomorrow. Oh, and I have that $300 that Sarah left here for you. Said you knew about it?"

Joe nodded, "Payment on what I loaned her. Apparently George gave it to her to give to me. Said she'd have the rest next month."

"She sure didn't have that kind of money, did she?"

Joe shook his head.

"So, what is George doing to make all that money? Robbing banks?"

Joe was amused by Adam's questions. "What I asked her, too. She said he scouts land for the railroad."

"If you don't mind me askin', what about you and her?" Adam said in a low tone.

"I do mind," Joe said.

That evening before Joe went on rounds, he pulled the ten gauge off the rack and loaded it with two brass shells. He made sure the back office door was barred and gave Adam instructions to keep the shotgun handy while he was gone. He also instructed Adam to lock the front office door. Joe knew that he might have to enlist some extra help to guard their "famous" guest until he could be transferred to Omaha where the federal court was.

At the far east end of the block, Joe shook doors starting with

Iain McNab's furniture store. When he got to the Texan, he noticed Siegler and Jarvis at the bar. As he turned to go inside he heard someone calling for him. It was Eli across the street.

"Have a message for you!"

Joe walked across and went inside the office. Joe shook his head as he read it. It was from the fort. "Seems the army is too damned busy to come and get their prisoner."

He returned to the Texan to talk to Siegler.

"Joe, have a drink on me," Jarvis said.

"No thanks, not right now," Joe said.

"You look like something is on your mind, Joe," Siegler said.

"Got a message here, the army wants me to deliver Private Thackett to the fort. I'll leave first thing in the morning and be back by late afternoon. I want two guards at the jail while I'm gone."

"Ah, yes, Doc Middleton! We heard. That Agent Langston is quite the man-hunter!" Jarvis said.

Siegler raised his glass, "To Mr. Langston." Jarvis touched his beer mug with Siegler's whiskey glass. "Do what's necessary, Joe."

Joe decided he didn't want to dive into the whole conversation about the real Middleton at that point and headed back to the office.

By midnight he had two extra men hired, courtesy of Budd Jarvis. One was Bony Wilson and the other was Tim Egan. Joe hadn't met Egan before but they were both trusted hands of Jarvis. They seemed capable enough to help Adam with guard duty.

"I want two men here at all times. Adam will have the ten gauge, the other man will have Smiley's sawed off," Joe ordered. "One man at a time can run over to the hotel for a meal, but be damned quick about it and get back here. You boys both have your carbines as well, good. Keep them loaded. Mr. Middleton's boys would like nothing better than to spring him if they find out where he is. He's escaped jails in the past, this won't be one of them." Joe finished giving instructions and turned in.

Chapter Thirty

Joe handcuffed Private Thackett and they left Taylorsville while it was still dark. They followed the Loup River until it started to make a slight northeasterly turn. At that point they rode due east, where they eventually picked it up again and headed south. The soldier hadn't said a word yet.

"Melvin, like to talk to you a bit," Joe said. He looked at Joe through terrified eyes as the horses plodded along.

"I know you don't like being in the army, but when you signed that paper, well, that's a binding contract. That is, you have to complete your time whether you like it or not."

"What difference does it make? They'll hang me or shoot me, anyway."

"I don't know what they'll do, Melvin, but I'll talk to the commanding officer. Tell him your pa needs help at the station being all alone out there. It's a fact, isn't it?"

Melvin nodded. "But he don't want me no more."

"If given the chance, you finish your time. Do your work first-rate, and when you get discharged, you go see if he hasn't changed his mind. I could see honor is a very important thing to him. And he's right about that, it should be," Joe said.

The first thing Joe saw was the tall flagpole. There was enough breeze to keep the 38-star flag waving. Joe believed it was the tallest flagpole he'd ever seen.

They crossed the river and approached Fort Hartsuff. Buildings made of lime and concrete were scattered around the parade ground, where the flagpole was positioned. The magnificent, 97-foot pine had been cut at the Niobrara River in northern Nebraska. Joe could see four blue army wagons parked near the stable. Their red wheels stood out.

Aiming directly toward the post headquarters at the southern corner of the parade ground, they rode past the guardhouse. A lone sentry waved them on. Two soldiers stepped out of the headquarters onto the boardwalk. These were the only soldiers Joe could see. Melvin stepped down as Joe tied up the horses. They both climbed two steps to the walk where Joe removed the handcuffs.

"Good day to ya, Marshal! Sergeant Edmund O'Malley, and this is Corporal Henshaw. Welcome to our little slice of heaven." Joe had already identified the men by their pale blue sleeve chevrons. The sergeant was a thick man, not fat, and almost a head taller than the corporal. Joe noted that the corporal's leathery face appeared to be a map of tough times.

"Joe Mundy, and I guess you know Private Thackett," Joe said.

"Oh, indeed we do, indeed we do!" the sergeant said. "That government horse is a mighty fine sight to be seein', I can tell ya that much!"

Joe thought the sergeant seemed like a jovial sort, at least he thought so for a short time.

"Corporal, would ya be handin' me your rifle?" The sergeant held out his hand. The corporal, who had been standing at port arms, thrust out the Springfield Trapdoor rifle. The sergeant inspected the rifle carefully, adding an, "uh-huh, uh-huh," then smashed the butt into Private Thackett's stomach. He bent in half with an "ugh," and fell to the boardwalk holding his middle.

The sergeant then jutted the rifle back into the corporal's hands. "Isn't it a beautiful day the Almighty has sent us?" he said. With hands on hips, he took a deep breath and looked into the distance.

"Yes, sir, it sure is," Joe said.

"Ah, now, Marshal, no need to be callin' me sir," the sergeant said, then added in a lower tone, "I work for a livin'!" and he winked.

Joe nodded. "Like a word with the captain about Thackett, is he busy?"

"Come right in this way." He waved at the closed door. "Corporal, show Mr. Thackett to his room in the guardhouse, if you please."

The sergeant stepped inside and knocked at an inner office door and opened it. He saluted and said, "Captain, the marshal would be likin' a word with ya."

Joe heard the captain's reply, "Send him in."

"That will be all, Sergeant," the captain said. He again saluted, stepped out, and closed the door behind him. Joe could hear his boots clunk down the hallway.

"Captain Carpenter, Marshal. Please be seated."

"Kinda dead around here, Captain," Joe said, as he glanced out the window.

"Yes, Lieutenant Lovell is out with a detail to search for that Sam Bass character," Carpenter said.

"Yeah, got a poster on him. They suspect him of robbing the U.P. down at Big Springs," Joe said. The captain nodded.

"I want to thank you for finding and returning Private Thackett, but most especially the horse. I've never had a deserter in my command before . . . and there better not be another." Before sitting down he offered Joe a cigar.

"No thanks. What will happen to Thackett?" Joe asked.

"There will be a court-martial. The final determination of sentence I could not say," Carpenter said.

"I wanted to explain something about Thackett. He lost his mother last month and his father is up in years and soon won't be able to handle the work at the stage station by himself. Probably kill him if he lost his only son."

"I understand what you're saying, Marshal. I command only one company of infantry here, Company K, with only fifty-five men. I need every one of them. But, they must be trustworthy men. Not that it should make a difference in my opinion, but since it's not wartime per se, it's unlikely that Private Thackett will face hanging," Carpenter said and leaned back in his chair. He gazed out of a window and said, "But he will do the work of three men around here. Heaven forbid should he desert again."

"I talked to him on the way here, about his commitment to the army, and honor. Hopefully he won't desert again," Joe said.

"That is my hope as well, because a second time will not bode well for young Thackett," the captain said, and puffed fire into his cigar. "I will venture a guess that you served in the war, Marshal. Officer?"

"I did. Corporal," Joe said.

"A horrible war. And now, still, the Indians."

"How are things with the Indian problems?" Joe asked.

Carpenter blew smoke toward the ceiling and studied it. "Many have been transferred to reservations, but some of them continue to be less than enthusiastic about moving. Soldiers had to kill Crazy Horse up at Camp Robinson. Progress is being made, though, Marshal."

The conversation continued for several minutes before Sergeant O'Malley knocked on the door, stepped in, and saluted. "Captain, sir, Lieutenant Jones has requested your presence at the post hospital." The sergeant stepped back into the hallway at attention.

"Very well. Marshal, would you care to have lunch before heading back?"

"I would, thank you," Joe said.

"Sergeant, instruct Corporal Henshaw to escort Marshal Mundy to the enlisted mess."

"Yes, sir!"

"Thank you for your time, Captain." The two men shook hands.

"Anytime, Marshal, and thanks again."

As they walked through the barracks, the corporal mounted his rifle on a round rack and continued into the mess hall. He instructed the cook to heat up a plate for the federal marshal and poured two cups of coffee. The corporal sat down across from Joe at a long table as he ate a plate of army beans, bacon, and biscuits. They talked about army service and where each had previously served.

"Back in '65 I was posted at Fort Mitchell. That was about a hunert mile east of Fort Laramie. On the coldest damn day of the winter, a bunch of Sioux and other breeds attacked a stage station called Mud Springs. I tell you what, I'd a rathered stayed in that warm barracks than treps' after Indians, but we done got ordered, so off we went."

"How many in your detail?" Joe asked.

"They was thirty-six of us. Plenty of men to scare off them red-devils. We's carrying Spencer carbines. Fire seven times 'thouht reloadin'. Each one of us freezin' our high-tails off. It was Feb-arry, ya see. Well, anyways, we no mores and got there when all hellfire broke loose. The Indians filled the horizon. I thought to mysef, 'shit oh dear,' got ourselves into something a might bigger'n us!" He stopped long enough to slurp some coffee and pinch his face as the hot liquid burned his throat. Joe was amazed how much the corporal talked, but enjoyed hearing about the battle.

"We fired and fired. We lost one man and another wounded. Guess we was lucky considerin' there was top side of five hundred Indians. That's official, too, no stretchin' that rope! Then, my eyes couldn't believe that Lieutenant Ellsworth ordered our horses be let out. Well, I thought, damned be if I'm *walkin'* back to the fort! The Indians quit the attack and went chasin' after our horses, then they left. When the attack was over, well, then we got time to cipher some numbers and it didn't take a pound of brains to hope they wouldn't come back."

Joe finished his meal, shoved his plate away, and concentrated on the coffee.

"Next day, we got reforced by about one hundred and forty men from Fort Laramie. I remember thinkin' to myself, ya didn't bring enough! We got attacked again, shootin' the station to pieces and then a sky full of arrows fell on some of the new horses and men. A few more men and a small cannon got to us that night. The next day we was all ready for another attack, but the Indians quit the field. You can see that we was a might relieved that it was all over. Then the scouts reported to the colonel that they tracked a thousand warriors who rode off to a big encampment on the North Platte River."

Joe pulled out his pocket watch to check the time. "Well, I guess you were lucky there."

"So's you'd think, wouldn't ya? This colonel from Fort Laramie decided we'd take one hundred and eighty-five men and go after them Indians! I couldn't believe my ears, and thought the colonel needed *his* ears cleaned out. Didn't he hear the scout's report of a thousand braves? Well, we caught up with 'em by this crick off the North Platte. I wanted to ask the colonel if he had bad eyesight too, 'cuz I could see that we was terrible outnumbered. Let me say that catching them Indians was easy enough, but we had a terribly hard time lettin' 'em go!"

CHAPTER THIRTY-ONE

Joe kept the bay at a trot when he reached Taylorsville's main street. He noticed Adam pacing back and forth in front of the office and decided to tie up there instead of proceeding directly to the livery. When Adam saw Joe, he stopped and waited for him.

"Looked like you was tryin' to wear out the boards," Joe said, as he climbed onto the boardwalk.

"This is all my fault. It was my responsibility, I'm sorry, Marshal," Adam said.

"What is it?"

"This mornin', me and Tim Egan were on duty. I went for a quick bite, like you said to, and when I came back, Middleton was gone. *Your Middleton.* That Agent Langston ordered Tim to release him!" Adam took a breath. "Said he wasn't Middleton and he wouldn't allow a man to be held without charges."

Joe rushed into the office and saw for himself. Only the bearded man who Langston thought was Middleton remained in the cell, and Bony Wilson. Wilson didn't say a word.

"Marshal, I looked around for him but he lit out on one of Budd's livery horses as fast as the wind. Old Mose tried to stop him but Middleton knocked him down. I'm sorry, it's all my fault. I shouldna gone to breakfast."

Joe contained his rage. "Where is Langston?"

"We think he's headed for Willow Springs. He told Tim that it's your job to transport *this* Middleton to Omaha," Adam said.

"I'm sorry, Marshal."

"Adam, it's not your fault. I should have met with Langston before I left." Joe put a hand on Adam's shoulder. "Right now, I want you to send a telegraph message to Marshal Twilliger in Willow. Arrest Harper Langston for breaking a prisoner out of jail here." Adam stared at Joe. "Now!" That broke his daze and he dashed out the door.

Joe walked up to the jail cage and looked at the bearded prisoner. "What's your name?"

"I told that city fella a dozen times my name is Arthur Franke. But did he listen? Naw. He seemed to think I was some outlaw, that Middleton fella you all been whisperin' about."

"Where'd he arrest you?" Joe asked.

"Up near Long Pine. I come back from Dakota, dead broke, lookin' for a job. Some boys workin' cattle hired me on. Worked about two days until I seed they had a variety of brands on them cattle. Looked like them cattle had a calf every day! Weren't lookin' for no troubles like that, so quit 'em. Just quit 'em, and rode about three miles, headin' south when he come up on me sudden like, with a pistol in my face. Made me put on the manacles my own self . . . and here I am."

"He arrest you for anything other than being Middleton?" Joe asked.

"Never mentioned nothin' else. I didn't do nothin' else. He was happier'ana dog with two tails. This Middleton fella must be some catch?"

"He was in there with you until this mornin'," Joe said.

"You don't say? 'Spose there is a resembleness. Gonna have to shave this beard," Franke said, and stroked the growth. "You gonna let me out now?"

"Probably. Talk this over with the judge first."

★ ★ ★ ★ ★

"Well, why don't someone haul off and ask Joe about Sarah?" Hadley said. The morning coffee club was fully attended and anxious for Joe's arrival so their thirst for knowledge could be quenched.

"Yes, you go ahead and do that," Siegler said with a snort.

"Gentlemen, I think it best if you let me engage the marshal in private and see if he wishes to discuss this particular burden he's carrying," Pastor Evans said. "The Lord's light can ease a man's burden."

Jarvis was silent. Thoughts of how he would kill George Welby recurred on a regular basis. He considered that the "why" of it would have to be revealed then. He wondered if Joe would actually try to stop him.

"Budd . . . Budd," Siegler said. "You don't seem to be with the conversation at hand. Hate to interrupt your thoughts, but what's your opinion about Joe and Sarah?"

"Who gives a buffalo turd? Haven't you old biddies got anything better to think about?" With that Jarvis got up and stormed out.

The North Star was silent, all eyes fixed on the front door, which no longer held Jarvis's image. They broke their stare and looked at each other. Harold Martin looked frightened.

"Now, what's the bee in his butter?" Hadley asked no one in particular and glanced back at the door.

Siegler looked at his coffee cup. "There's been something on his mind for a while, won't say what. But it seems to correspond with the return of our illustrious former marshal."

Joe appeared at the front door, and held his gaze down the walk in the direction that Jarvis had gone. No one had yet spoken to him by the time he got his coffee and sat down. "Did I interrupt something?"

They heard Joe's razor-sharp tone, which seemed a bit unfriendly.

"Ah, ah, no," Siegler said. "There was a lull in the conversation."

"Lull like a gunshot!" Hadley said. They looked at him.

"It seems like Budd has had something on his mind that he won't talk about," Siegler said. "Have any idea what's bothering him?"

Joe shook his head and sipped the coffee. "No, but I'm glad you two board members are here so I can tell you about something that's happened—"

Before Joe could finish, the remaining four club members indicated their assent verbally, their quick, "yeses" and "okays" in a not-so-veiled anticipation of his words as they leaned closer to the table.

"—at the jail," Joe finished. The group sat back in their chairs.

He began by informing them of the arrest of Private Thackett, and *the* Doc Middleton at Brown's Station, and how he identified the outlaw. Joe's news of Harper Langston's order to release the real Middleton was met with groans.

"Well Joe, first, I congratulate you on arresting this Middleton," Siegler said. The others assented. "Good God, we toasted that fool."

"By who'n' hell's authority did he release your prisoner?" Hadley asked.

"*His* authority, I guess. Adam wired Willow to watch for him."

"Who did Mr. Langston arrest?" Harold joined in.

"Says his name is Arthur Franke. Haven't any poster on him so will release him soon as I talk with the judge."

CHAPTER THIRTY-TWO

That evening, Joe sat behind his desk sipping whiskey. He'd talked to Judge Worden about releasing Arthur Franke and the judge agreed. On the subject of swearing out a formal complaint on Harper Langston, the judge was less than enthusiastic. He agreed that Langston had acted illegally in releasing Joe's prisoner, but was savvy enough regarding the justice department to realize that the town could never sustain the process of prosecution. If Langston purposely dragged out the affair, it could break Taylorsville financially. Joe was not happy, but agreed with the judge's advice. Joe informed him that if Langston ever showed up again, he would discuss the matter. He sent Marshal Twilliger another message to disregard the arrest of Langston.

With the prisoner released and Adam in Gracie Flats on an errand for Siegler, Joe enjoyed the quiet, but only for a short time.

Jenny, the young lady who worked at Jarvis's Texan, gave a knock and walked into the office. Her five and a half foot frame, golden hair, and blue eyes caught men's attention. Joe was no exception. She wore a plain gingham dress with a blue ribbon tied around her neck.

"I hope I'm not disturbing you," she said, and placed a small basket on Joe's desk.

" 'Course not, Jenny, what can I do for you?"

"Drinking alone?" she asked.

"Care for one?"

Joe got out another shot glass and filled it, and pointed to a chair. She sat down, took a sip, then a second.

"Brought some fried chicken for you from the chophouse. It's not the best ever made, but it's not bad."

"Mighty thoughtful of you," Joe said. "Have you eaten?"

Jenny nodded. "How are you doing, Joe?"

"I'm fine. How are you?"

"You know what I mean. It's all over town. Sarah and George," she said and sipped the whiskey again, not looking at him.

"Sure lots of folks concerned."

"Aren't you? What are you going to do about it?" Jenny asked.

"Doesn't concern me."

Jenny stared at him. "It did."

"Don't anymore." Joe said.

"Good," Jenny said with a sly smile and sipped the whiskey. Joe refilled their glasses and recorked the bottle.

"You hear that Rose quit the Texan and went back east?" she asked.

"I did," Joe said. "I remember the day you both came in on the freight wagon with Budd's piano."

Nodding, Jenny added, "She did the upstairs work. I don't. I sing a little, dance with cowboys sometimes, and let them tell me their troubles."

Joe nodded, wondering why she told him that. They sat in silence, until a rider skidded his horse to a stop in front of the office. The cowhand jumped off and rushed in.

"Marshal! That big rifle has us pinned down. Johnny Fuller is wounded bad. Get Doc to come out to Edson's range, north side of the river, about six miles."

"Who are you?" Joe asked.

"My name's Clive, work for Mr. Edson. He told me to bring

you and the doc back right away. Can't be movin' Johnny. His leg looked busted near in half, looked to me!"

"Jenny, go tell Doc to bring his bag and some splints and meet us at the livery, then tell Byron what's happened," Joe said as he grabbed his saddlebags and rifle. Before leaving, he stuffed the cloth-wrapped chicken into one of the saddlebags.

At the livery, Mose hitched a horse to the rental buggy while Joe saddled the bay. Doc arrived only minutes later and Joe waved him to the buggy.

"Okay, Clive, lead on," Joe said and the little caravan started for the river.

Light was beginning to fade as they approached. Clive pulled up, stopped, and turned to Joe.

"Jus' past that little bunch of trees, right around that hill," he said in a low tone. Joe nodded and waved them forward.

"We'll tie up at those trees and walk in," Joe said. Doc gathered his bag and splints and followed Joe and Clive as they walked through the cool water of the Loup River. As they approached, Clive hunched over and gave a whistle.

"We'll be in the open for a quick minute, then run right to a low spot," Clive whispered. Joe and Doc nodded. As they reached the open place they ran one at a time around and to cover. Clive went first, then Doc. Joe stepped off to the side and fired two quick shots from his rifle. As Doc was caught in the open, he dropped the splints and kept running. The ground exploded behind him as he reached the shallow crevice where Tye Edson, Clive, the wounded Johnny, and another cowhand were lying almost flat. Joe grabbed the splints and made it to the crevice before the shooter could fire again.

Edson looked over at Joe and his '76 Winchester and nodded. "Nice to see ya, Marshal."

"Where are your horses?" Joe asked.

"All run off by the shots. Clive managed to catch one of 'em so he could go for help. We couldn't move Johnny like that," Edson said and glanced to the wounded hand.

Joe looked at the cowhand and noticed a large pool of blood had soaked into the grass under his leg. The top section of his leg was a bit askew from normal; a wild rag was tied high to help slow the blood loss. Johnny was barely conscious.

Edson looked at Joe and said, "We was comin' in to town for business. The first shot went through Johnny's leg and into his horse. Dumped him here and ran off to die I 'spose."

"Too dark to do much, and no moon. We'll have to wait 'til morning. I'll move off over there before daybreak and engage him so you all can load him into Doc's buggy."

Edson and the hands nodded. Doc worked on Johnny's leg.

"Heard you're a federal deputy. Guess you'll be helpin' us now," Edson said in a cynical tone.

"Plannin' to anyway. Trying to figure out how to find the shooter," Joe said.

"Seems you can find him by ridin' around out here like a sittin' duck."

"Have you hired anyone to ride your range?" Joe asked.

Edson shook his head, "Can't find anybody."

The crevice they laid in provided cover, but not for sitting or standing. Joe peered over the edge in an attempt to see movement but there wasn't enough light.

"How's he doin', Doc?" Joe asked.

"Not good, he's lost a lot of blood. His femur is broken. Got him to swallow some laudanum." Doc wiped Johnny's forehead and added, "If he makes it through the night, there might be a chance. Can't see my damned hand in front of my face now."

"Appreciate whatever you can do for 'im, Doc." Edson's voiced drifted through the darkness. No moon plus clouds made for a coal-black night.

CHAPTER THIRTY-THREE

A trace of light gradually showed itself on the eastern horizon, so Joe looked out of the crevice. It was still dark, but hill outlines began to appear.

Joe touched Edson's shoulder, which brought the rancher out of his catnap. "Send a man to bring the buggy over. You should have enough darkness to load him up and head for town. Be quick, though, he'll have enough light to shoot soon if he's still out there. I'm going across over to that rise and draw his fire when the time comes," Joe said.

Edson sent Clive for the buggy and Joe trotted away. He found a ridgetop about fifty yards west of the men and sat down. He looked east but could barely make out the men's figures. He heard the horse and buggy splashing through the river and watched until he saw it approach the crevice. By then, he could see the men's outlines. Once they had the wounded man loaded on the back of the buggy and started for the river, Joe ran over the top and climbed another hill a little closer to the shooter.

The direction of the gunshot revealed that the shooter had also changed positions. A pop sound made Joe suspect the bullet had found its mark. He hoped Doc or the others weren't hit. Joe turned and fired three fast rounds at the shooter's new location. He leaned down, looked, and saw movement. Joe heard another shot and saw the dust cloud hit the hill behind him. He couldn't find better cover without becoming a full target, so he aimed the rifle and waited. The two heavy caliber rifle shots

170

sounded like one. The shooter's head dropped down fast. Joe thought he might have hit him, but levered another round into the chamber, anyway, and watched. He aimed the Winchester at the same place as the last shot. Two full minutes had gone by when Joe thought about taking a look. He scanned the hilltops to each side of the shooter in case he had changed position again but saw nothing.

After another minute, Joe decided to take a look. Fully exposed as he descended the hill, Joe got to the bottom and trotted an indirect course toward the shooter. The bullet that whizzed by his head answered the question at hand. Diving behind the only mound of dirt handy, Joe was now in a worse location. Not only was he at the bottom of a small valley, below the shooter, but a large bullet could easily punch through the dirt mound once the shooter zeroed in on him. Joe cussed to himself as he waited. The closest hill was several yards away. If the shooter positioned himself on the top of it, Joe was dead.

Several minutes went by as Joe watched in every direction. Thirty minutes ticked by with no more gunfire. Joe wondered if the shooter had ridden out and how long he should lie there if he was gone. *Sure could use a drink of water.* The cloud cover had cleared off with the new day bringing warm sunlight. Joe thought about the canteen on the bay and the river, which were both about a hundred yards behind him.

Movement! Dirt covered his face when the bullet plowed through the mound inches away. He fired and levered another round as soon as he saw movement again. *Has me sited in . . . that didn't take long. Should run for that hill, but he'd probably like that. Better than sittin' here waitin' for it.*

Joe was soaked by sweat as he laid in the sun. A glance at his pocket watch revealed that it was almost 10 a.m. He didn't realize that so much time had gone by. Another boom from the shooter and another face full of dirt. This time the dirt stung his face and right eye. He let the Winchester rest on the mound while he wiped his eye. Still somewhat blurry, he saw his old army pal, Derwin Foster, lying next to him with his head down staring at Joe. His blue uniform, like Joe's, was filthy. Usually ready with something laconic to say, Foster was oddly quiet. Joe shook his head and wiped his eyes again. His pal had vanished.

As soon as he could sight clearly he aimed and held his finger steady against the trigger. Joe fired again when the head popped up, but even though his bullet hit inches from the shooter, he could see him reload and fire again. Joe fired, levered another round with the shooter still in his sight, and pulled the trigger. The metal on metal snap of the empty chamber seemed as loud as a fired shot. Knowing that he had left the canteen behind, he then realized that he'd brought no extra rifle ammunition either.

The next bullet that the shooter sent his way plowed through the mound and gashed his left shoulder. Blood appeared and soaked into the white shirt. Joe removed his bandanna, wrapped it around the wound, and tied it tight. Another shot hit almost the same spot, missing him by inches. Then another, closer. Soaked with sweat and blood and covered with dirt, Joe tried to make as small of a target as possible. Another lull. More minutes went by. With the sun almost directly overhead, there was no call to check the pocket watch.

Joe had laid there for what must have been at least an hour without any further shots. He raised his head and peered over the mound but saw no movement. He waited and then looked again. Nothing. He raised his hat up above the mound and held it there. Nothing. Tired of lying in the dirt, Joe picked up his rifle and stood. He didn't take off running for cover, he just stood there. No more shots were fired. He checked the cavalry Colt and started walking with it in his right hand, the empty Winchester in his left.

When he reached the hill from where the shooter had been

firing, Joe put down the rifle and approached the position. He took short steps until he was on the back side. Grass was smashed down where the shooter had been. Joe found a pile of cartridge casings in the grass and inspected one. It was a .45-90. He remembered that the Sharps hunting rifle stolen from Harper Langston was the same caliber. He slipped it in a vest pocket and stepped back down the hill. A few minutes of looking revealed prints and droppings, a spot where a horse had been standing for a while. Unable to learn anything further, Joe started the walk back to the river and the bay.

Doc Sullivan could do no more for the wounded cowhand. He had stopped the bleeding, but there was nothing left to do but sit and watch Johnny's chest rise slightly, and then recede. He didn't want him moved any more than necessary so they left him on the examining table in the front room of Doc's house. Tye Edson had sent Clive and the other hand to the hotel while he sat and waited with Sullivan.

"Johnny worked for you very long?" Doc asked. He continued to watch for chest movement. He knew the cowboy was dying.

"Two years. Good man. Was gonna be my foreman." Edson looked down. "Soon as I know he's okay we'll head back out and meet Joe."

"What do you think is happening? With that maniac around shooting people?"

"Wick Canfield. I think he means to run me off," Edson said and glanced at Doc.

"Don't suppose you can prove that?" Doc said.

"No. When our cattlemen's meeting ended he walked out kinda muttering under his breath. My wife overheard him say, 'see how long he'll stay here,' or words to that effect."

"He is no good, to the core no good," Doc said. Edson started to nod when Doc got to his feet and approached Johnny. He leaned over his face and then rested an ear on the cowhand's chest. A minute later he straightened up and pulled a sheet over him. "I'm sorry, Tye, he's gone."

Edson stood, walked over the table, and pulled the sheet back. He studied Johnny's tan, leathery face for a moment and then replaced the sheet.

Joe opened the door and walked in. He glanced at the sheet and then to Sullivan.

"He passed," Sullivan said. "You are a mess. Let's have a look at that arm."

"Did you kill that bastard?" Edson asked.

Joe shook his head. "There'll be another time."

"Another time? You mean another of my men has to die? Another time! Why don't you do your damn job?" Edson said and slammed the door on the way out. Joe watched him leave and then took off his hat while Sullivan started to work on his shoulder.

"He's upset losing his man, Joe. He doesn't mean anything personal."

"Mr. Edson is right. It *is* about time I do my job. The job you all pay me for," Joe said. The icy tone had returned.

CHAPTER THIRTY-FOUR

With his left arm in a sling, cleaning the big Winchester was awkward. Joe sat in a chair beside the cold stove and sipped whiskey while he watched Adam work over the rifle at his desk. He periodically glanced at Joe's white sling as he worked.

"Sure is dirty," seemed to be the only words Adam could think to say. "Sure is dirty."

"Want you to know something," Joe said. "Soon as this shoulder heals I'm going to be gone awhile. Until I kill him."

"What happened, up there on Edson's range?" Adam asked, and glanced at the sling.

"Suspicion he ran out of cartridges. Good thing."

Adam nodded and glanced at the Regulator. "We goin' to service?"

"Believe we will."

Joe wore his suit coat draped over the wounded arm. He and Adam sat in the back row of benches, to the far right next to the wall, even though there were empty places ahead of them. Pastor Evans was talking to people in the front row.

Churchgoers filtered in and found seats as Joe and Adam watched. It was nearly time to begin when Joe noticed Sarah walk in, arm resting on George's. Many in the congregation watched them as well. They found seats three rows ahead. Joe found himself staring at Sarah. Her brown hair glistened and she wore a dark-green parlor skirt, a black paletot, and a velvet neck ribbon adorned with a cameo brooch. The same attire that she'd worn when Joe first took her to the hotel for a meal.

With his attention still on Sarah, Joe didn't notice Pastor Evans move to the lectern to begin the service. He wondered how George had smoothed over his infidelity and deserting her some three years before. *Must be quite the talker.*

"*. . .thus man joined in league with hell, against Heaven . . . !*" Evan's animated sermon disrupted Joe's thoughts for a moment, but they soon resumed. Joe figured that George's confession of his cheating would have been an interesting listen.

"*Man is a hard-hearted and stiff-necked sinner, loving darkness rather than light . . .*"

He, for one, would not be discussing the matter with anyone, for Budd Jarvis if for no other reason.

"*. . . eating sin like bread, drinking inequity like water. Holding fast deceit and refusing to let it go . . . !*" Evans had the flock spellbound as usual. His short fan-shaped beard held fast as he drove home his message.

Joe wondered if George listened to the aim of today's sermon or only heard the pastor talking. He remembered thinking that anyone who abandoned his wife should have no mercy shown him. He wasn't in the judgment seat, though, was he? He knew that his own life hadn't always followed a righteous line.

"*. . . because his deeds are evil . . . his heart wicked, full of pride, vanity, hypocrisy, covetousness, hatred of truth . . .*" Evans slowly raised his arm and shot an index finger skyward. "*. . . and hostility to all that is good!*" The words shot out like bullets. Perhaps the message was hitting home with some folks, who shifted in their seats. It could have been the hard wood, too.

Joe thought that this could be the most appropriate sermon the illustrious Pastor Cadwallen Christmas Evans had delivered to date. Glaringly appropriate. Joe saw that Jarvis was in attendance, seated near the aisle, straight down from him on the other side, without his wife. Jarvis had George fixed with an angry stare.

"... *the whole world lieth in wickedness!*"

Joe glanced at Jarvis again and this time noticed a small pistol in his waistband, in front of the suspender buttons. He refused to believe that he would shoot George inside the church. But what about outside?

"... *these glorious truths represent the great evil of sin, the infinite mercy of God . . .*"

It was a bit warm in the church with a full house, but Joe noticed that Jarvis's face was apple red and drenched in sweat. Jarvis reached a hand and touched the pistol butt as if to confirm it was still there and glanced around. Joe met his nervous eyes. Jarvis jerked his head away and looked at Pastor Evans.

"... *must accept him or be cast into hell!*"

Joe sat rigid in his seat wondering if he would have to defend George's life. Jarvis would have to stand up, then he would have a clear shot. It wouldn't take long for a determined person. Joe looked at Sarah sitting next to George, maybe hand in hand. *I can't be expected to save everyone who's in danger. Would be a shame, but it's not that he doesn't deserve it, cheating on and then deserting Sarah.*

"... *their sins and lawless acts I will remember no more . . .*"

Joe looked at Adam, whose attention was fixed on Evans, and glanced at Jarvis again. His hand was now on the pistol butt. Joe looked away and then downward where he noticed one point of the silver star on his vest peeking out from under the arm sling. He sighed, stood up, and moved past the others on the same bench. Genteel manners out the window, he stepped on more feet than he missed in his rush. A series of "ouches!" and "heys!" and "well, I nevers!" erupted from the row. Others ahead of them turned to see what was causing the disturbance.

Joe stepped past one elderly woman, who kicked him in the leg as he reached Jarvis. Had it not been for his tall boots, it would have left a nasty bruise.

"I want to see you outside, *right now!*" Joe's words seemed harsh to the lady kicker. He received another, "I never!" from her, too. By this time half the congregation had turned away from the pastor and gawked. Joe leaned over Jarvis until he nodded and stood up. As the two walked out of the church, Joe heard Evans's shouting words behind him, *". . . the inflexible character of the law, and the incalculable preciousness of the gospel!"*

"What the hell's wrong with you?" Joe reached out and jerked the little Smith & Wesson revolver away from Jarvis. "Don't you know Pastor Evans is desirous of no firearms in church?"

Jarvis was enraged by then for more than one reason. His right fist knocked Joe to the ground. A bit too slow getting up, Jarvis hit him again. This time he landed on the wounded shoulder. Pain-heightened anger got Joe up to return a right to Jarvis's chin, causing the big rancher to stumble backward. Being able to use only his right arm, Joe knew another quick hit was necessary. The second punch to the face still failed to down Jarvis, who came at him again. Jarvis's punch was more successful, sending Joe into the dirt. Not waiting until Joe got to his feet, Jarvis struck, which brought the same result. Instead of trying to stand up in front of Jarvis again, Joe went for his legs, which dumped the big man on the ground. Joe hit him in the face with three hard blows, which began to slow him down.

Joe then felt hands and was lifted off Jarvis. It was Siegler, who had stepped outside to see what was happening. "Joe! Joe, what in God's name are you doing?" Siegler yelled. "What's come over you?" Jarvis stood up but was done fighting. Both were panting.

"I want an explanation for your behavior, Marshal Mundy!" Siegler said in an official tone.

Joe used the back of his hand to rub away blood in his moustache. He looked at Jarvis and then to the door of the church where a few curiosity seekers stood, mouths agape. He could hear their whispering.

"Budd, what's this all about?" Siegler was a dog after a bone. Jarvis stared at Joe, who read the apprehension in his eyes. "Good God, look at you both! I am not one damned bit happy about this, and at church!" Siegler stared at Joe as if waiting for an explanation.

Joe leaned down, picked up his hat, and slammed it against his leg. "It's only a misunderstanding, Byron." He offered Jarvis his hand. Jarvis hesitated, then shook it, at the same time showing immense relief. Joe left the Smith & Wesson revolver on the ground but picked up his coat and ambled back toward the main street.

Chapter Thirty-Five

Back at the office Joe scooped handfuls of water from the washbasin in his sleeping room on his face and bare arms. After scrubbing away the street dirt, he toweled dry. He eased a clean white shirt over his head, tucked it in, and pulled up the suspenders. The shoulder was sore, but he was able to complete the task. The arm sling was too filthy to wear again so he left if off. The task of brushing the dirt from his coat was more of a challenge with only one good arm, however.

Adam returned from church and noticed Joe struggling with the chore. Without a word, he took the coat and started brushing it himself.

Joe walked over and sat down at his desk. "No curiosity, no questions?"

Adam didn't look at Joe, his attention on the brushing, "You mean the fistfight over at church? And with Budd, a town board member, who's got some sort of secret problem, or you have maybe. Figure you'll tell me if you want, but you probably won't. Not privy to much that goes on around here."

"It was a misunderstanding between Budd and me," Joe said.

Adam shot him a quick glance and continued brushing the coat.

"Some things are better and safer for you not knowin'," Joe said.

Adam finished the coat and hung it on a peg on the wall. "I'm not as smart as you, or tough as you, but what I hear you saying is I can't be trusted on certain things."

"No—"

Adam cut off Joe's reply. "Marshal, I was wounded once helpin' out, and stopped Smiley from shootin' you with his brother facin' you down in the street, and the board trusts me enough to take over when you're not here. Why is it you still don't trust me?"

Joe was quiet, surprised and pleased that Adam was standing up for himself. "Adam, you're right, what you said. You've earned my trust. I'll tell you about Budd's problem, and why it is between you and me." Joe explained the whole story, how Budd found George Welby with Rosella, and that was why Welby left town. The two were quiet.

"Budd wants to kill George? He'd go to prison," Adam said, as he thought out loud.

"That's correct," Joe said.

"So why did you start that fight with him at church?"

"Thought he might be fixin' to shoot Welby right there. He had his hand on a small pistol and was staring at Welby," Joe said.

"Why in front of all those people would he shoot someone?"

"Don't know. Guess the built-up hatred causes a person to think crossways."

"Byron is serious cross with you. You won't tell him why you took Budd out of the church." Adam stated this as fact.

"That's correct. I gave Budd my word, which I broke by telling you because I trust you. But it ends here. The disgrace Budd and Rosella would face . . . they'll have to work out their own problems, if he doesn't do something dumb."

"I understand. I hope they don't fire you over that brawl."

"If they do, they do. Doesn't change this matter," Joe said.

"How you gonna keep Budd from trying again? Can't be with him night and day."

Joe thought for a moment, "Don't know." He got up, stepped to the door, and looked down the street.

They moved chairs out onto the boardwalk and sat.

"How's the arm?" Adam asked.

"Sore."

They saw Dan Loman step out of the millinery and tack a pasteboard poster onto to the front. "What ya postin' up there, Dan?" Joe asked.

"Hello, Marshal, Adam. George Welby asked if I would put these up around town for him." Loman held one up for them to see.

Adam gave a low whistle and read aloud. "For Sheriff—Vote George Welby."

"George rode up to Gracie to hang them up there, asked me to do these here," Dan said. Joe glanced over at Sarah's bathhouse and saw a poster tacked to either side of the door.

"I'm sorry about, well you know, Sarah and you," Dan said. Joe gave a short nod. "Seems George is tryin' to be respectable. I told him I didn't think it was a real good idea, running against Canfield, I mean."

"Be real interesting to see what Canfield thinks of it," Joe said. They both nodded as Loman continued on his way.

"Think he'll try to kill George?" Adam asked.

Joe scratched his chin. "Hope not, for Sarah's sake, anyway."

Joe noticed the next visitor approaching from down the street. Byron Siegler stepped onto the boardwalk in front of the office. "May I talk to you, Joe. Give us a minute please, Adam," he said. Adam looked at Joe, who winked at him. Joe followed Siegler into the office and closed the door.

"I am calm now, but I want you to tell me what the hell that was all about at church. Damned Budd won't say a thing," Siegler said. Joe could tell he wasn't happy.

"Like I said, Byron, it was a—"

"Misunderstanding. Yes, I heard that part. What's the rest that I should know?" Siegler said. "What was it about, this *misunderstanding*? Several of those parishioners want your badge . . . today! What do I tell them, it was a—."

"Yes, Byron, tell them that," Joe said. "All there is to it."

"If you'd tell me what's it all about . . ." Siegler sat down.

"Byron, I ask you to trust me on this. It's something that will hurt some good folks if talked about openly, and I've given my word that I wouldn't. All there is to it," Joe said. He sat down on the edge of his desk. "If and when the time comes, I'll tell you."

Siegler stood up without looking at Joe. "Very well. I'll try to calm down the parishioners." He hesitated, "Oh, one more thing, there's growing talk and concern going on around town about this killer rifleman. People are afraid to leave town to visit friends and relatives."

"He's not after them," Joe said.

"I believe their concerns are legitimate." Siegler looked up. "I know you've tried to catch that man, but people say you're not doing enough. They know Canfield, or know of him, and believe you are the only real law around here. I agree. I wanted you to be aware of the talk."

Adam bolted through the door as soon as Siegler left. "They aren't going to fire you, are they?"

"Don't worry, Adam, there are worse things," Joe said as he stepped out and walked east down the boardwalk.

CHAPTER THIRTY-SIX

"Sheriff! Sheriff! There's a fight down at Avery's store, come quick!" The young woman who burst into Wick Canfield's office was gone as fast as she arrived. Nolan looked at Canfield as they both got up and trotted over to Nate Avery's general store.

On the boardwalk in front of the store, Avery was scuffling with another man, pasteboard posters strewn on the ground. Nolan pulled the two men apart as Canfield stepped up.

"What's goin' on here, Nate?" Canfield said.

"Sheriff, this fool wanted to put one of them posters on the front of my store. Just look at them. And I said 'No, sir! We want Wick Canfield for our sheriff!' He wouldn't take no for an answer," Avery said, still very excited.

Canfield picked up one of the posters and read it aloud. "You this George Welby?"

"I am, Sheriff. Meant no harm here, wanted to put up some posters is all," Welby said. "I apologize to Mr. Avery, who wasn't very friendly toward me, I'm afraid."

"That right, Nate?" Canfield asked.

"We have a sheriff, don't want him around," Avery said and glared at Welby.

A small crowd had gathered, watching with interest. One older man scooped up the posters and piled them on the boardwalk at Welby's feet.

Canfield stepped in front of the crowd and looked them over. "I want everyone to know that this will be a clean election. Mr.

Welby, from—" he turned and asked Welby where he was from "—Taylorsville, is welcome to place his signs around town here."

Deputy Nolan stood silent, somewhat spellbound by the seeming generosity of his boss, and puzzled by it. He didn't know this Welby character, but was amazed that Canfield was okay with this.

Canfield looked at Welby. "As long as a business owner says it's okay, you can nail up your posters." He said it loud enough for the growing crowd to hear. "Competition is good when it comes to political contests. It's the way our country is meant to operate. It's plum healthy for our newly forming county, and it's good for Nebraska and our country!" Some members of the crowd shot a nervous glance at each other as if he spoke a foreign language. A brave few clapped, which encouraged the rest to follow.

"We should all welcome Mr.—" he turned and read from a poster on the boardwalk "—Welby, to the race, and let the best man win!"

The crowd appeared stupefied by what they were hearing, especially from Wick Canfield, who some were very afraid of. They did demonstrate their elation with applause . . . not enthusiastic, but applause nonetheless.

"Now, with my experience here, I hope you'll vote for me, of course!" Canfield said. The crowd laughed with him. "Let the best man win!" With that, he shook hands with Welby and Avery. He stepped off the boardwalk and shook a few more hands. The facial expressions of many looked as if they were trying to decide between a bullet and a new rope. Canfield and a bewildered Nolan walked back to the sheriff's office.

CHAPTER THIRTY-SEVEN

Joe walked into the Texan and saw that there were a half dozen men sipping drinks and talking; only two of them stood at the bar. Ham Bluford glanced at Jarvis's office door as he approached Joe. "What'll ya have, Marshal?"

"Whiskey."

When Bluford served the drink, he studied Joe's face. In a low tone he asked, "What's goin' on between you and Budd? I heard about the fight."

"What did Budd tell you?"

"He won't say nothin'. I had to hear it from the boys here," Bluford said.

"It was a misunderstanding, that's all."

"Okay, I know when my nose is into it too far."

"He in his office?" Joe said.

Bluford nodded and gave him a wave.

Joe knocked on the door at the end of the bar with whiskey glass in hand. As he stepped inside, Budd shot him a surprised look, but waved him to a chair.

They sat staring at each other until Joe spoke. "You were going to shoot Welby right in church?"

Budd looked down at the papers on his desk and back at Joe, saying nothing.

"You know you could have hit one of those people? Whoever you'd hit, I'd have arrested you and you'd go to prison. What about your ranch and the Texan? And your wife. Ever give those

186

things a consideration?"

"I wasn't thinkin' right," Budd replied after a few moments. "In Texas . . . what he did . . . no one would blink if I killed him."

"That may be, but this ain't Texas. If that . . . thing, that happened with your wife, was a day or two ago, a jury might see fit not to convict you. It's been three years and you can bet they wouldn't be so understandin'. And neither would I."

Budd sat stone silent. He looked down again, and said, "I hate him so much, I . . . ."

"I do understand your feelin' that way, all things considered. I do. He's come back to his wife and is trying to make amends with her. It's time bygones be bygones I guess."

"Don't *you* care that he took up with Sarah?" Budd raised his voice. "She was *your* woman, everybody could see that!"

"She's his wife. She never ended it, legally," Joe knocked down the whiskey without a grimace. "We have to have an understanding, Budd. I know you didn't like me much when I came here, but I guess I've earned some respect from you after that shootin' last winter. I was downright heart-warmed when I found out you'd been guardin' me and Adam at Doc's while we mended."

"So?"

"Well, if you still hold any of that respect for me, I'm asking you, not as the marshal, but as a friend, don't do something that will force my hand. That's all."

Budd stood up with a bottle in his hand and Joe tensed out of habit. He refilled Joe's glass and poured himself one, but said nothing. Returning to his chair at the desk, the silence continued.

"Wonder if he ever told her about, about why he left?" Jarvis said.

"She told me he did."

"And she still wants him?"

"Still her husband she says," Joe said. He finished his drink and stood up to leave. "I hope we have an understandin' about this."

Budd looked at him and threw back his whiskey, but said nothing.

When Joe walked through the open office door, Adam was ready. "Listen to this." He held up his book and read, "Why are clouds like coachmen?" He closed the book and looked at Joe. "When it rains!"

Joe ignored him and started gathering his saddlebags, rifle, and ammunition.

"Goin' somewhere?"

"Gonna ride out to Edson's ranch and see if they've had any more trouble. Maybe I can spot the shooter out there somewhere," Joe said.

"Your shoulder healed up enough?" Adam asked.

"Enough." He handed Adam the special deputy badge and added, "I'll be back soon as I can."

Joe followed the Loup northwesterly, along the same route he had taken to Brown's Station. Under the fierce sun, hot air was moved by a friendly breeze. It was refreshing for both the bay and Joe when they splashed through the river and headed north. Although he'd never been to Edson's ranch before, he knew approximately where it was.

By midafternoon, Joe passed by small groups of cattle in the flats and gullies as the bay trotted past them. He could see Edson's brand on the nearby ones. Soon he guided the bay up an embankment and down the other side and observed a log house within a quarter mile.

As he walked the bay through a shallow canyon, two riders

appeared, one on either side with rifles pointed in his direction. "What's your business?" one of them yelled. Joe recognized the other, Clive, whom he'd met before.

"It's okay," Clive told the other hand. "Howdy, Marshal. This other yay-hoo is Raney," Clive said.

Joe shifted in his saddle slightly, "Raney. Clive, good to see ya again. Come to see Tye."

The riders reined up behind Joe with rifles in hand, pointed at the sky. "Straight ahead, Marshal, we'll follow you in," Clive said.

When they reached the long log house, one of the riders jumped down and went inside. He appeared again at the door with Edson. "Surprised to see you clear out here, Marshal. Step down and we'll have a drink." Edson nodded at the hand and went back inside and brought a bottle and two glasses.

Edson sat on the porch near a stump that served as a table. As Joe approached the other chair, he stopped and inspected ugly holes, some with chunks knocked out, in the logs by the door. He stuck his finger in one and looked at Edson.

"We get a night caller, every few days or so. Leaves a few gifts in the logs for us," he said and motioned toward the holes. "One night, that big rifle almost got Raney there," he said, nodding at the mounted rider. "You boys better go back out, and keep your eyes open." They rode out as Joe sat down.

"You can't see him in the dark, of course," Joe said. Edson nodded.

"Sometimes right after sundown. Shot out that window two different times."

Joe glanced at the window. "Almost hit my wife once. She's plum rattled most of the time. We sent Trudy away to stay with relatives in Lincoln until this thing ends."

"How many men do you have?" Joe asked.

"Only four now, with Billy and Johnny gone. Try to have two

keeping an eye out around here as much as possible, but we have ranch work, too. Can't be on guard all the time or we don't get nothin' else done," Edson said and took a drink. "I think Canfield is behind it, or one of his men, as I told you before. I've also lost six head. Believe he doesn't like me much, especially after the cattlemen's association meeting."

"Bet he'd like this spread."

"That's a fair bet," Edson said. "If I get scared and leave . . . so, what do you want?"

"I'd like to get some feelin' for where this shooter is, so I can kill him." Joe glanced at Edson and corrected himself, "I mean *arrest* him."

"You're welcome to stay the night, maybe we'll be lucky with another visit."

Joe accepted and after supper they returned to the porch to visit. Edson's wife hadn't extended any extra friendliness toward Joe, which made him a bit uncomfortable.

Edson fired up his pipe and watched the surrounding hills. "I'll apologize for my wife, she thinks you're not doing anything about this rifleman."

"And you agree . . ." Joe said.

"I reckon you wouldn't be here if you weren't. But remember, Marshal, I've had to bury two of my hands because of him. Patience has run out."

"You weren't thinkin' of a run for sheriff, were you?"

Edson studied Joe for a minute. "Be lyin' if I said I hadn't thought of it. No, I'm a rancher, third generation. Not a lawman."

Joe nodded. "In the morning, I think I'll ride over to Gracie Flats. If it's one of Canfield's men, I might accidentally run across him there," Joe said.

"How would you know him?" Edson asked.

"Wouldn't, unless he has that big Sharps hangin' on his horse."

At dark, Joe declined an offer to throw his blanket on the floor of the log house, opting to stretch out in the haymow of the small barn. Considering Edson's wife, he thought it a better decision. He led the bay to the safety of a stall but left him saddled just in case. With rifle within easy reach he drifted off to sleep.

Joe awoke as the sun eased over the horizon to fill the loft with light. He'd slept well through the uneventful night. Edson insisted that Joe share their breakfast before he left, which he did.

"Thank you, Tye, and Mrs. Edson, for the meals and stay, sure good to have home cookin' for a change," Joe said as he returned the rifle to the scabbard.

"Good luck hunting, Marshal," Edson said.

Mrs. Edson surprised Joe by stepping up beside her husband with glassy eyes. "I'm scared, Marshal, can't you stay another day?"

In fact, they were both surprised by the outburst. Edson turned toward her and put his arm around her. "Dear, we'll be fine, we have help. Besides, Marshal Mundy has to find that man . . . and kill him." She wiped one eye and gave a brave nod.

Joe stepped aboard the bay, touched his hat brim, and rode east toward the Flats.

CHAPTER THIRTY-EIGHT

Joe approached the edge of Gracie Flats by 11 a.m. He avoided the main street and found a livery to leave the bay. He walked to a southwest corner of the square where he could see the little courthouse and surveyed the businesses nearby. He chose the narrow Gracie saloon with a "For Sheriff—Vote George Welby" poster tacked on front, where he could sit by a window to watch the street and courthouse.

He walked inside and ordered a beer from the young bartender. The three other customers returned to their card game after looking him over. Joe sat down at the window and watched daily life in Gracie Flats. The county seat was easily twice the size of Taylorsville and the activity proved it. It looked as though every building was occupied, unlike his town, which had some vacant ones.

As he watched people going about their business, some occasionally stopping to chat, he thought about Canfield. Some day he would make a mistake, and Joe hoped to be there when he did. He bet himself that the full extent of the nefarious sheriff's activities were not even known. He was surprised at Welby running against Canfield. He must know how dangerous the man was. As mounted men rode by, Joe looked for a rifle scabbard. Some had them, but those that did, so far, weren't big enough to carry the Sharps. He glanced over to the little courthouse, sitting by itself in a block devoid of anything else except short weeds. The front door opened and Joe recognized the man leaving. Harper Langston. Special Agent Harper Langston. He mounted a horse tied at the street and trotted south on the Taylorsville road. Joe looked forward to *visiting* with Langston and finding out if he'd met with Canfield after all. He finished his beer and sauntered over to the livery.

He kept the bay to a trot until he could make out a few features of the rider farther down the road. After that he shifted from a trot to a walk when he thought he was too close. Once they were approaching the river, and no other stops were likely, Joe loosed the reins and eased the bay into a canter.

Trotting by the North Star on his left, he guided the bay west around the corner and down the main street to the office. Langston's horse was tied up in front.

"Glad you're back, we should talk about a few things," Langston said, losing no time to initiate the conversation. He was sitting in the chair in front of Joe's desk.

"Believe that's an accurate summation, Mr. Langston," Joe said as he hung his hat on a peg and sat down. Adam had seen Joe ride in and followed him through the door. When he noticed Langston, he walked over and leaned on the jail cage. He was wearing his badge and Remington revolver.

Langston stood as he began his tirade. "I learned from Marshal Twilliger in Willow Springs that you had intended to have me arrested, until you wisely retracted that request. Explain! And I demand that you explain why you released my prisoner, a federal prisoner, who happens to be the most wanted outlaw in Nebraska!"

Adam's eyes were wide as he listened to the scolding tone of the special agent's voice. He eased his attention to Joe, who sat poised behind the desk and listened.

Joe said nothing, but motioned toward the chair behind Langston and waited. Flabbergasted, Langston sat down.

"I have similar questions. Under whose authority did you

release *my* prisoner?" Joe said.

"Why, you thought that innocent man was Middleton, when I already had him here in jail!"

"Harper, you don't mind if I call you Harper, do you? Regale me with your first meeting with Doc, before you arrested him, I mean."

Langston looked baffled only momentarily. "Well, I've never actually met him before that, but I had a poster on him with a rendition of what he looked like. Catching these crooks is not difficult if one works at it. It obviously was him!"

"First of all, we can rarely go by the renditions on these posters. Most of the time, they don't resemble the actual man. Second of all, I'd met Jim Riley, in person, when he first came up from Texas. I know what he looks like, and *you* let him out of my jail . . ."

"Who's Jim Riley? We're talking about Doc Middleton!"

"That's probably his real name, 'til he changed it. It seems the only way you can corner Doc is by accident, and that's exactly how I caught him while arresting an army deserter."

Adam was enjoying this so much that he licked his lips. He wouldn't have left the office for a twenty-dollar gold piece.

Langston was silent. "You'd met him before," he stated. His eyes searched the floor. "Well, why were *you* arresting a deserter? That's federal." Claiming the win.

Joe nodded. "Major Daily gave me a commission."

"U.S. Marshal Bill Daily?"

Joe nodded again. "You will never intervene yourself with my office again, or *I will* throw you in that cage. You may, Harper, take that to the bank."

Adam was so elated that he almost clapped.

"Now, why were you visiting with Sheriff Canfield?" Joe asked.

Langston stuttered, "How'd you . . . ?" He slumped back in

the chair, stared at the front of the desk, and grew a tiny smile. "I wasn't planning to, after our conversation, but with nothing new to go on, thought I might as well introduce myself and see if anything comes out of it."

"Did it?"

"Nothing at all. He's appears the ever-efficient sheriff, willing to help however he can. Told me to let him know what little bits I had, and 'he'd see if he could help make 'em grow a bit.' "

Joe smiled inside about that. "Don't know, if I was you, that I'da told him who I was. All of his men now know you are in the area. You may want to find an extra set of eyeballs for the back of your head. Course, might come in handy to feed him some bits now and then . . . to see if they grow."

Langston scratched the back of his head and nodded.

Joe proceeded to tell Langston that a long-range shooter was on the loose, and was probably using his stolen .45-90 Sharps hunting rifle. He added that he had no doubt Canfield was behind it.

"I think it started out to show the new cattlemen's association that he was trying to cut down rustlers to help win votes, but it's something more now. Trying to drive Tye Edson off his land for one thing," Joe explained.

"No luck finding the shooter, I suppose?"

"Oh, I've found him a couple times. There'll be a last time, I guarantee it," Joe said.

Langston nodded. "Well, I'm sure you won't lament my leaving. I'm being sent to Ogallala to assist in the hunt for a man named Sam Bass. He robbed a U.P. train at Big Springs."

"Heard about it. Hope you have some *better* luck with that."

"Sure would like my rifle back," Langston said and eased out of the office. He mounted and rode off. Adam stood there with a grin big enough to injure himself.

CHAPTER THIRTY-NINE

It was the first of October. The summer heat began to wane. Joe and Adam sat on chairs in front of the office and watched a group of men reassemble a small platform at the town's main intersection. It was the same platform used on statehood day for speeches, including Joe's. Iain McNab let the town store it in the lean-to where he kept his wagon.

"Reckin' we'll be hearing all sorts of speeches this evening," Adam said.

Joe turned his attention away from the construction gang. "Afraid we will." He thought about the election. All county officials would be formally elected now that the county was established. Loup it was called. After the river. The town board members would be elected, too. Three townsmen were running against Siegler, Martin, and Jarvis. Zachariah Anson, who owned the chophouse, and Hayden Ford, who'd recently moved into a small house a short distance north of the North Star saloon. No one knew who he was, but rumor was he would be president of the town's new bank. All that was hush-hush, at least until Byron Siegler gave his election speech. Siegler had leaked a little about it to Joe, who promised to keep the announcement quiet. It would be a boon to the town. The third contender for a town board position was Cleve Escott, owner of the new millinery store. The only one Joe knew at all was Zach, whom he'd met a couple of times. He wondered how they viewed their town marshal.

"So, who you votin' for, for sheriff?" Adam asked and grinned.

Joe looked at him for a moment and returned his gaze to the platform. When he looked back, he noticed George and Sarah, arm in arm, step out of the laundry and walk east. Sarah glanced at Joe, then drove her eyes into the boardwalk in front of her. When they walked into the hotel, Adam reported.

"Look's like George and Sarah are going in for lunch." With no reply from Joe, he pulled out his book of conundrums. "Why is an egg like a colt?" Adam looked at Joe and waited for an answer. "Come on, you can get this one."

"I don't know, Adam, but *please* tell me," Joe said.

"Because it isn't fit for use until it's broken!" Adam chuckled.

Joe close his eyes for a moment, then rubbed them with his fingers.

By early evening, a crowd of people had gathered around the town's intersection. Farm wagons, horses, and one buggy were parked along both sides of the main street with a few on the side street. Red, white, and blue bunting adorned the speaker's platform. Joe noticed that Booth and family were in attendance as well as the Forsonns, the Swedish family who had sheltered him and the bay during a blizzard the previous winter.

"Know what this reminds me of?" Adam asked.

Joe shook his head.

"The opening night of Budd's saloon."

"Hopefully this won't be as eventful," Joe said, remembering Adam's brush with death.

"Agree."

When they noticed Judge Worden step onto the platform, they decided to walk down to hear the speeches. They stopped on the boardwalk and leaned against the empty building on the northwest corner.

Everyone started clapping at Worden, who held his hands up

to request silence. "The contenders for various offices will make their speeches now, erring on the side of brevity we hope, beginning with the office of county sheriff. Mr. Canfield, we will begin with you," Worden announced and stepped down.

Joe and Adam hadn't noticed that Canfield was in town, and both were amused that the judge did not address him as "Sheriff." Deputy Nolan stood by and watched.

Canfield stepped onto the platform and several people clapped, most likely out of courtesy, if nothing else. "Citizens of Taylorsville, what a fine community you have here. We are all happy that our county is now official, and elections are only a week away. My hope is that the county commissioners, whoever they will be, will see fit to properly fund the sheriff's office, so that I, if elected, will be able to better serve this fine town. I appreciate your vote." The crowd clapped again as he stepped down.

Next was George Welby. The crowd's acknowledgment was even less enthusiastic than Canfield's. "I know most of you knew me—"

"Speak up!" someone yelled.

"I said, I know most of you knew me when I was the first city marshal of Taylorsville. For those who don't, my name is George Welby. This is my beautiful wife, Sarah." He motioned to her. She hiked her dress and climbed the few steps of the platform. He placed an arm around her and she smiled, which received a good round of applause.

Adam noticed a few in the crowd glance toward Joe, who kept his eyes on the Welbys.

"I am a man who has made mistakes. I ask no absolution, but I have seen my way clear to the right path. I give much credit not only to my wife, but Pastor Cadwallen Christmas Evans, a soul saver if there ever was one. I ask only what Christians believe in, and that is a second chance."

Joe wondered if the crowd noticed Welby's hand quivering as he stroked his chin.

"We have placed our roots right here in Taylorsville and, with your vote, I promise to be the best sheriff, to you, the people. Thank you." Respectable applause followed.

"What'd ya think?" Adam asked Joe as they both watched the Welbys walk over and stand in front of the hotel. Joe watched Sarah look up at George with a warm smile.

"They applauded him."

"Probably glad he was done talking," Adam said, not hiding a bitter tone.

Byron Siegler took the platform and received the best applause so far. He talked about the progress, slow but steady, that the town had made. He spoke of the new telegraph office and the hope for a railroad line someday. Then he made the announcement that he let Joe in on some weeks ago. "After months of meetings with different officials in the banking business, I have been able to secure a deal—" the crowd mumbled in anticipation "—for the first bank in our great community!" The crowd roared, and applause and whistles were heard for a minute straight.

"We're gettin' a bank?" Adam said. "Now if I had some money to put in it!" Joe looked at him.

"And if you will turn your attention to the too-long empty building here on the corner, you will see the location of the new Taylorsville State Bank!" Siegler pointed to the building that Joe and Adam were leaning against. The crowd roared again. It was a true sign of progress for any town and the people knew it.

When the noise abated, he continued, "And I would like to introduce to you the president of our new bank, Mr. Hayden Ford. Mr. Ford, Mr. Wesley Potter of Kearney City, and myself are the owners. Mr. Ford is also a contender for the town board." When Ford mounted the platform, he shook hands with

Siegler, who retreated to a raucous applause and much hand-shaking once he reached the street.

Ford talked briefly about the bank and then his own interest in becoming a member of the town board. Joe was not surprised that poor Harold Martin wouldn't be giving a speech, even though he was running for reelection to the town board. His nervous condition would never allow it. Politically, it was probably a mistake.

When Ford stepped down, Budd Jarvis was next. A polite applause. "As you all know, I own the Texan saloon and the livery. I ranch west of town and have had business here since the town was founded. I appreciate your vote. One free beer to everyone after the speech makin'!" That got cheers from the crowd.

Anson and Escott were the last to speak and climbed the platform together. "I'm Zachariah Anson. I own the Anson restaurant, who many call the chophouse. I settled here early as well, and my goal if elected to the town board is to make Taylorsville a peaceful place again. We've seen too much violence, and violence begets violence. This town, any town, cannot and will not achieve success while violence darkens our streets." He nodded to Escott.

"I am Cleve Escott. My wife and I recently moved our millinery to town. Mr. Anson and myself seem to be thinking the same about the prospects of Taylorsville. We were here only one week when my wife was hit by a stray bullet. Hard to convince more people and businesses to move here with these unfortunate events. I thank you for your vote. Oh, and one last thing, both Zach and I wish George Welby good luck and hope he is our next sheriff. Thank you."

The enthusiasm of the crowd to their words was not lost on Joe or Adam. Darkness had enveloped the town, so many climbed into their wagons for the journey home. Some walked to the saloons.

CHAPTER FORTY

The silence in the office hung like a dark cloud. Adam poured a cup of coffee and hesitated. Joe was seated with his boots on the desk. "Coffee?"

Joe shook his head.

Adam took the chair and looked at Joe. "Like to know what you're thinking right about now."

"Nothing special."

"You're thinking the same thing I am. That somehow those knotheads think all these things have happened here because of you. I remember some called you 'only a gunman,' when you came to town," Adam said.

"I think you have it about totaled up," Joe said.

"They don't have the brains God gave a sparrow. What do they think would have happened with some of those 'unfortunate events' if you wasn't here at all?" Joe was silent.

"Well, I guess come next week, we'll see how it all piles up," Joe said. "Goin' to take in some air."

"Want some company?"

"Not this time, thanks," Joe said, as he planted his hat and walked out.

The town was fairly quiet as Joe shook doors. The lamps in Sarah's house were out, as they were at Doc Sullivan's. He continued on behind the buildings and came out on the east end of the main street. He shook McNab's and peeked in the

Texan, which still had about a dozen customers. He approached the front door of the North Star when he heard a voice call him. He turned and saw Jenny approaching from the Texan.

"I saw you go by, thought maybe you might like some company."

"You shouldn't be out on the street at this time of night, Jenny, I'll walk you back," Joe said.

"I'm done for the night, let's go to your office for a drink." Jenny's blue eyes searched Joe's. "You were on your way back there, anyway, weren't you?"

Joe nodded and held out his arm and she took it. They crossed the side street and walked by the new bank building on the corner.

When they walked into the marshal's office Adam sat at Joe's desk reading from his book. He stood up, nodded, and stepped away from the desk, "Miss Jenny, nice to see you."

"You, too, Adam," Jenny said as Joe positioned the extra chair for her.

Joe poured two shot glasses of whiskey, and offered one to Adam. "Uh, no thanks Marshal. I just remembered that I plum forgot that Mose asked me to help him. With some work, at the livery, you know. I better go. Hope it's not too late, that work he wanted help with."

Adam pulled down the new green shades before he closed the door on the way out.

Jenny chuckled, "Why was he so flustered?"

"I guess since I don't get many women callers here," Joe said with a slight smile.

"Maybe I'll have to change that."

Early the next morning Joe sat a chair in front of the office, sipped steaming coffee, and watched the sun rise. He noticed Adam approaching from the west.

"You get lost?"

"Oh, uh, well that work at the livery took longer than I thought, so I sacked out there. Any coffee left?" Adam said, with a smile.

Joe looked at him, "Thanks. And yes, there is."

About seven o'clock, Joe decided to walk down to the North Star and listen in on the coffee club. All of the usual members were in attendance when he arrived except Harold Martin.

"We was just talkin' about you, Joe," Hadley said. "We're all in agreement that you're the cause of all the town's ills!" He was the only one who laughed.

"We were discussing the speeches made last night," Siegler said. "I wasn't at all happy with the implications made by Zach and Cleve."

"Oh, it's only talk, to help 'em get elected, I 'spose," Joe said.

Pastor Evans joined in. "How do you foresee the election results, Byron?"

"I think we're okay. But Harold should have given a speech. Some think it doesn't matter to him if he's reelected or not. I wonder myself."

"He could no more climb that stand and talk as spit flames, Byron, and you know it." A few couldn't help but glance at Joe.

"I think that George Welby's speech struck a cord with folks. There's a chance he might beat out Canfield," Siegler said. "I'm almost sure he'll get the Taylorsville vote."

"I wouldn't want that victory, knowin' Canfield," Hadley said and sipped his coffee. Most of the group mumbled and nodded.

"What about your friend Ford?" Jarvis asked.

Siegler caught the sour note, "I didn't suggest he run for the board, if that's what you're thinking, Budd. He thought he could be helpful. I don't think he will be elected because no one besides me knows him."

"Where's he from, Byron?" Joe asked.

"Kearney City, same as Wes Potter. I was able to obtain their funding for the bank on a three-way partnership. They're both respectable bankers down there."

"I don't trust damned banks!" Hadley blurted.

"Gib, we haven't even opened yet. And, I think you can trust me," Siegler said.

"Long as I can stroll into that bank and take a gander at *my* money sittin' there in the safe." Hadley leaned over and wide-eyed a spot on the tabletop to emphasize his point. Siegler rolled his eyes.

Joe looked at Siegler and Jarvis. "Since you two are here, I wanted to let you know I'm leavin' at first light, head back to Edson's range."

"Be damned careful if you find that man," Siegler said.

Jarvis joined in. "You want one of my boys to ride with you?"

"No thanks, Budd."

"Don't go gettin' that horse shot," Hadley said. The others glared at him. "What? It's a decent horse, hate to see it get all shot up."

"Your thoughtfulness knows no bounds, Gib!" Siegler shot out.

Joe smiled. "Hope to be back in a day or two."

"Good hunting, Joe," Jarvis said.

CHAPTER FORTY-ONE

Lying on Joe's desk were packed saddlebags, two full canteens, and the big Winchester, cleaned and loaded. Adam had insisted on readying Joe's gear. He'd already gone to the livery and saddled the bay and brought him to the office.

"You're very efficient this morning, may have to keep you around," Joe said as he finished his coffee.

Ignoring the offhand compliment, Adam launched into the conversation. "Let me go with you, to watch your back."

"Can't leave the town without law, you know that," Joe said.

Adam knew that answer was coming. "Talked to Mose when I got your horse. Something he said, didn't sit right. Did you know he was born and raised in Louisiana? Or Loosana as he calls it."

Joe shook his head. "Can't say that I did."

"He asked where you was goin' and I told him you're huntin' for that rifle killer. Know what he said? He said, 'I already knowed that.' "

"He just asked to get the talk goin' in that direction. He said, spirits told him you were leavin' this morning for that purpose—"

Joe interrupted, "They have a lot of that spirit and voodoo nonsense down there."

"Well, that may be. He said he was told that something bad would come from this trip. I asked if you would be hurt. He said all they told him was something bad would come from this.

A bad omen. And I never told him what you were doin', did you?"

"No, but one of the bunch at the North Star probably mentioned it to him."

"Well, I didn't like the way Mose said it. It was like he *knew*, he *knew*, without no doubt at all. Like it's a God-given fact."

"Don' worry too much about that stuff. Besides, you have a town to watch over 'til I get back."

"I know you'll be careful," Adam said. He busied himself with pinning on the special deputy badge.

Joe let the bay walk west down the main street and turn north. There was enough light to see building outlines. As he passed the livery he noticed a form standing out front. It was Mose. He could see the white hair. Mose ignored Joe's greeting. He stood there and stared at Joe as the bay walked north out of town.

Joe thought that was odd of him not to say something or even offer a wave. *Too many spirits talking to him right then!* Joe loosed the reins and the bay slipped into a trot.

They stayed on the south side of the river and followed it past Budd Jarvis's ranch house, barn, and corrals. Shortly after, he turned the bay north and crossed the river. A few miles into Edson's range Joe stopped the bay near a buffalo wallow half full of water and pulled out his telescope. He extended it and sighted in hills and valleys. Beautiful country. He heard the pleasant, flutelike whistle of a meadowlark nearby. But other than that, a peaceful nothing . . . which he liked. It was being spoiled by something more deadly than a rattler. He aimed to change that.

Their progress was slow, almost lingering. He spent a lot of telescope time. Joe hoped that he could catch a glimpse of the shooter *before* the shooter saw him. He proceeded north toward

Edson's home place. Following a shallow valley, he kept his eyes on the hilltops and thought about the upcoming elections, the town board, and Sarah. And George. Did he have a chance of being elected sheriff? If he was, would Canfield try something? Like kill him on a lonely road somewhere? What would Sarah do then? The town board was friendly to Joe, but he could see the possibility of that changing after the election. Siegler was right about the pointed speeches made by Anson and Escott. They clearly thought their town marshal was too violent and maybe caused more violence. He liked Taylorsville but if the board changed and fired him, he'd still have the federal job. But would he stay in town, or move on? The thought river flowed through his mind, considering all the possibilities.

He had Edson's house in sight and watched the hills, expecting Clive and Raney to meet him at any time. He slowed the bay to a walk as he approached the house.

"Hello the house!" Joe noticed a rifle barrel protruding from a slit in the front door and stopped. "It's Joe Mundy, Tye!" The rifle barrel vanished.

Tye Edson opened the door and came out with rifle still in hand. "Come on up, Marshal."

After greetings, Joe sat on the porch with Edson and talked. "I asked the boys to pick up some lemonade powder from the drug store. Would you like some, Marshal?" Mrs. Edson spoke with a shaky voice.

"Don't want to put you to any trouble, ma'am," Joe said.

"Yes, mother, we'd enjoy some of your famous lemonade," Edson told her. When she went back inside, he spoke again. "She's almost a nervous wreck. So scared she can't remember what she's doing half the time. I'm glad to see you, Marshal. Did you kill that cur?"

Joe shook his head. "Has he been here?"

"Not for four days now. Why I thought maybe you'd got him,"

Edson said.

"I'm still looking for him, Tye. I will find him."

The conversation weaved its way to the election. Tye was most interested in the sheriff's race. He'd heard Welby was running against Canfield. "You think Welby has a chance?"

"Seemed like his speech was well received. I don't know."

"Somehow, I don't think Canfield will let him win," Edson said.

Mrs. Edson appeared on the porch again and served them each a glass. "I have ham steak and potatoes about ready. Marshal, I insist you eat with us." Not waiting for an answer she disappeared inside the house.

Joe pulled his pocket watch out. It was 11:45. "Didn't realize it was almost noon already."

Edson's eyes constantly scanned the horizon. Joe felt sorry for anyone who had to live like that. Edson noticed Joe looking at him. "Done watching for Indians, and now this. No one's goin' to run me off. Too much invested."

"Didn't run across Clive or Raney on my way in," Joe said.

"They're putting together twenty head for Jarvis's auction. They should be camped southeast. You might check in with them on your way back to town." Joe nodded.

After Joe and the bay were fed and watered, he prepared to leave. "Think I'll move around this area for a while before I meet up with your boys."

"Kill that animal, Marshal, so we can live normal again," Edson said.

Joe touched his hat brim and road out.

It was midafternoon when he stopped the bay and dismounted. He led the horse into a deep cut of a hill and ground tied him out of sight. Joe carried the rifle and telescope to the hilltop and sat down in some tall grass. Not complete cover, but not bad, either. He could barely see the roof of Edson's house through the telescope. It was a warm day with no breeze. None that cut through the grass, anyway. It was 2:55 by the pocket watch. Joe was becoming impatient. He did enjoy the quiet of the prairie. He used it to think. The possibility of arresting the shooter was something he realized he had overlooked. Kill him, end it. But, he was a lawman and he had an obligation to arrest the person responsible, if at all possible. Visions of the bodies of Ike Raymond, Johnny Fuller, and young Billy Parker clouded his mind. Not to mention the three long-range duels he himself had already fought with the killer.

CHAPTER FORTY-TWO

Joe gave up by early evening. Nothing so much as a coyote passed through his field of view. He decided to find the camp of Edson's two hands before nightfall. As the bay walked, Joe wondered if George and Sarah were eating at the hotel and talking about his prospects of becoming sheriff. Irritated that his thoughts had drifted to them again, he loosed the reins and let the bay canter.

The sun was nearly touching the western horizon when Joe saw a rider. He withdrew the rifle from its scabbard and slowed the bay to a trot. Then he saw the second rider and relaxed a bit. He lost sight of the two when they rode behind a hill. He slowed the bay to a walk as he approached and could see Clive and Raney's campsite.

"Hello the camp!" Joe announced his presence.

It must have startled them, as both grabbed up Winchester carbines and dropped to the ground. "Come in with yer hands to the sky or we'll open fire and not stop!" Raney yelled out.

Joe replaced his rifle, raised his hands, and moved the bay forward. "Marshal Joe Mundy, boys. Don't be shootin'," Joe answered. As he got close enough to see, the two hands stood up.

"Come on in, Marshal. Sorry about that. It's just about nervous enough out here to make the hair on a buffalo robe stand up," Clive said. Raney went about starting the campfire.

"I understand why you feel that way. Mind if I share your fire tonight?" Joe asked.

"Mind?" Clive turned and looked at Raney, who had stopped what he was doing to stare at Joe. "Mind? Hell, no, we wouldn't mind! Not one damned bit, would we?"

"Marshal, truth be told, you's welcome to stay with us long's you want!" Raney joined in. "Ever' day we feel like that rifleman is watching us, tryin' to choose which one of us to drop first!"

"You boys don't look like you've been eating too well," Joe said and opened a saddlebag. "Got this salt pork here, more than I can eat."

"Much obliged, Marshal. We'll have us a regular feast tonight!" Clive said. "I've been worried about Raney here. Today he turned sideways and I plum lost sight of him!" He laughed, a little too much. "Thought there was just a pair of boots and chaps standin' there!"

"That wadn't funny the first time," Raney said as he watched the flames grow.

It was dark after the meal was finished and tin plates were put away. A coffee pot sat near the fire. A bright full moon lit up the landscape, which was a blessing under the circumstances.

"You boys get some sleep, I'll stand guard," Joe said.

"Well, thanks, Marshal. I'll relieve you later on." Raney looked at Clive for approval. The two spread out their bedrolls, and with Winchesters across their chests, lay their heads against saddle pillows and pulled hats over their faces.

Joe retrieved his rifle and walked out of the firelight near a small pine tree. He sat down, listened, and watched. He heard the high-pitched howl and yips of a coyote who failed to show himself during Joe's watch earlier that day. He could also hear the bawls of cattle nearby. The coyote was making them nervous. The expanse of the night sky seemed to be everywhere. It inspired a person to stare. His thoughts drifted to a conversation he'd had with Edson. The rancher told him that Clive and Raney trailed up from Texas on their fourth cattle drive when he met them. Edson told them he needed a hand to replace one who had returned to Austin. Joe was amused by their first conversation with Edson. "Sure be interested in that there job, Mr. Edson, but you see, me and Raney here come as a set, kinda like a horse an' saddle. We dun rode together too long to be a splittin' now."

The night went by fairly quick in Joe's estimation. The night sky began to fail, announcing the start of a new day. He decided to let Clive and Raney sleep, which he suspected was the only good night of sleep they'd had in a while. He got the fire perked up and sat the coffee closer. Sitting down, he rested the rifle against his leg. Clive and Raney snored on. Joe picked up a pebble and lobbed it onto Clive, who jerked awake.

"Oh, my, is it my turn to stand watch a'ready'?" He sat up and rubbed his eyes.

"It's morning. The coffee's on," Joe said.

"Marshal, you shoulda woke one of us. I'm real sorry to have slept through like we dun." Clive leaned the carbine across his saddle. "Thank ya, though, best sleep I've had in a durned month!"

"That's for sure." Raney stirred and found his feet. He stepped close to the fire, wrapped a rag around the handle, and poured three cups of coffee. As he leaned forward to return the pot to the fire, the coffee pot exploded. Hot coffee and blood doused Joe, who sat on the other side of the fire. Raney fell into the fire but rolled away.

"Raney! My God, ya hit?" Clive yelled and crawled over to him.

"It's ma hip! My damned sore hip!"

Clive pulled Raney's chap for a better look. "Well, sweet

Jesus. It's a clean wound, almost missed ya. But ya got another hole in yer worn-out chaps!"

"*Almost* is the important word there!" Raney screamed.

"You two stay down and be quiet," Joe said. He started for the bay and the ground exploded short of the camp by ten yards. Joe threw his saddle on the horse and with rifle in hand leaned forward. The bay knew to run. Joe wasn't thinking about the election, or Sarah, or her husband;he was going to kill a man or get killed tryin'. He had calculated the approximate area where the shots came from and he tapped the bay to get there as soon as possible. It was foolhardy to charge up and down each hill perhaps, but he planned to end this today.

As he cleared the top of another knoll a loud rifle exploded in his vicinity. He caught a glimpse of movement and rode hard toward it. He dismounted and ran to cover as another shot plowed dirt near him. The eastern sun showed half of itself and provided a good reflection off the shooter's rifle barrel. Joe pumped round after round at that glint until he saw the barrel flip over backward. He yanked three extra rounds from his vest pocket and rammed them into the loading gate of the rifle. Deciding that a good old-fashioned infantry charge was in order, he stood and ran toward the hill where he last saw the rifle barrel. As he neared the top, he fired twice more at the ridge, sending dirt clods flying. At the top he shouldered the rifle and held a finger against the trigger until he saw a man lying face down at the bottom.

He hesitated a moment, but the man didn't move. He glanced around and saw the rifle, which had slid part of the way down the hill barrel-first. It was a Sharps rifle. His senses on fire and the sound of a rider approaching behind him, Joe swung his rifle toward the new threat. It was Clive, who waved his hat like a madman. "Don't shoot, Marshal. Comin' to help," Clive yelled. Joe waved at him and refocused on the dead man. Clive joined Joe at the hilltop and went down the other side with him, pistol drawn.

The man was dressed in brown trousers and a lightweight brown jacket, a cartridge belt around his waist. The jacket had a bloody hole ripped through it. Joe knelt and eased the man over on his back. He was still alive.

"Mercy me of the highest! Ain't that . . ." Clive's mouth remained open while he further studied the man's face.

Joe was shocked as well. "George Welby." He'd shot Sarah's husband, and a candidate for county sheriff. He pulled one of the big cartridges from Welby's belt and inspected it. "A .45-90."

"Why in hell . . . well I guess I don't take all this in. Ain't he a runnin' for shurf? Why's he trying to kill us?" Clive stood up and shook his head.

Joe pulled open the coat, vest, and shirt, which were a bloody mess. He let go a shrill two-part whistle that drew the bay to him. "There's an extra shirt in my saddlebags, get it." Clive ran to the bay, mumbling something Joe couldn't understand.

Cutting the shirt into two parts with his pocket knife, Joe stuffed one half on the exit wound and the other in the front to try and slow the blood loss.

"Didn't know it was you, but I . . . knew, if caught . . . it'd be you," Welby said and groaned. "Who ever heard . . . of someone riding hell-bent, toward someone shooting at him?" His face was drenched in sweat. Joe pulled off his wild rag and mopped the wounded man's face.

"You mind tellin' us why you shot at us?" Joe asked. "You're the one who's been killin' out here?"

Welby shook his head. "It's a . . . long story, that . . . you probably won't believe, anyway," he grimaced.

"I've got time, but you don't. We'll get you horseback and to town."

Welby struggled to sit up, "No . . . I can't move my legs."

"Hellfire, Marshal, you can use Raney's horse, or we'll find his, but how'll he stay on?" Clive asked the obvious. "We could tie 'im on."

"I don't know, Clive," Joe assessed. "He bled a lot more when I moved him."

"Take care . . . of Sarah for me . . . please," Welby said, his quiet tone almost hard to hear. "I know . . . you can do that."

"Clive, go for Doc Sullivan. Ride hard, bring him back here pronto." The cowboy threw his hat on and was off.

"Thanks, for your . . . efforts."

"Why don't we talk. We have time before Doc gets here," Joe said. "And don't leave out one damned thing." He could see that the blood was soaking through the shirt already.

"I did something . . . real foolish. Wanted my wife, and . . . be together again."

"I already know why you left her, where'd ya go?" Joe asked.

Welby blinked a few times and said, "I didn't . . . mean that." He closed his eyes as if to hide shame. "Did odd jobs up in Canada. Lost what money I had . . . coming back, when I did that foolish thing. I was dirty, had a beard, no good clothes . . . I couldn't face her, like that, so at Gracie Flats, I broke into a general store one night. Canfield must have buffaloed me when I came out. He didn't . . . recognize me at first," he said, groaning.

"I'm more interested in why you took to shooting people with that Sharps rifle," Joe said. His patience was short with the rambling, but also frustrated that he couldn't do more for Welby. He wanted him to stand trial, but also return him to Sarah. *Hell, I don't know what to think.*

"Canfield . . . told me he'd hold off, on charging me for the theft. I was to work for him, whatever he wanted done . . . no questions asked, and pay well for my work." Welby coughed a few times and cleared his throat. Joe gave him a drink from his canteen. "I told him, I'd take my chances with the judge." He closed his eyes.

"What then?" Joe startled him awake.

"He said the only option I had . . . was to agree. He'd do things to Sarah, in front of me, kill her slow as he would me after. He said, if I took her and ran, his men would track us as far and as long as it took, just to prove his point. I couldn't see another way."

"So you took up ambushing honest men that easily? You know you killed three good men, one was only twenty-two years old?"

"Didn't kill . . . anyone . . . none," Welby sputtered.

"If Doc gets here fast enough, you might have a chance. But any way it shakes out, *now* would be a good time to tell the truth!" Joe tried to control himself.

"I replaced Canfield's man . . . I think his name was . . . Browning, or . . ."

"Banning? Courtney Banning?" Joe's excitement returned.

"Yes . . . that's the name. Don't know, but I think . . . Canfield killed him. Why he wanted me. Had to keep active, to keep him happy. He wanted some dead, like Edson, and his hands. He wanted Edson's place . . . so I shot up Edson's house. I could have shot Edson, but didn't. I shot a horse that one of Edson's hands was riding . . . that was as far as I would go. That's when you came and we traded shots . . . 'til I ran out."

"Johnny Fuller."

"Who?" Welby asked.

"Johnny Fuller. You got his horse, but the bullet went through his leg first. He died at Doc's."

"Oh dear God . . ."

"You got me, too, in the shoulder," Joe added. "You ever shot a Sharps like that before?" He glanced at the big rifle still lying where it fell.

Welby opened his eyes and gently shook his head. "Canfield provided the gun and ammunition. Told me to practice . . . I didn't know about . . . Fuller."

"You'll have to stand trial for him," Joe said. "And then you can testify against Canfield and I can arrest him."

"Wish I could . . . but I think we both know how this ends up . . ."

"You'll make it," Joe said, not really believing it. "You should have come to me." He didn't know what else to say at that point.

"Would you have believed me? Or even . . . tried to, after taking my wife back, from you? I know what you think of me, fooling with Rosella, and then . . . running out on Sarah. I . . . don't blame you . . . for feeling that way."

Joe thoughts were whirling now. "Guess we won't know now."

"Canfield told me when he was reelected . . . he'd let me go . . . and tear up the theft complaint."

Joe churned his thoughts over and over.

"He said after that . . . I, we, would live as long as I kept my mouth shut."

"You mighta beat out Canfield," Joe said.

"No. He said . . . my running would make it obvious, that he and I, weren't associated. He owns the clerk who counts votes. It was going to be a close race, but he'd win." Welby coughed.

All Joe could do was shake his head. He believed Canfield was as ambitious a criminal as Doc Middleton, maybe more so.

They had been silent for a few moments when Welby chuckled.

"What?" Joe asked. His thoughts still whirling.

"It's funny. I thought . . . that when I died, I'd be old and gray haired, and sitting in a rocking chair . . ." He feigned a little grin as tears coursed down to his ears.

Joe didn't see the humor in the situation. He leaned him up

217

slightly and gave him another swig of water from the canteen. If everything Welby had told him was true, and he believed Welby had no reason to lie at this point, the man was nothing but another pathetic victim of Wick Canfield. If Welby didn't live, Joe knew that he would be back to square one in nailing the murderous sheriff.

Chapter Forty-Three

Doc Sullivan threw the whip as his buggy rolled at high speed. Clive led the way. Adam rode in the buggy with Doc.

"It's got to be close now!" Clive yelled at Doc.

It was late afternoon as the men searched for Joe. Clive rode on ahead and was the first to spot Joe sitting on top of the hill. He waved his hat at Doc and Adam.

With the buggy stopped, Doc grabbed his bag and jumped down. Adam raced up to Joe.

"You okay? You have some blood on your face."

Joe nodded. "Leave your bag, Doc. No hurry now."

Sullivan hesitated and sat the bag back in the buggy. Clive tied his horse to the buggy and joined the others on the hill. Sullivan stopped at the top, looked, and stumbled down to the figure with a hat on his face. Joe remained where he was.

Adam stood beside Joe and watched Doc remove the hat to see Welby's face. He sat down beside Joe while Doc directed Clive to bring his buggy around the hill to a cut where the bay and now Welby's horse were standing so they could load the body.

"Can't believe this. Why was Welby shooting people?" Adam said. "Comin' out here, though, how it's goin' to look to folks in town. You shootin' George, and you and him, and Sarah."

"I'll tell you what all he said on the way back to town. A sad story," Joe said and stood. "Would have been better to have someone with me to hear it I 'spose."

They proceeded to the cowboys' campsite where Doc Sullivan fashioned a temporary bandage for Raney. They sat him in back of Doc's buggy with Welby. It was cozy, but better than horseback for now.

"Clive, like to have you boys tell Judge Worden what took place here today," Joe said.

"Be happy to, Marshal. Then we'll have to report to Mr. Edson." Joe thanked him and they set off for town at a walk. Joe told Doc, Adam, Clive, and Raney everything that Welby said before he died. Doc and Adam realized what the situation looked like for Joe.

"Isn't there any way to stop Canfield?" Doc asked.

"Don't know of any at present. I'll tell the judge what he said, but it's my word against his, is all it amounts to." The men were silent on the rest of the trip.

When Taylorsville came into sight, Adam said that he would take Welby to McNab's after they left Clive and Raney with Doc.

Mose met Joe as he walked the bay inside the livery. Joe handed over the reins to the bay and Welby's horse, pulled out the rifle, and untied the saddlebags. Before leaving Joe turned to Mose. "You were right." The old Negro offered a single nod.

"Reckon I better gather up Byron, Budd, and Harold."

As Joe walked onto the main street, he stopped, then continued on to Sarah's bath business. He saw her and leaned the rifle and saddlebags against the door frame.

"Oh, Joe. You are a mess, are you okay?"

Joe pulled off his black hat and nodded as he entered. His mouth became dirt dry as he tried to talk.

"I assume you want a bath. Wouldn't look good, so I'll leave for a while." She started for the door.

"Stop. Sarah. Don't want a bath . . . well, I guess I do but, I have things to say. Bad things you gotta hear."

"Why, what's wrong!" Sarah blurted.

"I was camped with two of Tye Edson's hands, on their range last night. Early this morning, that rifle shooter I've been after . . . well he opened up on us. Nicked Raney Miller's hip pretty good. I went after him . . . and I . . . I killed him."

"Well, that's certainly not bad news, you scared the dickens out of me. Congratulations!" Sarah said, relieved. "Wonder what made him kill people like he did?"

"Stop talking, Sarah! I talked with the shooter before he . . . before he passed on. Canfield was forcing him. It was George, Sarah."

She froze and gently shook her head, "That's absurd. What are you up to?" A stern look replaced her smile.

"He replaced the first man Canfield hired for the job, that man actually did the killing. George only killed one man, by accident really. But I didn't know all this 'til I shot him, Sarah. I wanted you to hear it from me. Clive and Raney can tell you what I'm saying is true."

Tears welled up in Sarah's eyes. "Where is George? Where is he? I want to talk to him right now! This instant!" Joe grabbed her by the shoulders when she charged him. "Where is he, damn it?"

"He's at McNab's."

She hit him on the chest with both hands, screaming *"No!"* and ran out. Joe stood there a moment and stepped out onto the boardwalk. He watched her grip her dress as she ran down the street toward McNab's. Martin and Jarvis were standing in front of the marshal's office watching as well.

Siegler was already standing inside the office, no doubt wondering what this was all about, when Joe walked in. Martin and Jarvis followed him inside and closed the door. Joe remounted the rifle into the wall rack, dropped the saddlebags on the floor, and sat down at his desk. He pulled out the bottle from the bottom drawer and took a long pull, swallowed, and took another smaller swig.

"Joe, what's going on?" Siegler asked.

"I killed the shooter." The three board members cheered. "I killed Welby." Silence shattered the office. Harold Martin glanced back and forth at the others, wrung his hands, and sat down in the extra chair.

Several minutes later when Joe stopped talking, the silence continued. No one had a word to say. They didn't know what to say. Joe poured whiskey into a tumbler this time. He motioned them to it. None accepted. Adam stepped into the office long enough to receive his next chore. "Adam, take Pastor Evans down to McNab's right away." His deputy bolted out the door.

Jarvis broke the silence. "You just told Sarah, didn't you?"

Joe nodded, and took another drink.

"I'll have that drink," Jarvis said. Joe set out another small tumbler and poured. Jarvis downed it and Joe refilled it.

"Damn." They all looked at Harold. "No one, other than Joe, witnessed what George said. People are going to think Joe killed him for revenge . . . for taking Sarah away from him."

Siegler looked at the floor, deep in thought. "I don't know what to say. You carried out your duties, Joe. You couldn't have known it was George. None of us would have. He fooled all of us. I do wish this had happened after the election."

CHAPTER FORTY-FOUR

Late that evening Joe and Adam sat in the office. Adam put his book down and lit the lamps. He pulled down the green shades and returned to his chair. The Regulator rang nine bells. After the meeting with the town board, Joe had gone to Judge Worden's office and told him every detail he could remember. Clive Adler had already been there and the judge had written down his statement as well. He would forward his written records of the shooting to the prosecutor in Gracie Flats once Raney gave his statement. Worden told Joe that he would include his recommendation that the shooting was self-defense, and, in his opinion, no charges were warranted. The prosecutor would read them before the coroner's inquest was held.

They soon heard voices outside. Then more voices, as a crowd gathered in front of the office. Voices turned into angry shouts. The angry shouts were directed at Joe. Adam got up and peered out behind a window shade. "There's a crowd out there. Two of 'em holding torches and bottles."

They listened to the angry shouts. "Mundy! Why'd you murder George?" Another voice, "You expect us to believe he was the assassin?" And another, "He made up the story, for vengeance, everybody knows that!"

"No, he didn't, he's honest!"

"Shut up! Only Mundy heard what he said."

A deep voice added, "Edson's two hands were there, and saw the shooting. One of them got hit. They told the judge what happened!"

"He could have arrested him! But he only knows how to kill. Now, where's that leave Sarah? Without a husband!" The yelling became general.

Adam looked at Joe. "What are we going to do?"

Joe stared at the Regulator. Then they heard another voice. A familiar one.

"Men, this is enough of this idle talk, go on home," Siegler announced.

The crowd ignored his request, repeating and adding to their accusations. "We want him fired and arrested for murder. He's not above the law!" Several in the crowd cheered and continued yelling.

The yelling lowered in intensity when Joe and Adam stepped onto the boardwalk. "What's this all about?"

"You know what it's about, Marshal. It's about you murdering George Welby!" The crowd cheered.

"I'm sure Judge Worden will let you read Clive and Raney's statements if you really want the truth, or is it a witch hunt you're on?" Joe said.

"You're just a gunman. Killing is all you've done since *he* brought you here!" The man pointed to Siegler. Cheers again. "How many have you killed in the time you've been here, Mundy?"

Siegler jumped in again, "You should all be ashamed of yourselves. If you'll put down the whiskey and think. Think about the fact that Joe, and Adam, were nearly killed protecting us and this town—"

The yelling drowned him out. "That was trouble that followed him here from his gun work in Kansas! Yeah! He's a killer." Cheers again.

"What do you want? Do you want our town to be at the mercy of every outlaw and bully that rides through here?"

Siegler had to yell to be heard. "Anyone here want to risk his life for fifty dollars a month? Well? We must have law here."

"Fire him! He draws the bad element like flies to cow shit!" The crowd roared. "Make Adam marshal. Then the town can settle down and not have all this killin'!"

"He didn't draw George Welby back and force him to ambush people, did he?!" Siegler was caught up in the argument.

"That's what Mundy claims. Anyone else hear Welby's story?" The crowd roared, "No! No! He killed George for taking Sarah away from him! The real killer is still out there!"

"That's enough! Look at you God-fearing citizens of Taylorsville, with your blind judgments. What is wrong with you people? I didn't see any of you volunteer to track down that assassin. You're sure brave enough now, though!"

A man Joe didn't know stepped onto the boardwalk and launched his bottle at Joe. It missed but went through an office window. "Let's haul him out of town!" The crowd cheered again.

As the man advanced, Joe hit him on the side of the head with an open hand, sending him crashing to the boardwalk. The crowd started for the walk and Joe pulled the cavalry Colt. "I'm willing to die doing my lawful duty. Are you willing to die to stop me?" The crowd hesitated and retreated. It didn't stop them from insults and various comments, however. Joe grabbed the dazed man by the back of the vest and dragged him inside to the jail cage.

When Joe returned to the boardwalk, he saw that Judge Worden had joined them on the walk.

"I heard what was going on here, so I've come to watch the proceedings. Gentlemen, I can assure you that your next actions will be judged harshly . . . *by me,* in my court! How many of you will I have to send to Sheriff Canfield's jail in Gracie Flats? How many of you want that experience?" A near hush enveloped the crowd. A few mumbled. A few broke off and walked away.

"That's what I thought! You all should be ashamed of yourselves. Now, go home!" Worden ordered. A few more ambled off, then a few more until the front row of men realized that there was no one behind them. They walked away at a brisk gait.

"Judge, you'd make a good lawman," Adam observed.

"I am a man of the law, Adam Carr," he retorted.

Adam opened the door and Siegler, Worden, and Joe walked inside, broken glass crunching under their feet.

"Well, that was exciting," Adam said.

Joe offered his desk chair to Judge Worden, who took it. Siegler sat in the extra chair. Joe got the bottle out of the drawer with two glasses and sat them on the desk next to a pair of tin cups Adam had moved there.

After a drink all round, Siegler spoke. "I didn't expect the people to react this harshly. Not good, not good at all." Joe nodded his head toward the jail cage. Siegler caught the hint and was quiet.

"I hope they heed what I said, because I have no tolerance for the actions of a mob. I will have no qualms with sending some of them to Canfield's hoosegow, by God!"

The prisoner spoke, "Judge, I didn't mean—"

"Quiet!" Worden yelled. "The next time I talk to you, *you* will be standing in front of my bench!" The prisoner wilted onto the bottom bunk from the thunderous tone of Worden's voice.

After they had a second drink Joe announced that he was going on rounds.

"I'm going with you," Adam said and stood up.

"You have to stay with the prisoner," Joe said.

"Joe, considering what's happened here tonight, don't you think—" Siegler was interrupted.

"Appreciate your concerns. A mob feeds on their perception

of fear. I won't feed them, for their own good." Joe stepped out, with Siegler and Judge Worden following.

CHAPTER FORTY-FIVE

The start of a new week followed an uneventful weekend. The election was two days away and townspeople had shifted some of their attention from Joe to the candidates. Joe sat at his desk filling out returns on federal papers he had served the day before. He thought about Sarah, whom he hadn't seen since Friday when he had told her about George. He trusted Pastor Evans to take care of her. Joe sent Adam to deliver George's personal effects and gear to Sarah, everything except the Sharps rifle, which sat in the wall rack. He would return it to Agent Langston if he ever saw him again.

Joe finished the paperwork and glanced at the Regulator. It was almost 10 a.m., time to be at Judge Worden's office and the coroner's inquest. A buggy and two horses were tied in front of the judge's office when Joe arrived. Inside were Sheriff Canfield, Deputy Nolan, and the prosecutor who came down from Gracie Flats. He also saw the three town board members, the candidates for the board, along with Gib Hadley, Iain McNab, and about ten other townspeople. Joe was surprised so many people were there. He did notice a few stink-eye looks when he entered.

"Good morning, Marshal," Judge Worden greeted. "We are still waiting for Doctor Sullivan, Clive Adler, and Raney Miller." The front row of seats was reserved for the witnesses to be questioned.

"Marshal, it distresses me that yet again there is another killing here, and—"

"Why don't we save this for when we are in session?" Worden said. Canfield stopped talking. "Marshal, do you know Mr. Van Horn?"

"William Van Horn, Marshal. County Attorney." Joe shook his hand. "My assistant, Steven Harding, who will be keeping an account of this process."

"You're not the one who prosecuted our meat theft here last winter," Joe stated. He looked over the attorney, who was tall and rail straight, taller than Joe. A neat, close-trimmed beard and moustache concealed a weak chin. But as Joe would soon learn, his chin was the only weak thing about him.

Van Horn shook his head, "No, that was Mr. Albright. He moved on to Denver." Van Horn returned his attention to the papers he was reading.

Doc Sullivan and Adam arrived only moments before Clive and Raney.

"Very well, gentlemen, we will get started." Van Horn took the floor. "This coroner's inquest is regarding the death of George Welby, local resident of Taylorsville, and candidate for sheriff. We will begin with you, Doctor Sullivan. Would you tell us how, when, and where you became involved?"

"Well, Clive Adler rode into town and told me that George had been shot, and that he couldn't be moved without a wagon and that Marshal Mundy had sent him for me. I was to proceed quickly with him leading the way. This was Friday last, in the afternoon."

"And where was it that Mr. Adler led you?" Van Horn asked.

"It was across the river, northwest about three or four miles, maybe. On Tye Edson's range."

"And when you arrived at your destination, who was there and in what condition did you find Mr. Welby?"

"Well, Joe, Marshal Mundy was there. He said we were too

late. I examined George, and he was deceased. There was a large amount of blood on the chest and on his back." Sullivan explained.

"Did you examine him further?" Van Horn asked.

"Not until we returned to town. I did the examination at undertaker McNab's."

"And what was the cause of death?"

"A large caliber bullet had penetrated the chest and exited out the back near the left scapula," Doc said.

"So, it is your professional opinion, then, that the bullet struck front to back, and not entering the back and exiting the front?"

"That is correct."

"Very well, thank you, Doctor," Van Horn said. Clive was questioned next and then Raney.

"Mr. Miller, tell us what happened as you saw it."

"Yes, sir, that's my name. Well, it was 'bout breakin' day, we was gettin' up. I stepped up to the fire to pour my coffee, and wham! The coffee pot jus' exploded in my hand, at the same time I fell into the fire. I didn't know right away I was shot, 'til I rolled out of the fire."

"Where were you shot?" Van Horn asked.

"It was up on boss Edson's range!"

"No, no, I mean where on your body."

"Oh. Uh, right here in my darned sore hip. I'll show you." Raney started to stand up but was stopped before he unbuttoned his trousers to exhibit the wound.

"No, no, there's no need for that. We know Doctor Sullivan treated your wound," Van Horn said. "Thank you, that's all, Mr. Miller."

"Marshal Mundy, you admit to shooting George Welby in your statement made to Judge Worden. Why did you shoot Welby?" Van Horn's tone turned suspicious.

"As stated here, because he shot Raney and kept shootin'. Been after a man for some while who had already killed three with long-range rifle shots."

"Marshal, do you know Sarah Welby?"

"Yes, everybody knows that," Joe said.

"What did you think of George Welby?" Van Horn continued.

"Think of him?"

"Yes, did you like him. Did you dislike him?"

"Didn't really know him, only what Sarah, uh, Mrs. Welby said about him."

"You must have held some opinion as to his manner of leaving town some three years ago."

"Yeah, thought it was about the lowest thing a man could do to his wife, leave her like that." Joe said.

"So, the fact is, you didn't like Welby very much, maybe even hated him? Would that be fair to say?"

"Didn't know him enough to hate him, only what he did to Sarah."

"And what exactly has been your relationship with Mrs. Welby?" Van Horn asked.

"We were in company with one another. I took her to meals at the hotel."

"Did you love her Marshal Mundy? Was it an intimate relationship?"

"That's none of your damned business," Joe spat, and gave Canfield an eye. He could see that the prosecutor had been well informed by the famous sheriff, no doubt with help from Dan Loman's secret reports.

"I'm afraid it is my business, as this is an official coroner's inquest, Marshal, you should know that. And in case you don't know, the purpose here today is not only to find the cause of death, but to examine the circumstances surrounding the death and to thereby determine if criminal charges should be filed against a culpable party or parties."

Joe stared at Van Horn.

"So, I will ask that you answer the question, Marshal. Were you having a physical relationship with Sarah Welby?"

"Yes." Joe's face reddened with anger.

Van Horn continued. "So for the record, you were having a physical relationship with Mrs. Sarah Welby, a married woman. Married to George Welby . . . the man you killed on the past Friday."

"She had filed a paper to end her marriage because George abandoned her near three years ago," Joe said.

"A disillusionment filing that she never signed, according to Judge Worden, isn't that correct, Marshal?" Joe started to answer but Van Horn wasn't finished. "You knew that Mrs. Welby had not signed the paper, didn't you?"

" 'Spose so." Joe looked at the floor and then back at Van Horn.

"How long had Mr. Welby been back, until his death, I mean?"

"I don't know exactly, maybe six, seven weeks."

"And how long ago, in your best estimation was Billy Parker murdered?"

"About two months I guess."

"It could have been a little longer then? Maybe a little more than two months?" Van Horn asked.

"Maybe, but not much more."

"So, Marshal, I think it's safe to say that this so-called assassin had been carrying out his nefarious deeds *before* George Welby returned to his wife?"

"I could not say that for sure. Maybe Sheriff Canfield can add something here." Joe was angry, and wanted Canfield to answer for Welby's deathbed confession.

"Well, Sheriff Canfield is not a witness in this inquest, but I understand your contention. I also understand that you and the sheriff aren't of the same mind, so to speak. Copies of statements from Judge Worden, convey a confession of sorts, that Welby made indicating collusion, and, in fact, stating that he worked for the sheriff in scouting around the ranges for the purpose of killing people . . . and to take over Mr. Edson's ranch?"

"That's what he said before he died," Joe said.

"And that scenario doesn't sound a bit preposterous to you?" Van Horn's voice elevated.

"Didn't make that judgment. It's what he said before he died. And last winter Mr. Canfield's deputy tried to kill me and my deputy. I guess not being of the same mind would be accurate."

"That was not Sheriff Canfield, however, was it? It was his deputy. So, back to the subject at hand, correct me if I am mistaken, but you were the *only* witness to hear this confession that Mr. Welby espoused . . . before he died? Is that right?"

"That's right."

"When George Welby returned to Taylorsville, his wife, Sarah, left you and returned to her husband, isn't that correct?" Van Horn asked.

"Yes."

"That would anger even the stoutest of mind, don't you think?"

"Just what the hell are you diggin' at?"

"We've established that the assassin had already been at work *before* Mr. Welby returned to town." Van Horn let the statement hang in the air.

"He said that he replaced a man who was doing the same kind of work for Canfield," Joe stated.

"Oh, yes, I am aware. More of the statement that only *you* heard," Van Horn said. "To be clear, Marshal, there isn't anyone else who can verify your statement?"

"My word's been good enough so far," Joe said. "And why would he lie at a time like that? He knew he was dyin'."

"Indeed. Fairly obvious that you and Mr. Welby didn't always agree, either." Van Horn paced and scratched his chin whiskers. "A person with even a little sense could possibly think that you were upset with Mr. Welby's return, and Sarah's leaving your bed to return to her husband."

Joe stood up and faced Van Horn. "Marshal Mundy, please take your seat," Judge Worden commanded. Joe stared at Van Horn and sat down.

"To continue, the assassin running around the country might offer a convenient opportunity to track down Mr. Welby and kill him, for taking away your lover, would it not?"

"A sensible person would know that Raney didn't shoot himself. And that the .45-90 cartridges in Welby's belt were the same caliber I found after an earlier shootin'," Joe said.

"Now that Mr. Welby is dead, we don't know that his target was Raney Miller. Maybe it was you, Marshal. Maybe he knew you were trying to kill him and it was a scenario of he gets you before you got him, eh?" Van Horn shoved an unlit cigar between his lips. "And a .45-90 cartridge isn't exactly a rare cartridge, is it?"

The inquest finished at 1:30 p.m. Everyone headed to the hotel or chophouse for a meal. Joe and Adam went to the North Star.

Chapter Forty-Six

Gib Hadley followed Joe and Adam into the North Star and served up three whiskeys. "Thanks for watchin' the place, Jack." Hadley's part-time bartender stepped out from behind the bar after pouring himself a beer.

"What kind of a horse's ass does he think he is, anyway?" Hadley said. "He purty much blamed you of murder!"

Adam joined in, "That fancy lawyer can sure twist up a story 'til juice comes out."

"I heard he come up from Kansas City, Missouri," Hadley said. "He oughta go right back down there and stay!"

Joe was silent, rerunning the inquest through his mind.

"Well, what in hell do you think about it?" Hadley asked.

"He certainly is athirst with his job, Gib," Joe said. Adam and Hadley looked at each other.

"That's all ya got to say? He's tryin' to put a rope around your neck!" Hadley said.

"Everyone will see the ambushes have stopped," Adam said. "More proof that Joe got the right man, even though it surely was a surprise to all of us that it was Welby."

"That's a straight-arrow observation right there," Hadley said.

After the public left, Van Horn discussed the inquest with Judge Worden while Canfield, Nolan, and Harding looked on.

"I understand your line of questioning, Mr. Van Horn, but I

don't see any cause for charges against Marshal Mundy. From what I've seen of him, he's certainly not to be trifled with in the execution of his duties. He's law through and through," Worden said. "They were shot at by Welby, Joe returned fire. It cannot be proved any other way."

"Perhaps, Your Honor, once Steven transcribes the inquest, I will study it. I still feel that it's possible that Mundy planned to kill Welby over the woman. I'll let you know what my decision is."

"I agree with Mr. Van Horn. He was mad at Welby for taking Sarah back," Canfield said. "Plain as a tail on a horse."

"That was enlightening, Sheriff, but loose talk is not proof," Worden said, dismissing him. Canfield's face reddened.

"We'll ride back to Gracie Flats then," Van Horn said. "Be in touch, Your Honor."

Worden nodded.

"Dick can ride along with you, Mr. Van Horn, I want to make some inquiries here before leaving town," Canfield said, as they walked out.

"See you back in Gracie, Sheriff," Van Horn said. He climbed into his carriage and shook the reins.

Wick Canfield walked his horse behind the hotel and west past Doc Sullivan's and on down past Sarah's house. He thought as he walked along. Turning north, he walked across the west end of the main street and on up to Loman's meat market. He decided a visit was in order.

Dan Loman was startled enough at the sight of Canfield that he dropped a knife he was using. "Oh, a good day to you, Sheriff. Nice to see you."

"No reason to be nervous, Dan, we're friends, aren't we?" Loman nodded too many times.

"I wanted to tell you that I was disappointed to hear of the . . . *accident* with your finger. You should know that I fired Mr.

Banning. I won't tolerate that kind of thing."

"Uh, uh, okay. Thank you?" Loman couldn't figure out what he should say.

"I want to know everything Mundy does until after the election tomorrow. Then we can return to the old schedule. My deputy, Dick Nolan, will be by, so have something for him."

Loman nodded again, "Okay, yes, sir. I'll do that."

"Suppose you heard that Mundy killed George Welby?"

"Yes, yes, I did. Turned out he was the one shooting at folks. Good thing it's all over. They got him, so no more ambushes out on the range."

Canfield was lost in thought, *They got him, so no more ambushes.* He smiled to himself. *Another shooting would make it obvious that Welby wasn't the assassin. Maybe that would strengthen the case against Mundy.*

"Dan, sell me a couple of those beef steaks!"

Loman was startled by the sheriff's gleeful outburst. "Oh, ah, yes, sir." He wrapped up the steaks and handed them over. "No charge, Sheriff, no charge."

"I wouldn't hear of it," Canfield said, and dropped a five-dollar bill on the counter.

"Oh, ah, you have change coming!" Loman said as his customer walked out.

Canfield trotted his horse north until out of the town's sight, then turned northwest. He sported a wicked grin and wiped his black moustache one way and then the other. He kept to the ravines as much as possible. About an hour later he was on Tye Edson's range. He could see cattle in the distance, so slowed his horse to a walk. He thought he could see a rider coming south toward him so he dismounted and unsheathed his '73 Winchester rifle. He left his horse hidden in a deep ravine and found a spot in the tall grass at the hilltop. He knew he wouldn't have the range that the Sharps .45-90 had, but he didn't want the rider to get close enough to identify him in case he got away, either. He sat patiently and brought up the rifle. His target was a cowhand, someone he didn't know. As the rider came within range, he held his breath and squeezed the trigger. The rider jerked and hunched over the saddle horn, which told Canfield that his .44-40 bullet found its mark. He levered another round as the rider kicked his horse into a dead run. Canfield believed his second shot had missed and now the rider was out of range. *Someone will find his carcass baking in the sun.*

CHAPTER FORTY-SEVEN

Joe and Adam sat in the office without talking. Adam wasn't even reading his book. He sat and stared at the Sharps rifle in the gun rack. Joe sipped another whiskey and watched the Regulator. He wasn't particularly interested in the time, it was something handy to fix on.

The door banged open and both men jumped a bit. "I apologize if I gave you boys a start!" Pastor Evans said. Adam got up and gave the pastor his chair.

"Care for a drink, Christmas?" Joe asked.

"I would have one, filled to the rim, please."

Joe poured and handed it over. "I hoped you'd let us know how Sarah is doing."

"Precisely my reason for visiting, Marshal, and the drink, of course." Evans looked upward before taking a drink. "Mrs. Welby is a brave soul, as we—"

"Don't mean to interrupt, Christmas, but how is she?" Joe said.

Evans ignored the transgression. "She is in rough condition, Joe, poor soul. I poured her a drink of whiskey, as a medicine you know, to settle her nerves. She took to it heartily. I thought, if it could subdue her pain for a little while at least, the Almighty might overlook it." Evans finished his glass and waved off Joe's offer of a refill. "She's sleeping now, so I'll check back in on her later." Joe nodded.

"If I may speak frankly?" Evans asked as he studied Joe's

face. Joe nodded again.

"Sir, you look like hell. You mustn't blame yourself in this matter. George Welby was the offender here and you did the job you are required to do, no matter how distasteful it becomes at times." Joe glanced at Evans and back to the Regulator. Silence followed.

A loud voice, then two, could be heard in the street. Then some lower, urgent sounding ones.

"You gotta' be kiddin' me. Think that mob is—" Adam was cut off when the door slammed open. Sarah pushed through the doorway holding a small pistol with both hands and began firing. The chimney on Joe's new desk lamp exploded on the second wild shot. He dropped behind the desk and Pastor Evans froze with mouth agape. Three quick rounds were fired before Adam grabbed her and took the pistol away.

"You shum' bitch . . . kill you . . ." Sarah sputtered. She looked faint so Adam held onto her. Joe stood up and Adam threw the pistol to him. It was a Smith & Wesson .32 rimfire. It was engraved, *For my Dear Sarah, from George.*

"Bashterd . . ." Sarah sputtered again. She had difficulty forming words and swayed back and forth even while being held upright by Adam.

"Adam, would you assist the pastor in returning Mrs. Welby to her home?" Joe asked. Adam held her up by one side and Pastor Evans held the other.

"I'll stay with her, Joe," Evans said on the way out.

Joe stood behind the desk and surveyed the damage. Beside the lamp, he found two bullet holes in the wall behind where he sat. Only one had come close to his head. He started to pick up broken glass from the desk when Byron Siegler entered the open doorway.

"Good God, we heard the shots . . . thought some dumbbell had tried to kill you! And then I saw Adam and Pastor Evans taking Sarah home. She tried to kill you?" Siegler took a breath.

"She was drunk," Joe said and finished the cleanup.

Siegler gawked at the bullet holes with mouth open.

"Wanna close the door?" Joe asked. Siegler reached back and closed it, without taking his eyes from the lamp with no chimney and the bullet holes in the wall.

Joe had no more than offered Siegler a seat than a rider skidded his horse up in front of the office. The rider was leaning over the saddle horn and Joe could see blood on his calico shirt. They bolted out of the office to help the rider.

Joe grabbed the reins. "Bony, what happened?"

"I'll be damned if someone didn't haul off and shoot me again! I wasn't doing nothin' to be shot fer. I wasn't doin' nothin' but attendin' my own business. I was shot by ambush, coming back to Mr. Jarvis's ranch. He'd sent me to Tye Edson's place to return a saddle we barred."

"Hold on, I'll get you to Doc's." Joe led the horse, and sent Siegler to find Jarvis.

"How bad is it?" Joe asked.

"Not bad, hurts like a lightnin' strike, though. At least it wasn't muh sore ribs agin. They hurts just fine without any extra help." Joe was glad to hear Bony complain all the way to Doc Sullivan's.

Sullivan gave Bony a spoonful of laudanum and began the examination. He probed for the bullet, which had entered the right side of the chest under the shoulder blade. There was no exit wound.

"The back of muh shoulder hurts, if that helps any, Doc." Sullivan gently explored his shoulder and upper arm with his fingers and when Bony yelped, he knew he'd found the bullet.

"It's lodged in your upper arm. I don't think it's worth the risk of taking it out, unless you really want me to try?"

"I'd jus' a soon have no more holes in me than I already have if it's all the same to you, Doc," Bony said.

"Very well. It'll be sore for a while, but I'll clean it up and dress the wound. You are a lucky man."

While Doc worked, Joe took the time to question the cowhand. "Bony, tell me what happened, everything you can remember."

"Well, like I said, I'd taken a saddle back to Mr. Edson, and was on muh way back to Mr. Jarvis's when I heard a rifle shot and plum as fast, felt the bullet hit me."

Jarvis and Siegler arrived. "Are you okay, Bony?" Jarvis asked.

"Sho am, Mr. Jarvis, a bit sore, but Doc says I'm lucky!"

"He'll be fine. Leaving the bullet in because of where it is. It's not a large caliber or it would have done more damage. It would cause more problems than necessary to remove it," Doc said as he wrapped Bony's shoulder. "Would like him to stay here a day or two so I can watch him."

"Oh, now, Doc, I got plenty of work awaitin' on me, ain't that right, Boss?"

"You'll do what Doc says," Jarvis barked and turned to Joe. "What in hell is this? I thought Welby was the assassin?"

Joe ignored him and continued with Bony. "Did you see anyone, Bony?"

"No, sir, I sho 'nuff didn't," Bony said with a wry smile. The laudanum was working. "I kicked the nag into a run and headed for town."

Joe saw the look Jarvis and Siegler were giving him. "Welby *was* the shooter. The second shooter. Someone wants me to look bad, like I did kill Welby because of Sarah."

Siegler responded, "Joe, we agree with you. We're worried how all these idiots around town will see it."

"Are you thinkin' Canfield or his deputy shot Bony?" Jarvis asked.

"That's my summation," Joe said. "Easy to do on their way

back to Gracie. Not real far out of their way."

Jarvis nodded, "Whether Welby was or wasn't the shooter, the fact is, he shot Raney and you shot back. Clear self-defense."

CHAPTER FORTY-EIGHT

The next morning the entire coffee club was gathered at the North Star. It was election day and the major topic of conversation. The shooting of Bony Wilson was as well.

"Soon as I knew about Bony gettin' shot, I knew Canfield did it to shed a dark cloud on Joe," Hadley declared. "Ain't that right, Joe?"

"I agree, Gib, but once again, provin' it is another thing," Joe said.

Harold weighed in. "And he will be officially elected today since there's no one running against him." His cup shook as he raised it to drink.

"When I go to the church to vote, I ain't givin' him the benefit of my vote," Jarvis said, and received several "hear, hears."

"I'm a little worried about the town board race. Maybe we can talk His Honor into overlookin' some of Zach and Cleve's votes!" Hadley said and grinned. Joe looked at him. "Hell, I was only addin' some humor. Our meetin's haven't much been enjoyable since all these tryin' times."

"And with Welby's funeral tomorrow," Harold said and shook his head.

"That was a Godly thing for you to have done Joe, paying for Mr. Welby's funeral," Pastor Evans said. Jarvis glanced at Joe.

"How is Sarah this morning, Pastor?" Siegler asked. Everyone turned and looked at Evans.

"She's overcome. Very sick this morning after her bender yesterday. Doctor Sullivan gave her something to help with the after-effects of the alcohol," Evans said. "She hasn't mentioned shooting at Joe. I'm not sure she remembers it."

"Well, sure thing Joe remembers it!" Hadley said and laughed. All of the others grinned, except Joe.

"I asked Judge Worden if he'd bring the town board results to the Texan this evening and announce them there. Ham has tacked a few signs around to let folks know," Jarvis said.

After leaving the coffee club, Joe stopped in at Siegler's general store and bought a new chimney for his desk lamp. Earl was going to wrap it up so it wouldn't get broken, but Joe told him he thought he could carry it across the street and to his office without that happening.

Adam had swept out the office and was almost finished with the boardwalk when Joe returned. "When you goin' down to vote?" Adam asked.

"Whenever you're ready, might as well get it over with."

As they walked across the street, it looked to Joe that Sarah's laundry and bath business was closed. They turned the corner and went south.

"Maybe I should walk on this side of you, in case Sarah takes a shot at you as we walk by her house," Adam said. Joe glanced at him to see if he was being funny.

It was almost eleven o'clock and there were already several people in line at the church to vote. Deputy Sheriff Nolan was standing near the ballot boxes. There was one for county office ballots and one for the town. Joe would carry the town box to Judge Worden's office to be counted when the voting ceased at eight o'clock.

"Deputy Nolan," Joe said. "Everything in order?"

"Good day, Marshal. Keeping an eye on the county box,"

Nolan said. "Here to pray or vote?"

"I think a little of both wouldn't hurt."

Nolan smiled.

Joe and Adam saw some of the people in line ahead of them turn, offer a glance, and turn back. Some faces were friendly and nodded, some were decidedly not. As they neared the table, they could see the volunteers handing each person two ballots. Once they had theirs, they stepped into makeshift booths rigged with hanging blankets that afforded privacy.

Joe read that another man was running against William Van Horn for county attorney. He voted for the other man and skipped over Canfield's and Welby's names. After marking Siegler, Martin, and Jarvis's names for the town board, Joe folded his ballots, stepped out of the booth, and dropped them into the appropriate boxes. A minute later Adam stepped out and did the same with his. They nodded at Nolan on the way out.

Joe and Adam were silent as they walked down the main street. The town was crawling with people. Everyone seemed to be out with an air of election-day excitement. A couple of men were drinking from beer bottles in front of the North Star. It was becoming a festive atmosphere.

"Hope everyone behaves today," Adam said.

"Looks like people are enjoying the day." Joe thought about the town getting a bank, and talk of a railroad line was floating around. And, he wondered how Sarah would be once the pain of losing George subsided. It was obvious they would never be together again. Things had changed there.

"Let's stop in and see the judge," Joe said and they rounded the corner of the hotel and angled across the street.

After greetings, Worden gave some instructions. "Marshal, I'd like you to meet me at the church no later than eight o'clock. We'll bring the ballot box back here where I'll do the counting.

You'll stand by while I complete the task."

"I'll be there, Judge," Joe said.

"Then we'll stop by the telegraph office and wait for the results from Gracie Flats before announcing them at the Texan," Worden said and sat back in his chair. "Should be quite a crowd. Folks seem to be excited over their first election."

"Yes, sir, they do," Joe said. "Too bad we already know some of the results."

"Canfield," Worden stated. "Yes, I know what you mean. I have to keep my mind open as a jurist, but frankly, he bothers me. I don't need to tell *you* to never turn your back to him."

Joe nodded. "He'll get caught someday, and I hope I'm the one doin' the catchin'."

Adam went back to help Siegler with some work at the general store while Joe made rounds and watched for anyone over-imbibing. He sat with Gib awhile in the North Star before returning to the office.

By seven o'clock Adam had finished his work and they met for supper at the hotel. Several customers were finishing their meals and anxiously discussing the election. All were friendly toward Joe and Adam. One man Joe didn't know was leaving but stopped by their table and offered a greeting. "Don't let them get to you, Marshal. We know you did what you had to do." He continued on to the front door.

"Nice to know some people around here have brains," Adam said. He slurped his soup and glanced at Joe.

"We finish here, I'll go over to the church," Joe said. "You can go on down by the Texan and keep an eye on things." Adam nodded and finished his meal.

It was dark as Joe walked by Sarah's house. There was a single lamp burning. Activity at the church was nil. One volunteer remained seated at the table; Judge Worden and Deputy Nolan each occupied a chair. Joe walked in and took a seat on a bench. Every few minutes Judge Worden took out his pocket watch. After the fourth time, he stood up and said, "That's it, gentlemen. Eight o'clock on the dot. Deputy, you may take custody of the county box and return it to Gracie Flats."

"Thank you, Your Honor. Marshal." Nolan picked up the box and walked out.

Joe picked up the town box and followed the judge to Sarah's house, then on east past Doc Sullivan's and across the street to Worden's office. Worden opened the padlock and sat down at his work table. Joe wondered how long it would take to count the votes for a town of about 200 people. He listened to the pronounced "tick-tock" of Worden's new wall clock to pass the time. Every so often, the judge would make scratches on a piece of paper, and then go back to unfolding ballots. Joe noticed how careful and deliberate he was in carrying out his task.

Joe started to doze, but pried his eyes open, hoping this was the first time he had nodded off. He looked at the clock, which read 9:25 p.m. He glanced at Worden, who was making scratches again behind a huge pile of ballots. He dropped the pencil and picked up a new cigar, lit it, and leaned back in his chair.

"The job is finished, Marshal," Worden said with a frown.

"Thought you'd be glad to be done?"

"Finishing the chore is good. The result of my work is not." Joe guessed that he'd have to wait to know what the judge meant by that.

Worden folded up a piece of paper and slid it into an inside coat pocket. "Well, shall we?"

Joe and Worden watched Eli, who watched the telegraph key.

"I didn't know Gracie Flats had a telegraph," Joe said, more to make conversation than anything.

"They do, but there's only a line from Willow Springs. They will resend to us when they receive from the Flats." Eli returned his gaze to the key.

Joe checked his watch and it was after ten o'clock when the key started to click. Eli tongued his pencil and jotted down each letter. Minutes later the message ended. He stood up and handed it to Judge Worden.

"What a surprise, Canfield is sheriff," he said with a low tone.

They marched across the street and entered the crowded Texan. It was decorated inside and out with red, white, and blue bunting. Joe stopped beside Adam as the judge stepped in front of the bar. He pulled the paper from his coat pocket.

"If I can have your attention, gentlemen, the election results are in!" Worden had to yell until the noise died. "For county attorney, winner is William Van Horn. For sheriff, Wick Canfield . . ." He continued through the county offices and then on to the Taylorsville town board. "The new town board is, Byron Siegler, Zachariah Anson, and Cleve Escott." The crowd became noisy again.

Joe and Adam stepped up to the bar and Jarvis served them each whiskeys. Siegler, Martin, and Gib made their way over to them, all silent.

Siegler spoke. "I hate this. I'd hoped we could have kept the board as it was. I thought we worked together well. Hard telling what Zach and Cleve are wanting to do." The little group mumbled and sipped from their drinks.

"They best not get too hog-wild with their ideas, by God!" Hadley said and downed his whiskey.

"Will you still be the head of the board, Byron?" Adam asked.

"The first meeting of the new board will be in the morning, Adam. The three of us will vote on it. The position is now called 'mayor.' "

Zachariah Anson stood on a chair. "I have a toast! If I can have your attention!" The crowd quieted. "I would like to offer a toast and a thank you for the work Budd Jarvis and Harold Martin have done to help this town progress and only hope Cleve and I can do as well." The crowd cheered and raised their glasses.

"Ass," Jarvis said and smiled as he met Zach's eyes and raised his glass.

Judge Worden approached the group and offered his free hand to Siegler, Jarvis, and Martin. He downed his whiskey and said, "Have to admit that I didn't want to see a change in the board. You men did fine with it and I salute your work." They thanked Worden before he left.

Jarvis refilled their glasses as Anson and Escott squeezed through the crowd. They shook hands with Jarvis and Martin. "I meant what I said up there, men. Congratulations on your work," Anson said.

"Yes, I will try to meet the expectations you men set," Escott said.

After they returned to their table the group was silent until Hadley spoke. "Is it just me, or are those two horses' asses tryin' to sound like politicians?" The glumness seeped away and they all laughed.

Except Martin. "Well, I guess I'm no longer a member of the town board." They realized at that moment how important it was to Harold and how genuinely saddened he was at the loss.

Jarvis broke in, "Don't worry about it, Harold. You and me will run against 'em next time. How's that sound?" The group voiced their agreement and patted Martin on the back. Joe was sometimes amazed at the compassion that the rough-hewn Jarvis showed on rare occasions. His timing on those occasions was usually just about right.

CHAPTER FORTY-NINE

Joe laid on his cot thinking about the previous day's election, the surprising, and the not surprising, results. He hadn't felt the joy most did during the festive celebrations at the Texan. He'd returned to the office well before the celebration was over, but he was glad he did. Someone had followed him to the office and he could still smell her on his blanket. Adam didn't know she was there with Joe when he came back, so early this morning when Jenny left, she was extra quiet not to wake him. Joe started to smell coffee, which told him Adam was up and busy. He stood, leaned over the basin, and splashed water on his face. After dressing he poured coffee and sat at the desk. Adam was busy reading from his book of conundrums.

"You're up early to have been out so late," Joe said. "Have a good time?"

"Yes. No. I don't know," Adam said, and pocketed his book. He offered a thoughtful look at the floor.

"What's wrong?"

Adam thought a moment. "I don't know. Everything seems, I don't know. Beside the mark."

" 'Cause of the board changes?" Joe asked.

"I don't know, maybe. Everything that's gone on around here." Adam refilled his cup and Joe's and sat down.

"Maybe things will settle down again," Joe offered.

"What if someone else gets ambushed?"

"Well, then I go hunting, again," Joe said.

"Canfield may have already hired someone to replace Welby, like he did with Banning." Joe hadn't considered that. He was stuck on the belief that Canfield had shot Bony to help the prosecutor's case, and his own interest in getting Joe out of his way.

"That is possible. Hopefully the fire that was started with Welby's statement will keep him low for a while," Joe said. He sat with his thoughts and stared at the Regulator, but not the time.

Adam said, "It's about time for the board meeting. Should we go down there?"

Joe withdrew from his thoughts and read the clock this time. "Let's go."

They met Jarvis and Hadley and walked along to the church together. Inside, Siegler, Anson, and Escott were seated at a table near the lectern with about a dozen people looking on. Joe, Adam, Budd, and Gib took their seats.

Anson was the first to speak. "We'll bring this meeting of the Taylorsville town board to order. For this first meeting of a new board, we decided that we would let the citizens in attendance today decide for us who will serve as mayor. Slips are being handed out to everyone to mark one of our names on; then they will be collected."

Joe marked down Siegler's name as he was sure Budd and Gib did as well. A volunteer gathered the slips, sat down next to Escott, and counted. He then stood up and announced that Zachariah Anson would serve as mayor. Jarvis glanced at Joe and Gib.

"Very well, thank you. We will push some of the more mundane items to the end of the meeting and start with what I believe is the most pressing," Anson said. "As most of you know, my main interest in running for the town board was to push this town forward, and I believe to do that, we have to attract more folks to live here, and draw more businesses to town. We have empty buildings from the first boom and bust, and we must have them filled. But folks aren't going to come to a town that is becoming known for violence. No one wants to take up roots in a town like that. And with no malice, but only the town's progress in mind, I think the first step to take is a change in our marshal's office." The audience talked amongst themselves. "Therefore, I am putting forth the motion that Marshal Joe Mundy be relieved of his position, and Adam Carr appointed to replace him. Discussion is open before the board votes on my motion."

Adam looked at Joe and mumbled, "Son-of-a-bitch!"

"With all . . . due . . . respect, Zach. Uh, *mayor,*" Siegler thundered. "Do I have to remind you and the townspeople what our marshal has done to protect us from those who would run wild here? Do we have to consider what would have happened had he not been here? I'll remind you of a few things. Lucy Sauter—" The crowd groaned. "I know, I know, a soiled dove, but a human being. She would have been beaten to death if it wasn't for Marshal Mundy. He would have done the same to protect any one of us. Who would those scoundrels have attacked next if Mundy hadn't stopped them at the Palace. Maybe it will be one of you. And, the Palace, a den of inequity if there ever was one! Who keeps that place under control? We cannot regulate who comes and goes through town. Some come here with evil intent and you all know it. You've seen it! Our very safety is at risk without someone who can handle these outlaws! If you remember, I brought him here because it was vital that we employed someone like him and we couldn't depend on the sheriff." A few in the crowd agreed. Cleve Escott scratched down the proceedings in the book Harold Martin had used.

"If I may, gentlemen," Judge Worden stood.

"Please, proceed, Your Honor," Anson said.

"I have been a jurist for forty years, in three different towns. I have seen and judged those who care little about law. Some towns are fortunate, and only require the mild touch of a lawman. This is *not* one of those towns. This is a town that needs the type of man who uses an iron hand to keep the peace. Maybe, I'll even say, probably, in the future such strong law work will no longer be a necessity here. *But!* That time has not come yet. You will rue the day you released Mundy as your marshal." Worden sat down.

"Thank you, Judge Worden," Anson said. "Does anyone else wish to offer an opinion before the board votes?"

Jarvis leaned toward Joe, Adam, and Hadley and whispered, "Cleve will vote to keep you after his wife was shot."

"Very well, board members, with a show of hands, who approves my motion of relieving Joe Mundy as marshal and appointing Adam Carr in his place?" Anson and Escott raised their hands.

Hadley stood and yelled, "You had that planned all along! No matter what anyone said!" The crowd became noisy, but it was not clear if they liked the board's decision or not.

"Order, please," Anson banged the table with his new gavel. "We thank Mr. Mundy for his work here, and as I said, hold no hard feelings against him. We believe this is a benefit to the town as it moves forward."

"Who's gonna tell the curs that when they ride into town, you?" Hadley yelled again.

Joe put his hand on Hadley's shoulder. "It's okay, my friend."

"Adam, would you step forward and receive your oath?" Anson said.

He stood, "No, I will not!"

Joe stood up beside him and said in a low tone, "Yes, you will. You are the only one in this town who can do the job." As he talked, Joe unfastened his badge and pinned it to Adam's shirt. "You go up there now. Don't make me tell you twice." Adam stared at Joe, who nodded.

Adam marched up with a sullen look and raised his right hand before Anson told him to. Siegler nodded his approval.

"Ah, well, then. Adam Carr, do you swear to uphold the laws of Taylorsville and the state of Nebraska, so help you God?" Anson read from a paper.

"I do!" Adam spat. Anson offered his hand but Adam ignored it and walked back to Joe, who was already gone.

When Adam reached the office he found Joe organizing his belongings on the desk. He stormed in and kicked over the extra chair. "Those goddamned sons-a-bitches!"

"Sit down, let's have a drink," Joe said. He pulled the bottle out of the drawer and poured two tumblers.

Adam stared down at the upended chair with hands on hips. He bent over, righted it, and sat down.

"To friendship," Joe said. Adam took a heavy gulp and sat the glass down.

"You are my friend," Adam said.

"I know," Joe said. "Like you to have my '66 Winchester, sort of a token of friendship." He handed Adam the brass-framed carbine that he'd ridden into Taylorsville with.

Adam took it and looked it over. "This means a lot to me . . ."

"There should be a box of cartridges in the desk somewhere," Joe said, as he packed his saddlebags.

"What will you do? Where will you go?" Adam began firing questions. "You'll stay in town, right?"

"Don't know yet. 'Spose I'll get a room at the hotel for the night," Joe said. Adam could see that Joe had pinned on the federal badge.

"You don't *have* to leave, do you?" Adam continued. "Don't want to lose my best friend very much." His eyes became glassy so he looked away from Joe.

"Hell, Adam, don't worry about me," Joe said. "I'll always be around."

ABOUT THE AUTHOR

Monty McCord is the author of *Mundy's Law: The Legend of Joe Mundy* (Five Star, 2013), which won a Peacemaker Award and was a finalist in two other competitions. The book also received an excellent review from *Publishers Weekly* and a starred review from *Booklist*.

A retired police lieutenant and graduate of the FBI National Academy, McCord writes books about lawmen and outlaws from the Old West period to the mid-twentieth century. *When I Die* is the second installment in the Legend of Joe Mundy series.

Additionally, McCord has six published nonfiction books.

The employees of Five Star Publishing hope you have enjoyed this book.

Our Five Star novels explore little-known chapters from America's history, stories told from unique perspectives that will entertain a broad range of readers.

Other Five Star books are available at your local library, bookstore, all major book distributors, and directly from Five Star/Gale.

Connect with Five Star Publishing

Visit us on Facebook:
   https://www.facebook.com/FiveStarCengage

Email:
   FiveStar@cengage.com

For information about titles and placing orders:
   (800) 223-1244
   gale.orders@cengage.com

To share your comments, write to us:
   Five Star Publishing
   Attn: Publisher
   10 Water St., Suite 310
   Waterville, ME 04901